REVENGER

REVENGER

A WESTERN DUO

COPY 1

FRANK LESLIE

FIVE STAR
A part of Gale, a Cengage Company

GALE
A Cengage Company

Farmington Hills, Mich • San Francisco • New York • Waterville, Maine
Meriden, Conn • Mason, Ohio • Chicago

LIBRARY OF CONGRESS CATALOGING-IN-PUBLICATION DATA

Names: Leslie, Frank, 1963– author. | Leslie, Frank, 1963– A bullet for Sartain. | Leslie, Frank, 1963– Death and the saloon girl.
Title: Revenger : a western duo featuring Mike Sartain, the Revenger / by Frank Leslie.
Other titles: A bullet for Sartain. | Death and the saloon girl.
Description: First edition. | Waterville, Maine : Five Star Publishing, a part of Cengage Learning, Inc., [2017] |
Identifiers: LCCN 2017018154 (print) | LCCN 2017024028 (ebook) | ISBN 9781432837235 (ebook) | ISBN 1432837230 (ebook) | ISBN 9781432837228 (ebook) | ISBN 1432837222 (ebook) | ISBN 9781432837358 (hardcover) | ISBN 1432837354 (hardcover)
Subjects: | GSAFD: Western stories.
Classification: LCC PS3552.R3236 (ebook) | LCC PS3552.R3236 A6 2017d (print) | DDC 813/.54—dc23
LC record available at https://lccn.loc.gov/2017018154

First Edition. First Printing: October 2017
Find us on Facebook–https://www.facebook.com/FiveStarCengage/
Visit our website–http://www.gale.cengage.com/fivestar/
Contact Five Star™ Publishing at FiveStar@cengage.com

TABLE OF CONTENTS

★ ★ ★ ★ ★

Revenger #1
A Bullet for Sartain

★ ★ ★ ★ ★

CHAPTER 1

Buffalo McCluskey set his shot glass on the bar with a solid thump, ran a bear-sized paw across his beard, and turned angrily to the tall, dark man leaning against the bar beside him.

"I'm ready for another drink, Sartain!"

Mike Sartain, known from one end of the frontier to the other as "The Revenger," sipped his own whiskey and regarded the burly man humorously from beneath his sand-colored Stetson's flat, salt-crusted brim. He hadn't shaved since leaving the 55-Connected, where he and McCluskey had played at wrangling for the past seven months, as a change of pace from Sartain's bloody vigilante ways. His cobalt-blue eyes were set off by the rich black beard shadow and the sun-seared skin drawn taut across his high, chiseled cheeks.

"Well, why don't you buy yourself one, you old black-hearted malcontent? While you're at it"—Sartain finished his own whiskey and skidded the glass down beside McCluskey's with a glassy clink—"you can buy me one!"

McCluskey bunched his lips inside his curly, salt-and-pepper beard sprinkled with seeds and coated with trail dust and blood from the venison haunch he'd consumed half-raw around last night's campfire. "Damn you, Mike—you know it's your turn to buy."

"Beg to differ with ya, partner," said Sartain in his slow, Cajun drawl, shaking his head slowly. "I done bought the last round. Seems to me I'm two rounds ahead, as a matter of un-

9

contestable fact."

McCluskey squared his shoulders at Sartain and dropped his chin, fashioning a look that said he couldn't believe what he'd just heard. "You owed me three shots, Mike. Don't you remember how I staked you to that poker game at the 55-Connected? I staked you 'cause you told me you'd buy three rounds—*three rounds*—soon as we hit town!"

Sartain's face colored as he turned to face the big man before him. Sartain was as tall as Buffalo, but Buffalo was as broad as a barn door, with a hard, rounded paunch. His voice grew in volume as the other voices around the saloon fell silent, the other customers and the whores turning to regard him and Buffalo warily.

"You got one hell of a selective memory on you, my addle-pated old pard. I told you I'd buy you three rounds if I couldn't pay you back."

Sartain pounded his right fist on the mahogany. "But, damnit, I filled an inside straight and done *paid you back*!" He gave a slow, menacing smile. "But I got a feelin' your memory's better'n you're lettin' on, old man."

Buffalo bunched his lips. His voice rumbled up from deep in his chest, filling the entire saloon and even drowning out the thunder of an approaching rainstorm. "You're the one with the selective memory, *old friend*! You said you'd buy me three shots of good whiskey even if you paid me back—'as a token of your appreciation.' "

He spoke this last with mocking exaggeration, twisting his broad, warty face bizarrely.

Sartain slapped the bar. "Consarn you, Buffalo! I swear—!"

"Hold on there, fellers." The small, bald bartender had moved down the counter to stand before them, holding both small, pink hands up, palms out. He was so short that the top of his head rose only a foot above the mahogany. "No need to bust up a good friendship over whiskey. Surely there's a way to settle this without fisticuffs."

"I'll buy the boys a drink," piped up a man sitting with two others near the piano. He and his friends were decked out in business suits and bowler hats, fat stogies in their mouths sending thick smoke ribbons up from ash trays arranged beside their beer mugs. "Anything for a little peace and quiet."

"Hell, I'll chip in," said the man across from him, scowling toward the bar and dipping two fingers in a vest pocket.

"That won't cut it," Buffalo objected sharply. "Me and my old buddy Mike here's gonna have to settle this ourselves. He's gonna buy me a drink, or I'm gonna pound his Cajun head down so flat, it'll do me for a stool for mountin' my hoss!"

"I know, I know!" A red-headed whore with a mole on her chin ran up beside Buffalo, the purple feathers in her hair dancing around the big man's right ear. "Why don't you arm-wrestle for it? Two such big, brawny men as yourselves can certainly arm-wrestle!"

Sartain and Buffalo studied each other in angry silence.

"That sounds like a good idea," chirped the little bartender. "A good, fair way to settle this matter"—he swallowed, taking in the impressive sizes of both men—"without bustin' up my place."

A man to Sartain's right cleared his throat. "My money's on the bearded *hombre*. I got five dollars says he can take the younger man any day of the week!"

Another voice rose from the other end of the smoky, shadow-swept room. "I got a three-ounce nugget that says Sartain can take the mossyhorn!"

Then the others jumped up, waving greenbacks or gold pokes or fistfuls of coins, and a few minutes later it was agreed that the redhead, Arliss Dupree, would hold the bets. As Arliss strode about the room, taking money and writing names on a note pad, Sartain and Buffalo stood at the bar, facing each other, glowering, upper lips curled.

When the pretty saloon girl had slapped the greenbacks on the bar top, announcing that all bets had been placed, the room grew silent once more.

Buffalo grinned at Sartain, who stood unmoving before him, and began untying the whang strings holding the right sleeve of his smoke-stained buckskin tunic closed. "What's the matter, Mike—yalla?"

Sartain raked his gaze from Buffalo to the saloon girl, who was staring up at him, eyes wide, lips slightly parted. Her well-filled corset rose and fell heavily. Sartain said shrewdly, "Winner gets a quarter of the kitty and a bottle of Royal Oaks."

The redhead glanced around the room. The other customers nodded, shrugged, or grumbled their agreement.

"What the hell, then?" Sartain snarled at his big friend.

He whipped off his pinto vest, slung it onto the bar, and rolled up his shirtsleeves. As he headed for a table, the men who'd been sitting there promptly gained their feet with drunken uncertainty and scrambled away with the same uncertainty, freeing their chairs.

"Ready to have your arm wrenched out of its socket, Buff?"

Buffalo doffed his ragged leather hat and plopped down in a chair across from Sartain. "Ready if you are, ya damn Loozy-anna sharpie!"

The challengers got comfortable, squirming around in their chairs and rolling the kinks out of their necks and shoulders. The other customers left their own chairs to scramble around Sartain and Buffalo. Both men eyed each other with barely restrained fury.

Finally, when they'd planted their right elbows on the scarred tabletop, which Arliss had efficiently toweled dry, they each got a good grip on the other's hand.

The room fell silent.

Distant thunder rumbled beyond the night-black windows. A lantern sputtered. Someone spat anxiously into one of the sand boxes haphazardly placed around the saloon. The redhead, obviously accustomed to such contests, appraised them both, making sure their free hands showed above the table, that neither concealed a pig sticker or a derringer, then laid both her own hands over the fighters' entangled fists.

"Good luck and giddyup, gents!"

Arliss lifted her hands away, and both fighters stiffened and locked eyes. One of the onlookers goosed the whore's ass. She flicked an angry hand at him, whispering, "Quit!" as she backed away toward the bar.

Neither Sartain's nor Buffalo's hand moved for nearly five minutes. Then Sartain's knuckles began sagging toward the table. When they'd gone halfway down, the Cajun bit his lower lip, the color rising in his sunburned cheeks, the old bayonet scar above his right eyebrow turning paper-white, and fought the hand back up. His right bicep bulged like a wheel hub through his shirtsleeve.

Swallowing, he bent Buffalo's ham-like paw down toward the table.

A devilish light flashed in Sartain's cobalt-blue eyes.

Buffalo's rugged features turned crimson. He glared at the Cajun, squinting one eye and groaning softly, his chair squeaking beneath his two-hundred-plus pounds. He bit his cheek as he fought Sartain's hand back up. They held there, deadlocked, glaring and sweating, for another ten minutes.

Outside, the storm rumbled louder. Somewhere in the town of Navajo Wells, a dog barked. Coyotes yipped in the hills.

The onlookers gaped at the fighters, taking occasional drags from stogies or cigarettes and intermittently sipping whiskey or beer. Otherwise, they were as still and quiet as pallbearers.

Back in the shadows a whore whispered to no one in particular, "They're going to grind each other's knuckles to *powder!*"

Someone told her to shut up. She glowered at him.

Buffalo's eyes widened, boring into Sartain's. "You son of a *bitch!*"

Lines spoked around Sartain's eyes as he balled one cheek with a lopsided grin. He canted his head, bent Buffalo's fist over to his left. Buffalo's head sagged sharply as Sartain drove the bearded man's knuckles into the table.

The room erupted with applause, cheers, and groans.

Men clapped Sartain on both shoulders, popped the cork on a bottle of Royal Oaks bourbon, and assured him that drinks were on them for the rest of the night. Others converged on the redhead, Arliss, who hiked herself onto the bar, crossed her legs importantly, grabbed the kitty, and began flipping through her notepad.

Buffalo, his right cheek resting on the tabletop, glared up at Sartain and raised his voice loudly enough for only his partner to hear. "It was your turn to lose, ya son of a bitch!"

Sartain smiled woodenly as one of the well-dressed gents pumped his hand. He said out of the side of his mouth, "Shut up, you horse's ass, and *maybe* I'll buy ya a drink."

Several hours later, when the last of the other customers had left the bar, Sartain leaned back in his chair. He dug his winnings out of his shirt pocket, flipped half onto the table amidst the dozen or so empty shot glasses and beer schooners.

"There's your cut, pard. Twenty-five dollars. Not bad for a slow Tuesday night."

Buffalo stuck his quirley stub between his lips and counted the small wad of bills, glowering across the table at Sartain. "It was your turn to lose, damn ya, Mike."

"Who cares who wins or loses as long as we make a little extra drinking money?"

" 'Cause I don't like lookin' weak. And that's how you made me look." The burly man leaned over the table toward Sartain, casting a furtive glance at the redheaded whore wiggling her fanny as she sponged off the bar top. *"Weak!"*

Sartain chuckled and stuck his half of the winnings back in his shirt pocket. "All right, all right. I was just gettin' you back for that water bucket trick you pulled on me back at the bunkhouse. Tell you what. You can win the next two times. I don't mind losin'. Some girls feel sorry for losers."

He canted his head toward the redhead. "Ain't that right, Marliss?"

"That's right, honey. But it's Arliss . . . and I set even more store by winners." She turned to give him a flirtatious grin. "You spendin' the night, Mike?"

Sartain grinned back at her. "With you, sweetheart. All night long. And, uh, thanks fer helpin' us out. I know it wasn't much of a take for ya, but me an' ole Buffalo find our little hornswogglin' routine cuts the boredom."

"When you spend six years in the cavalry, you'll do anything to cut the boredom," said Buffalo, throwing back his last whiskey shot.

"You two in the service together?" Arliss asked.

"Opposin' sides during the Fight Against Southern Rebellion," said Buffalo. "Me a blue-coat, him a mangy Reb. Then scouts at Fort Beckett over New Mexico way, off an' on."

"So what brought you to cattle wranglin'?"

"Boredom . . . for me, at least. Change o' pace for ole Mike." Buffalo sauntered toward the stairs at the back of the room. "I'll take leave o' you two lovebirds. See ya in the morn . . ."

Boots thumped on the boardwalk outside the saloon. The silhouette of a hatted head appeared over the batwings. A young man's voice said, "Would there be a Mister Sartain hereabouts?"

Arliss glanced at the Cajun still leaning back in his chair. He glanced at Buffalo, then brought the front legs of his chair back down to the floor, edged his hand toward the big, pearl-gripped, silver-plated LeMat revolver thonged on his right thigh.

"Who wants to know?"

The batwings squawked. Boots raked the puncheons and spurs chinged as the short, slender figure entered the saloon, dragging his pant cuffs.

A kid with long, stringy hair. A bracket lamp shone on a charcoal smudge of a mustache mantling his upper lip. He wore a ratty shirt, vest, and a plainsman hat.

Mud spotted his baggy duck breeches. A Russian .44, positioned for the cross-draw, graced the worn holster on his left hip. Sartain had spent enough time around ranch hands the past half-year to know right off that this kid had mucked around in cow shit aplenty.

"Names Marty Calloway, Mr. Sartain. I just come from Black Bird Gulch Roadhouse. There's a man there. Says he needs to see you real bad." The kid hesitated. His voice quivered slightly. "If'n . . . if'n you're the one they call The Revenger, that is."

Chapter 2

Arliss gasped at the moniker mentioned by the kid.

The redhead looked in surprise at Sartain. "That you, Mike? You The *Revenger*?"

Sartain didn't go around announcing himself. He placed ads in newspapers when he felt inclined to hire out his guns as well as his razor-edged sense of right versus wrong, but he didn't use a trumpet to announce his comings and goings. He was wanted by the law for his vigilante ways, so he tried to keep as low a profile as possible for a man of his size and passionate, blue-eyed gaze.

"The Revenger—that'd be him," Buffalo said with a dry chuckle, standing at the bottom of the stairs, one hand on the newel post and casting his gaze toward the lanky kid at the front of the room. "Just hope you ain't a bounty hunter, sonny, or you'll be ruing this night!"

Arliss stood with her back to the bar, staring in awe at the tall, dark Sartain.

"Who is this *hombre* that wants to see me so late?" Sartain asked, still slouched in his chair, his right hand resting on the pearl grips of his fine LeMat.

Distant thunder clapped again, the storm unable to make up its mind where exactly it wanted to unleash its fury.

"Said his name was Ubek, er . . . somethin' like that. Said he needed to see you real bad. Said it was somethin' about someone named . . . umm . . ." The kid snapped his fingers to

17

jog his memory. "Phoenix."

"Phoenix?"

"Who's Phoenix?" Buffalo asked.

Sartain kept his eyes on the kid. "Describe this pilgrim for me."

The kid flushed slightly and looked around, as if looking for a picture of the man on a wall. "Uh . . . under six foot, I'd say. Very skinny. Dresses kinda dandified. Wears a thin beard, one o' them . . . whadoya call 'em . . . ?"

"Van Dykes?"

"Yeah, a Van Dyke beard. And small, round specs . . . sorta like a schoolmaster. Two guns." The kid glanced at the ceiling, squinting his eyes with concentration. "One with walnut grips, the other with pearl." He offered a wan, sheepish smile. "Purty poppers."

"Sounds like Ubek, all right. Why in the hell didn't he come to me?"

The kid hesitated, flushed. "Said he couldn't be seen in town," he explained, his eyes crinkling a little as he added wryly, "Law trouble."

"Law trouble—Jeff?" The description had sounded like Jeff. The law trouble did not. Sartain kicked his chair back, stood, and crossed the room to the boy. He towered over the lad, his shadow falling across the kid's skinny features. "How long's he gonna be there?"

"The rest of the night. Said he had to leave before sun-up."

"He pay you?"

The kid smiled, showing several half-rotten teeth and tobacco-blackened gums. "He said you'd probably throw some-thin' in . . . fer the information. Maybe . . . ?"

Sartain fished in his pocket and flipped the kid a gold piece. "Run on back to your spread, boy. You should've been in the mattress sack hours ago."

The kid pinched his hat brim. "Thanks, Mr. Sartain."

He turned and pushed through the doors. His spurs chinged. Tack squawked as the kid climbed onto a horse. Hoof thuds sounded, dwindling off in the damp night, distant lightning flickering above the silhouetted hill on the other side of Navajo Creek.

Sartain stared over the batwings at the black, starless sky.

Phoenix . . .

"I reckon I best go check it out first, partner." Sartain hadn't heard the burly oldster lumber up beside him.

Buffalo stared at him gravely. "You've made quite a few enemies over the years. Could be a trap."

"Not too many people know about Ubek . . . and Phoenix."

"Can't say as I've heard you mention them names. Just the same, wouldn't hurt for me to scout the roadhouse. Black Bird Gulch is known for its owlhoots and drygulchers." Buffalo patted Sartain's shoulder. "I'll ride in, have me a drink, ride out. Meet you on the trail. Give me a fifteen-minute head start."

He gave Sartain another pat, then pushed through the doors and crossed the wide dirt road toward the dark livery barn fronting the creek, abutted on both sides by corrals and parked wagons in various states of disrepair. Navajo Wells had been a boomtown at one time. No longer.

Only a handful of people remained—those who'd come to support the boom but were still too poor to head elsewhere.

Or didn't have anywhere else to go . . .

When Buffalo had led his saddled sorrel out of the livery barn, mounted up, and galloped south along the road, Sartain pushed out onto the saloon's rotten stoop and rolled a cigarette. He'd fired it with a lucifer, taking the first deep drag, when the batwings squawked behind him. Light footsteps sounded, and the smell of ripe cherries rose to his nostrils.

Sartain glanced left. Arliss appeared, wrapping a cloak about her slender shoulders. She stood beside him, her head rising only to his shoulder, and took the quirley from his fingers. She placed it between her lips, drew a shallow puff, then returned the cigarette to Sartain.

"Helluva night to be out." She shivered, holding the cloak taut about her shoulders. "A night like this, a man needs to curl up with a warm woman." She rubbed a shoulder against his. "A woman needs a warm man."

"I'd like nothin' better."

"Won't this keep till tomorrow? Black Bird Gulch is a dangerous place in the daylight. Night . . ." Arliss shuddered again.

"Don't look that way."

Arliss looked up at him, her brown eyes reflecting the saloon's wan lamplight pushing over the batwings. "That shavetail saddle tramp was spoutin' names from the past, wasn't he? A painful past."

Sartain glanced at her, offered the cigarette. "You a witch?"

"Don't take a witch to read a man's eyes." Arliss took the quirley, held it before her lips, and studied it for a time. "Nothin' like names from the past to call up dark haunts." She took another shallow drag off the cigarette and coughed. "Phoenix. Pretty name." She looked up at him, arching one brow. "Pretty woman?"

"How'd you know it's a woman?"

Arliss smiled bemusedly. "A man named Phoenix couldn't get you out on a night like this." Her smile broadened. "Not when you got me here, ready and willin'."

Sartain snorted.

"You really The Revenger, Mike? The one we hear so much about—rightin' wrongs for folks who can't right 'em themselves?"

"One an' the same."

"Well, I'll be damned."

"You just never know about folks." Sartain gave her a quick, affectionate squeeze and kissed her cheek, genuinely wishing he could stay with her this rainy night.

But those two names from his past had him on edge and feeling anxious.

"I'll be headin' out," he said as he dropped down the porch steps.

"Want the quirley?" Arliss asked behind him.

Sartain was striding toward the livery barn. "Nah, you finish it."

Thunder rumbled and lightning flashed. Rain began falling, lightly pelting the rutted, hard-packed street. In the hills, several coyotes yammered maniacally, as if to be heard above the storm.

Arliss huddled within herself and, letting the gusting wind rip the cigarette smoke from her lips as she turned back through the batwings, yelled, "You be careful, Mike!"

Sartain threw out an arm, then drew one of the barn's front doors open and stepped inside, where Buffalo had left a lamp burning on a stanchion post. The tall, dark-haired man took his time, saddling his lean, muscular buckskin stallion named Boss, his bushy brows ridged with thought and, as Arliss had guessed correctly, dark hauntings from his past.

When he'd unwrapped his yellow slicker from his bedroll, he donned it and crawled into the hurricane deck. He gigged Boss toward the front of the barn, leaned over to blow out the lamp, ducked through the door, and spurred the stallion into the rain-splattered street, the hooves making sucking sounds in the manure-laced mire.

He put the big stallion into a trot, sitting stiff-backed in the saddle, reins held high. When the ruined shacks of Navajo Wells receded behind him and he'd climbed the first rocky hill to the south, lightning flashed in earnest and thunder echoed around the high, rocky ridges to the east and west.

21

"He-yah!"

Lowering his head against the rain, Sartain gigged Boss into a ground-eating lope. Horse and rider couldn't ride fast for long, however, as the rain fell in sheets, sluicing off Sartain's hat and the horse's head and cutting gullies across the narrow, rocky wagon trace.

The rider cursed a blue streak when he found the trail cut off by a flooded arroyo, the muddy waters running too fast and deep between willow banks to risk traversing even atop a sure-footed stallion like Boss. It took him a good twenty minutes to find a shallow place to cross, another fifteen getting back to the main trail, which was as much a creek now as a passable wagon trace.

Thunder rumbled like the Navajo gods beating on giant war drums, and sharp witches' fingers of lightning cut the velvet sky silvered by the rain coming down like javelins.

Lightning flashed off the high, craggy peaks surrounding Black Bird Gulch, telling Sartain he'd reached his destination. Water roared in the creek beyond the cottonwoods and willows to his right.

As he steered the jittery stallion around a trail bend, a blur of orange light shone about fifty yards ahead. Cottonwoods, willows, and boulders fallen from the surrounding ridges made the trail a vague, black corridor.

Good place for an ambush.

As Sartain lifted a corner of his oil slicker above his holster, he touched his LeMat's pearl grips and wondered why Buffalo hadn't met him.

The horse slogged through the mud. Sartain swung his head from left to right, using the intermittent lightning flashes to scour the nooks and crannies for drygulchers. As the trail began opening ahead like a tunnel mouth, something obscured the lighted windows of the roadhouse—a branch hanging from a cottonwood. Probably broken off by a lightning strike or the wind.

As Sartain drew closer, it became more and more apparent that what hung from the cottonwood looming blackly on the right side of the trail was no broken branch. An icy knife stabbed his bowels.

He reined the horse up before the tree, stared up at the object. Lightning flashed and thunder cracked like simultaneous Howitzer blasts. The sudden, brief illumination showed Buffalo McCluskey hanging from an arching branch of the cottonwood, boots turning slowly three feet above the muddy trail.

Buffalo's face and beard were a wet, bloody mask, his hair curling straight down the sides of his head. The big man's eyes were open, staring down, his tongue protruding from the right corner of his mouth.

The hemp noose shone like a corded muffler around his neck.

The lightning had no sooner flashed than Sartain, shucking his Henry rifle from his saddle sheath, swung his right leg over the stallion's head and dropped straight down to the ground. His boots splashed mud around his shins. He flicked the back of his right hand against the horse's shoulder, turning the mount and sending it splashing back the way it had come.

Levering a fresh shell into the rifle's breech, Sartain bolted off the trail's left side, bulling through shrubs and stumbling over rocks. Whoever had shot Buffalo had hung him there for a reason. It'd be a good way to freeze a rider—to see his dead friend hanging from a branch like that, Buffalo's face obliterated by several well-placed rifle shots.

While Sartain's heart leap-frogged around inside his chest and his gut burned with the bile of rage, he'd been an army scout and tracker too many years to freeze up at the sight of a dead friend—even as good a friend as Buffalo. He wouldn't make himself an easy target.

He'd search out a target of his own . . .

Sartain hunkered down beside a boulder, glanced back toward the trail, where Buffalo's bulky silhouette slid this way and that, turning in the wind. He bunched his lips, fought back a curse, and flicked rain from his cheeks. He turned back to the roadhouse, crept to the edge of the yard, hunkered down beside another cottonwood, and rested the Henry across his thighs.

Before the low-slung, adobe-and-brick roadhouse, only one horse stood tethered to the hitchrack, hanging its head against the rain streaming off the porch's shake roof. Odd that the owner hadn't put the animal in the barn, out of the weather.

Unless the horse was Buffalo's sorrel. The mounts of the killer or killers could be in the corral on the other side of the yard. On the other hand, after killing Buffalo, they might have lit a shuck.

Only one way to find out.

Blinking water from his lashes, Sartain took another cautious glance around the yard, then sprinted out from the trees, tracing a zigzagging course in case someone were laying for him with a rifle. Ahead stood the rock ruins of an old Spanish trading post.

Sartain hunkered down behind a three-foot-high rock wall, took another glance around the yard, scrutinizing both the front and back corners of the roadhouse, then leapt the crumbling stones. He ran to the near wall of the roadhouse and pressed his back against the bricks just left of a lighted window.

The perfume of burning mesquite, ripped and torn by the wet wind, touched his nostrils.

Sartain edged a glance through the nearest window. Inside, four men in various styles of rough trail garb played cards around a table, their faces hidden by shadows. None looked even remotely like the saloon-owning businessman, Jeff Ubek.

Behind the bar, a burly man with a long, bib-like beard stood cutting up a javelina carcass with a stout cleaver. The bar was comprised of three whipsawed planks laid across beer kegs. The voices of the other men were a low murmur below the wooden plunks of the barman's cleaver.

Sartain pulled his head back from the window. Taking the rifle in both hands, he ducked under the window frame and slogged through the mud to the front. He stopped at the corner.

Before the hitchrack, Buffalo's sorrel gave a start, pulling back from the rack as it turned its gaze to Sartain and whickered.

Mike pressed a finger to his lips, shushing the beast. He met the sorrel's miserable gaze. *Who shot your master, Buck? And why?*

Where's Ubek—if he was ever here?

What about Phoenix?

Sartain wasn't getting any answers to his questions standing around out here, staring at the roadhouse's sagging front porch. Squeezing the Henry in both hands, he headed for the door.

CHAPTER 3

As Sartain stepped onto the half-rotten stoop fronting the roadhouse, he looked down at the rough pine boards.

Several sets of fresh mud tracks angled from the steps to the front door, glistening faintly in the lantern light falling from the front wall's single window.

Sartain followed the steps to the doorframe over which a beaded curtain had been closed to keep out the rain. He swept the curtain back with one hand, holding the Henry straight out from his right hip, and stared over the batwings.

Chop-chop-chop, came the solid reports of the bartender's cleaver. *Chop-chop-chop.* The man, spying Sartain in the doorway, halted the cleaver and stared at him, narrowing one eye. He was fat with long, cottony hair falling to his shoulders, while the top of his head was bald as a plucked chicken and of similar texture. The end of his long beard was stained with the blood of the javelina he was butchering.

The barman glanced at the four men sitting at a table on the other side of the narrow room. They seemed intent on their card game, none glancing at Sartain.

The apron looked back at the newcomer. His cheeks flushed, but he gave a casual nod. "Come on in outta the rain, feller. I got meat roastin' aplenty."

Sartain said nothing. Rifle aimed straight out from his hip, he stared at the card-players who still hadn't turned toward him, but toward whom the fresh, overlaid mud prints led.

"I always roast a pig on a rainy night. The weather tends to drive the prospectors in from their diggin's. I'll probably have a full house by noon tomorrow!" The apron smiled, but his small eyes remained edgy as they darted back and forth between Sartain and the card-players.

The Cajun canted his head slightly, slitting one eye.

Curious.

If these were indeed the crew that killed Buffalo, they seemed in no hurry to ventilate Sartain.

He cast a quick glance behind and around him, then lifted the Henry's barrel and stepped inside, dropping the curtain back into place behind him. The four at the table—a roughshod crew if he'd ever seen one—all wore pistols on their hips. From his angle, he could see only two faces—one Mexican with mare's-tail mustaches and a steeple-crowned *sombrero,* and a half-breed with belligerent blue eyes, long black hair, and a knife scar down the entire right side of his face.

None were Ubek.

Sartain stretched a glance to the rough-hewn second-floor balcony, the railing built from peeled pine poles. There appeared to be four or five small rooms up there. Ubek could be in one of those, but Sartain doubted he was here. Jeff was a New Orleans businessman, and these five just didn't seem cut from Ubek's fancy southern cloth.

Unless, like Buffalo, Jeff was dead . . .

"No food," Sartain said, resting the Henry's barrel over his right shoulder as he turned casually and sauntered to a table near the front of the room, keeping the ticking wood stove between himself and the tough-nut card players.

They wanted to play it like poker, so he'd play it like poker.

Let them make the first move . . .

"Bring a drink." Sartain set his Henry on the table and kicked out a chair. "Maybe a deck for some solitaire."

"Sure, sure." The bartender nodded, set his cleaver down, and scrubbed his hands on his bloody apron. "Whiskey and solitaire. Sounds like a good way to spend a stormy night."

As he brought the bottle and a glass, one of the men at the other table sang in a desultory, dissonant tone, "Oh, Susannah, I'm comin' home to you . . . to fornicate in your old pop's barn . . ." He spread his cards on the table. "There you go, Alejandro. There's that jack you was lookin' fer."

He laughed.

"Shut up, *gringo* pig, or I put out your other eye!"

As the bartender glanced warily at the gamblers, he set the bottle and shot glass on Sartain's table.

"No, you shut up, ya stinkin' bean-eater, and toss that gold thisaway!"

The winner of the hand guffawed, glancing casually between two of his compatriots and Sartain as he puffed the fat stogie in his teeth. When Sartain met the man's glance, the man dropped his one good eye to his own table and continued singing his nonsensical song.

The other hardcases threw down their cards, several groaning, the half-breed complaining there was only one whore in the place, and a skinny one at that . . .

The bartender stood before Sartain, rubbing his hands up and down on his apron and shuffling his weight from one foot to the other. "Uh . . ."

Sartain glanced up at the man. "Somethin' wrong?"

"Uh . . . well . . . I was hopin' maybe . . . you'd pay up front?"

Sartain glanced at the hardcases, one of whom was shuffling the cards, then returned his gaze to the apron. Obviously, the man didn't think Sartain would be around to pay him later.

The Cajun smiled, stretching his lips back from his strong, white teeth, then casually reached into his shirt pocket. He flipped two gold pieces onto the table. "Leave the bottle."

The man nodded, tried another nervous smile, then shambled back behind the bar, where he dropped the coins in his cashbox and resumed chopping the javelina.

When Sartain raked his gaze from the bartender to pour a drink from the bottle—it was likely brewed out back with snake venom and panther piss, but he doubted the barman stocked his favorite brand of tangleleg, Royal Oaks bourbon—he caught the half-breed's furtive glance. The big breed looked away quickly, flushing slightly, and Sartain calmly picked up the bottle and splashed whiskey into his shot glass.

Somewhere upstairs, a woman laughed softly, intimately.

"Those whoremongers are havin' a real good time," said one of the hardcases as he threw several coins onto the table. "I'll see your five, Cayuse, and I'll raise you fifteen."

"Christ, McDade, where in hell you get this kinda money?"

"Some men work fer a livin', you lazy bean-eater."

Chuckles.

The man called Cayuse cussed and said something Sartain couldn't hear.

Sartain sipped his whiskey and kicked out the chair beside him, crossed his boots on it.

How did these men know about Ubek . . . and Phoenix . . . ?

Why did they want Sartain dead? Maybe they didn't. Was there someone else here, separate from this crew?

The Cajun took another sip of his drink and absently shuffled his cards. He had a feeling he'd find the answers to his questions real soon . . . if he kept his mouth shut. Keeping the card players in the upper periphery of his vision just beyond the smoky wood stove, he laid out a game. The Henry repeater lay across the table's far right corner, in front of the whiskey bottle and shot glass, but within easy reach for when he needed it.

Outside, the thunder rumbled infrequently. In the windows to Sartain's right, lightning flashed once every five minutes or so. Upstairs, the woman groaned with pleasure as bedsprings squawked.

The bartender had raked the chopped meat into a stew kettle and sat back on a high chair, rolling a cigarette. His eyes continued to dart to the hardcases' table, his pupils dilated. His hands shook as he built his smoke.

Sartain had just set down a greasy eight of clubs when one of the outlaws made a soft popping noise with his lips. Someone else snickered. The white man called McDade—red hair, bowler hat with a feather in it, and long, bushy sideburns—elbowed him hard.

"Ow!" raked out the man who'd made the popping sounds, grabbing his arm and choking down a laugh.

Sartain shuttled his glance back to his cards. Holding the deck in one hand, a single card in the other, he stared hard at the four of clubs. His jaws tightened, and he fought back the burn welling up from his gut.

Buffalo was dead, hanging by his neck outside in the storm from a mangy tree, and the hardcases were laughing about it.

Not for long . . .

Sartain snarled as he flipped down the card. In the corner of his right eye, something moved. He turned his head that way. An arm had snaked down from an unused chimney hole above the bar. The fist of the arm gripped a Schofield .44. The barrel was angled toward Sartain.

The Cajun threw himself forward, slapping his left cheek to the table and making the cards bounce as flames stabbed from the belching six-shooter.

Bang! Bang! Bang-Bang!

The reports rocked the room as the slugs sizzled about Sartain's head like lightning, one plunking into the wall behind him, the other three chewing wedges from the table on either side of his splayed hands.

One of the hardcases threw his head back, guffawing. Sartain kicked his chair back against the wall. Clawing his LeMat from its holster, he flung himself forward and dropped to one knee.

The shooter had withdrawn most of his arm from the hole and was trying to work the pistol out, as well. The pistol had gotten stuck on the edge of the hole, and the hand frantically jerked it. The hardcase on the other side of the wood stove was still laughing when Sartain fired three quick rounds into the ceiling around the hole.

The laughter stopped abruptly.

Upstairs, a man cried, *"Aye, caramba!"*

The hand in the hole released the .44, which tumbled onto the bar. There was a loud thud as a body hit the floor above, and the warped wooden slats around the hole shuddered, sending dust sifting over a large jar of pickled pig's feet at the bar's right end.

Sartain didn't see the thick, red blood dribbling down through the bullet holes in the ceiling.

Shouts rose to his left as all five hardcases moved at once, throwing their chairs back and bounding to their feet, several twisting toward Sartain as they filled their hands with iron.

Sartain swung the gun toward the crowd and emptied it, one shot flying errant while one clipped an ear and the other plunked through the middle of the half-breed's chest. The half-breed stumbled straight back from the table, dropping his arms and his chin to stare dumbfounded at the hole in his striped wool poncho.

At the same time, Sartain dodged two bullets as he slipped the LeMat back into its holster and grabbed the Henry off the table.

The whiskey bottle shattered as Sartain thumbed the repeater's hammer back and again dropped to a knee. Two men fired at him at once, the bullets slicing the air on both sides of his head to shatter an unlit bracket lamp on the wall behind him.

As the redhead in the feathered bowler extended a long-barreled Starr .44, gritting his teeth around a brown-paper cigarette, Sartain fired two more shots and then levered the Henry quickly before diving left.

McDade's slug whistled through the air where Sartain had been standing, and crashed into the same bracket lamp that had been hit before.

Sartain's shots blew the top of one man's head off while plunking into a chair another man had thrown himself behind. Sartain rolled off a shoulder, took quick aim at a shadow sliding through the heavy powder smoke, and fired.

"Christ!" came the bellow as a big man in a deerskin vest grabbed his ruined shoulder.

A gun popped twice from the other side of the wood stove, and Sartain kicked down a table to absorb both shots.

"Sartain, I presume?" shouted an Irish-accented voice that likely belonged to the redhead. "No way out of here, boy-o!"

Shadows moved through the gun smoke, boots pounding the puncheons, spurs jangling raucously. Three guns thundered—a rifle and two pistols. The near-simultaneous flashes spread out across the room before Sartain.

The Cajun ducked as the slugs slammed into the table, one punching through the wood and slicing a neat furrow across the top of his right shoulder.

Gritting his teeth against the pain, Sartain raised his head, snaked the Henry's barrel over the top of the table, and fired through the smoke, two shots plunking into the floor and a table, the third spanging off the iron stove with an ear-ringing clang.

"Got you now, ye son of a bitch!" the Irishman's voice punctuated the shots.

"Who are you and why'd you kill Buffalo?" Sartain bolted to his feet, fired blindly into the heavy, pungent powder smoke to his left, and sprinted forward.

Two shots barked at him, pounding the front wall. A third clipped his neck. As he neared the bar and lofted himself into a dive, a bullet seared across his left thigh.

"Shit!" he complained as he flew over the top of the bar, kicking the jar of pickled pig's feet, which plunged from the bar and landed with a strident roar, instantly filling his nostrils with the smell of pork and vinegar brine.

He landed hard on his left shoulder and hip, pain lancing him. He twisted around, looked to his right. The barman was cowering on hands and knees, looking sour.

" 'Preciate the warnin'!" Sartain exclaimed sarcastically, clamping a hand over his bullet-burned thigh.

The barman just covered his ears and shook his head fatefully, as though awaiting the inevitable.

CHAPTER 4

The Irishman's voice boomed from the other side of the bar: "Sartain?"

"What?"

"Yep, that's him, boys!" the Irishman bellowed, laughing.

Sartain yelled over the top of the bar, "You chicken-livered sons o' bitches got me at a disadvantage!" He pumped a fresh round into his Henry's action.

The Irishman only laughed and said, "And we're about to kick you out with a cold, shovel, Mr. Revenger, sir!" He laughed again.

Sartain shifted his knees to avoid pickled pig brine. The bald, bib-bearded barman sat with his back to the wall, one leg curled beneath his butt, his giant belly and chest heaving, his terrified face streaked with sweat.

"Sorry, mister," he groaned. "They said if I warned you, they'd kill me and burn my place, kill my whore."

"No need to apologize," Sartain raked through gritted teeth, pushing himself to his knees while pressing a fist against his wounded thigh. "They're probably *still* gonna kill ya and burn your place." He winced. "Killers of this stripe don't leave witnesses."

The barman groaned.

Sartain clutched the Henry in both hands and edged a look over the bar. Three figures moved slowly toward him about six feet apart.

They stopped suddenly. Guns flashed and popped.

Sartain ducked back behind the bar as the shots chewed up wood from the bar planks and pelted the back wall with slivers.

Sartain pressed his back to the bar, easing his butt to the floor, clutching the Henry straight up and down before him. Sweat streamed down his cheeks, dripped off his curly, black hair, and speckled the floor.

The shooting stopped.

The silence that followed was nearly deafening.

Sartain was breathing hard, his chest rising and falling sharply. He held his breath and pricked his ears, listening.

Above the ringing in his head, he could hear soft foot thuds. The three remaining bushwhackers were moving toward the bar, their spurs ringing faintly, broken glass crunching beneath their boots.

Sartain glanced at the bib-bearded barman. The Cajun held a finger to his lips and then, taking his Henry in one hand, began crawling slowly on hands and knees toward the end of the bar nearest the front of the place. He winced with the effort of trying to move as quickly as he could while also trying to make little noise and not give away his position.

"Hey, boyo," said the Irishman, the man's voice cleaving the room's heavy silence. "Where are ya, boyo?" Grit continued crunching softly under slow-stepping boots. "Why don't you just come out of there, now? Make this a whole lot easier on all of us . . ."

Sartain gained the end of the bar. He peered around the corner toward the main drinking hall. He could see none of the three from this vantage.

When he slid his gaze around the bar's front corner, he saw all three just as the Irishman, apparently anticipating Sartain's move, swung his two pistols in his direction.

The Cajun jerked his head back around the bar's front corner as the Irishman's pistols thundered, the slugs loudly hammering the corner of the bar and flinging slivers in all directions. After the Irishman's first two shots, Sartain bounded off his boot heels and launched himself into a dive straight out into the main drinking hall.

He hit the floor on his left shoulder and hip, firing the Henry from over his belly.

Boom! Boom-Boom! Boom-Boom! Boom!

As Sartain pumped and fired, pumped and fired, he watched the three gunmen twist around and holler and fly back, screaming, shooting their pistols into the ceiling or into the front of the bar or the floor. By the time the Cajun's Henry's hammer had clicked benignly on an empty chamber, all three men were down and writhing, groaning.

Smoke wafted as thickly as gathering storm clouds.

One of the writhing men kicked over a chair that fell with a bang resembling another pistol shot.

Peering through the smoke, Sartain spied movement on the stairway rising to the second floor at the rear of the room, just beyond the bar. He rolled behind an overturned table as the man on the stairs extended a pistol in one hand. The pistol popped, driving a slug into the far side of the table. Tossing his empty Henry aside, Sartain clawed the LeMat from its holster, thumbed back the hammer, and extended the gun over the rounded edge of the table.

The man on the stairs—his unbuttoned shirt hanging open to reveal his longhandle top, a shell belt and holster hooked over his left shoulder—triggered his pistol once more. At the same time, Sartain's LeMat leaped and roared in his outstretched hand.

He fired twice more, saw the shooter fall back against the rail, stretching his lips back from his teeth, and then twisted around and ran awkwardly back up the stairs. Sartain emptied the pistol at the man, but his slugs only hammered the railing and the wall on the other side of it, blowing out chunks of adobe.

The shooter disappeared up the stairs. Sartain could hear him running back toward him on the second story. The Cajun gained his feet. The bullet crease across the outside of his left thigh burned and barked at him. Blood bubbled out of the cut in his tweed trouser leg.

He cursed as he quickly emptied the spent shell casings from the top-break LeMat and replaced them with fresh from his shell belt. When all the chambers were filled, he closed the gun, spun the cylinder, and strode toward the stairs, half-dragging his left foot and sucking sharp breaths through his teeth.

To his right, the barman peeked over the top of the mahogany, his eyes wide.

"Sorry for the mess, *amigo.*"

The barman's eyes widened.

Sartain spied movement to his left. He turned to see the Irishman using a chair to regain his feet. The man's shirt was bloody, and blood dribbled from between his lips. His eyes were opaque, the light dying in them, as he heaved himself off the chair.

Sartain swung the LeMat toward the snarling man. The gun barked hoarsely. The bullet plunked into the middle of the Irishman's forehead. Blood and goo sprayed out the back of his head. The Irishman nodded his brainless head as though in vigorous agreement with something Sartain had just said, and sagged back off the table to the floor, boots quivering.

Sartain continued to the stairs. He used the rail as he climbed, keeping his left hand clamped over his bloody left thigh. At the top he edged a look down a dingy hall lit by two guttering candle lanterns, one bracketed to each wall. He stretched his gun hand out in front of him, along the right wall.

Something moved on the hall's left side, in a half-open doorway. The Cajun shunted the Colt toward the girl who'd just poked half her head, a bare, tan shoulder, and one round, brown, fear-bright eye into the hall. That eye snapped wider when it found the LeMat. The girl jerked her head back inside the room with a muffled gasp.

At the same time, a man leaped out of the room directly across the hall from the girl's. Sartain pulled his own head back into the stairwell as the killer's pistol spoke twice. In the hall's close confines, the reports sounded liked twin howitzer blasts. Sartain jerked his pistol into the hall and fired once as the man leaped across the hazy, smoky corridor in a brown blur of fast motion, and disappeared inside the girl's room.

The girl screamed shrilly. There were foot thuds and sounds of frantic jostling.

Sartain cursed, ran down the hall, only slightly hobbling on his bad leg, and used his good foot to kick the door open. As the door slammed off the inside wall and lurched back toward Sartain, the Cajun stopped it with his right boot as he aimed the LeMat straight out from his shoulder, tightening the tension in his trigger finger.

He held fire. His heart thudded.

"I'll kill her!" the killer taunted him, grinning.

He was a tall, slender Mexican with short curly brown hair and a thick mustache drooping down both corners of his mouth. Another small patch of hair sprouted beneath his lower lip.

He held his cocked pistol to the girl's left temple. She was also Mexican. She wore only a sheer, cream wrap. The killer held his free arm tightly around her shoulders, holding her fast against his gun barrel.

"I'll kill her!" he repeated, desperately.

In the heavy silence beneath the rain's patter against the window flanking the killer, another pattering sounded. Sartain glanced down to see blood dripping down the outside of the right leg of the killer's deerskin pants and onto his brown boot adorned with gaudy white stitching over the pointed toe.

Drip, drip, drip. They came as regularly as the ticking of a clock. Each drop beaded on the boot's worn leather and rolled off to the floor, staining the rug behind the girl's delicate, bare right foot that shifted position as she struggled against the killer's savage grip.

The killer showed his teeth beneath his mustache. "I will kill her!" He pressed the barrel of his cocked revolver tighter to the girl's head.

She groaned. Tears glazed her chocolate eyes. She gritted her teeth as the killer clamped his hand around her shoulders even more tightly.

"Don't kill her," Sartain said. His heart was drumming in his ears.

"Kindly ease the hammer down, *amigo*. Toss the pistol on the bed, or I will splatter this pretty little *puta's* brains all over you!"

The girl's head was tipped back against the killer's chin. Her breasts rose and fell sharply as she breathed. Her flat belly expanded and contracted and her small, delicate bare feet shifted slightly on the rug, looking delicate and fragile against the killer's leather boots.

Sartain looked at her face. She stared back at him, brown eyes reflecting the umber glow of two lit lanterns. She couldn't have been twenty. Her skin was fine and smooth, like polished ironwood. Her hair, pulled back in a loose chignon, was the rich brown of roasted coffee beans.

She hardened her jaws and said, "Keel him, *Senor*! Send him to *El Diablo*!"

The killer narrowed an eye at Sartain and stretched his lips a little farther back from his teeth.

"Hold on," the Cajun said, depressing his LeMat's hammer

and raising the barrel. He tossed the pistol onto the bed, where it bounced and lay still.

"Let her go," Sartain urged the man.

The killer continued to hold the girl taut against him, pressing the revolver against her temple. *"Si,"* he said. "It would be a shame to kill one so young and pretty. I could get another round out of her tonight, maybe, no?"

He removed his cocked pistol from the girl's temple and thrust it toward Sartain, narrowing his right eye as he aimed at the Cajun's head. "Say good-bye to life, *amigo!*"

"No!" the girl shrieked, twisting around and throwing herself against the gunman's right arm.

The pistol exploded. Instinctively, Sartain ducked as the bullet plunked into the wall several feet to his right.

"*Puta* bitch!" the man snarled, using his left arm to fling the girl away from him.

She screamed as she flew against a dresser.

Sartain took one running step toward the bed and lunged off his heels. The Mexican gunman fired two more rounds, both slugs hammering the wall and knocking the cross of Saint Guadalupe off the wall over a chest of drawers.

Sartain landed belly down on the bed. Bouncing, he grabbed the LeMat and rolled to his right as another of the killer's slugs chewed into the bed after nipping the Cajun's left elbow. Sartain rolled onto his belly and extended the LeMat toward the shooter, who had turned around and was hurling himself through the window.

Sartain fired twice quickly as he glimpsed only the man's boots being drawn through the window after the rest of him had disappeared. Both the Cajun's slugs flew wild into the dark, rainy night from which came the thud of the Mexican's body landing on something outside.

Sartain fought his way off the bouncing bed, ran to the

window. Slanting down and away from him was a brush roof glistening in the steady rain, turning blue with sporadic lightning flashes. Sartain aimed the pistol out the window and slid it this way and that, looking for his target.

"Where the hell did you go, you son of a bitch?"

A shadow bolted out from under the awning—the silhouette of a horseback rider. Lightning flashed, limning the rangy Mexican riding Buffalo's sorrel. The man was hunkered low in the saddle. He was beating the horse's right hip with his holstered pistol and cartridge belt.

Sartain steadied his aim, fired. The rider glanced over his shoulder toward the roadhouse.

Lightning flashed again. Sartain triggered the LeMat and was about to engage the shotgun shell but held fire. Horse and rider had galloped into the chaparral beyond the yard, out of sight and out of range.

Behind them there was only the muddy, puddle-dimpled yard glistening with each flash of lightning, lurching with each thunderclap.

Sartain lowered his smoking pistol, the odor of cordite peppering his nose. Quickly, the chill, damp breeze erased it. The Cajun wrapped his left hand around the bottom of the window frame, dug his fingertips into the half-rotten wood. He gritted his teeth as he stared off in the direction in which one of Buffalo's bushwhackers had run off in the night.

"*Senor.*"

Sartain jerked around. The girl gasped, startled, and stepped back.

"You are bleeding," she said.

"Any more of 'em?"

She shook her head. "There is one more dead across the hall. The one you shot through the ceiling."

Sartain sighed.

"You are bleeding, *senor.*"

The Cajun looked down at his left leg. Blood was oozing out from behind the bandanna he'd tied around it.

"My partner got it a lot worse," Sartain said, holstering the LeMat and wrapping his hand gently around the girl's arm. "Are you all right, *senorita*?"

The girl nodded. "This is a crazy place, *mi amigo.* I am accustomed to such eruptions." She narrowed her eyes and hardened her jaws. Her brown eyes flashed beautifully. "You should have shot him when you had the chance."

"Oh, I'll get another chance," Sartain said, brushing his thumb across her chin and winking. "You can bet the seed bull on that!"

The girl nodded once, gazing up at the tall, blue-eyed Cajun appraisingly. "I bet you will at that, *amigo.* But, first, let me tend your leg . . . and make you as comfortable as I can on such a cold and deadly night, eh?"

CHAPTER 5

He woke just after dawn. While Esmeralda slept, curled on her side, snoring very softly, the Cajun gathered his clothes and dressed. He loaded his pistol and his Henry repeater and then he went downstairs.

The barman, Chico, sat in the misty dawn shadows, head down on a table. Around him were several piles of scrip and specie, all of the dead men's pistols and their rifles stacked across the arms of a near chair.

On the table, too, was a half-empty whiskey bottle.

The barman was snoring loudly, evenly, pooching out his lips with each exhalation. He did not awaken as Sartain walked past him on the balls of his boots.

The Cajun went out to the barn, found a pick and a shovel, and used both to dig a grave in a relatively high spot between two washes a hundred yards behind the barn. The rain had loosened the sandy soil, making an easier job of it than it otherwise would have been.

When he'd deemed the grave deep enough, Sartain returned to the barn. He saddled Boss and then he back-and-bellied Buffalo belly down over the saddle. He led the horse and his dead friend out behind the barn to the fresh grave, and gentled Buffalo, wrapped in a saddle blanket, down inside.

Grimly, the Cajun shoveled dirt back into the grave, rounded the top, and arranged large rocks over it and along the edges, to hold the carrion-eaters at bay. He'd have fashioned a cross, but there was no time for that. Maybe he'd return at some other time to pay his respects and put the finishing touch on the mossyhorn's grave.

For now, with the sun beginning to climb, he was burning daylight. He needed to get after the rangy Mexican while the man's trail was still relatively fresh despite the rain. Carrying the pickax and the shovel over his shoulder, he led his horse around to the front of the barn. When he'd returned the digging implements to the little side shed in which he'd found them, he walked back outside and closed the doors. He heard soft footfalls on wood and turned to see Esmeralda descending the steps of the roadhouse's front gallery.

She walked across the yard toward Sartain, holding a croaker sack by its rope-tied neck in one hand, a long, slim cigar in the other. The sun was up now, slanting its buttery light into the soggy roadhouse yard. It flashed blue in Esmeralda's black, freshly brushed hair.

She wore the same thin wrap she'd been wearing last night. It did little to conceal her. The cones of her brown breasts jostled as she walked in a pair of worn moccasins that were a lovely contrast to the fineness of the rest of her.

She stopped beside Boss, held up the sack to Sartain. "Food for the trail. Burritos made from beans and spiced chicken. And a bottle, as well. Chico's best stuff." She smiled. "He won't mind."

"Thanks."

"Good luck to you, Miguel," she said, using the Spanish translation of his first name, as she'd done last night in her room. "I hope you find your friend's killer."

"I intend to find out the what and why of it, too." He hadn't recognized any of the dead killers, had no idea why they set the trap for him or how they'd gotten the names of his friend, Phoenix and Jeff.

He stepped up to the girl, smiled down at her. "Thanks for the grub and everything else."

"My pleasure, *amigo.*"

Sartain took the girl in his arms and kissed her. He gave her a long, passionate kiss. He had a feeling it was the last bit of real tenderness he'd be displaying for a long time, and he wanted to enjoy it, as he'd enjoyed her the bittersweet night before.

"You kiss a *puta* on the lips?" she said, blinking, startled.

"Best lips I ever tasted." He winked at her.

She smiled, sandwiched his long, tapering, unshaven cheeks in her hands. "You are a lover, Miguel Sartain." She narrowed her eyes with a grave befuddlement. "But you are a killer, too. *Hombre de la Venganza.* The Revenger."

"You know?"

"Who has not heard? I certainly never expected him to be a man like you."

"This life is full of surprises, *senorita,*" Sartain said, pecking her cheek and then toeing a stirrup. He cheeked Boss as he stepped into the saddle and settled his weight.

"I put some extra bandages in the bag," Esmeralda said. "A tin of poultice made from prickly pear blossoms and bacanora. My mother's concoction."

"*Gracias.*"

"Stop again sometime," she urged with a smile.

"Wild horses couldn't keep me away."

Sartain pinched his hat brim to the girl and then "Tsucked" Boss into a lope, brushing his fingers across his holstered LeMat as he headed in the same direction the rangy Mexican had.

CHAPTER 6

Don Alonzo de Castillo woke to find himself lying in a wedge of lemon morning light pushing through one of the tall, arched windows of his sleeping quarters at Hacienda de la Francesca, in the foothills of the verdant Olvidado Mountains in northern Sonora, Old Mexico.

Don de Castillo blinked, lifted his regal, bearded head, groaned, and then eased his skull, with the tender brain residing inside like a violently beating heart, back down on his silk-covered pillow.

The don could hear the blacksmith, Rafael Loera, wielding his infernal hammer against his infernal anvil. The blacksmith shop at Hacienda de la Francesca was positioned back with the stables, a hundred yards from the sprawling main *casa,* of which Don de Castillo, *haciendado* of Hacienda de la Francesca, was *patron.* But this morning Loera and his heavy steel hammer and his stout iron anvil sounded loud enough to be stationed at the foot of the don's bed.

Clanggg! Clangggg! Clang-Clangggg!

"Oh, Mother Mary, please have mercy on this poor devil's soul!" the don groaned, pressing his beringed fingers hard against his age-spotted temples, trying to quell the hammering heart in his head.

Nearby, a girl grunted.

The don turned his head to the left. A perfectly round, naked brown bottom faced him from only a foot and a half away. The

46

don smiled, his salt-and-pepper bearded cheeks climbing up under his coffee-brown eyes.

Despite Loera's ceaseless hammering, despite all the Spanish brandy and Cuban cigars the don had consumed the night before, he felt better just staring at this girl's bottom.

The sweet bottom of the seventeen-year-old daughter of Don De Angelo, who owned the bank in Nogales, though of course there would have been no bank without Don de Castillo and Hacienda de la Francesca. That's why the girl, young enough to be the Don's granddaughter, was here. She'd been here for the past two months as the Don's "special guest."

Of course the arrangement, while sanctioned by the girl's father, was a sacrilege, and Don de Castillo had heard that the girl's mother had made a special trip to visit a Catholic cardinal in Mexico City to somehow get her daughter's sins expunged.

But what was the De Angelo family to do?

Don de Castillo and his twenty-odd gun hands pretty much had this corner of Mexico and even a good bit of southern Arizona in a stranglehold. He was the richest, most powerful man within several thousand square miles, and even the territorial governor of Arizona was at Del Castillo's beck and call. The governor of Sonora would have been, as well, if he didn't turn and run every time he heard the don's name spoken.

Yes, de Castillo was the wealthiest man in many a mile.

So why, behind the pounding in his head from too much brandy and mescal and the grating in his throat and lungs from too many cigars, did he feel so hollowed out?

Empty.

Sad beyond his ability even to describe it.

The don stared at the girl. But then she became another girl whose memory haunted him, and he felt that razor-tipped stiletto twist in his guts once more, as it had been doing regularly for the past two months.

The don groaned. His pain and sorrow acquired an edge nearly as sharp as that of the stiletto in his belly. Flaring his nostrils and hardening his jaws, he shoved his head forward and sank his teeth into the girl's plump right buttock.

"*Ohh!*" the girl cried, instantly lifting her head from her pillow and pulling her bottom away from the don's mustachioed lips. Flabbergasted by such poor treatment, she blinked at the don through the tangled screen of her chocolate curls, hiked a leg and rubbed at the marks of de Castillo's teeth, and said, "That hurt, *el patron!*"

"Oh, I hurt you, *chiquita*?" The don grinned savagely at the girl, though he rolled his words in sugar. "Please forgive me. I just woke feeling frisky, that's all."

He leaned forward. The girl jerked away, but he held her supple thigh with one hand and pressed his lips to the bite mark he'd left in her rump. He wasn't sure why he felt such savage urges toward De Angelo's simple-minded, full-busted, and round-hipped daughter, but he did. He supposed abusing the poor child was his way of getting back at the female who'd broken his heart, since she was no longer here to take the punishment herself.

Another woman, if only a silly girl, would have to do.

And for now, that "woman" was banker de Angelo's empty-headed but pretty and voluptuous daughter, Isabel.

"Lie down," the don said, pushing up onto his knees. "I will make it up to you, *chiquita.*"

The girl gazed fearfully into the don's eyes, and he tried to keep his voice pleasant as he said with a little more steel this time, "Lie down, *chiquita*. I told you—I woke frisky, and I am going to have fun with you now, whether you like it or not."

"But, Don," the girl said, crumpling her eyes, "I am only just awake. I was sound asleep!"

"*Chiquita!*"

"Yes, Don de Castillo," the girl said with a trill in her voice as she lay belly down on the silk sheets, placing her hands on either side of her head and resting her cheek against her pillow.

The don rolled onto her. He toiled, though his heart was not in it.

Why did anger and frustration and the compulsion to inflict pain always arouse him more than pure lust ever had?

Sometime later, the girl sobbed, her shoulders jerking. "Don Alonzo, why do you insist on treating me so poorly?" She cried into her hands.

She sounded so pathetic that the don almost knew the strange, unfamiliar feeling of sympathy. Staring down at her, he sighed.

"*Si*, why?"

De Castillo leaned forward and placed his mustached lips against the girl's back. She shuddered at his touch. That rankled him fleetingly, but still his marginal sympathy remained.

"I swear, sweet Isabel, I am a monster sometimes. To compensate for my savageness, I will send you into San Luis with Jacinta later, in my own private carriage. She will be instructed to treat you, on my behalf, to the finest dress that *Senor* Rincon can sew especially for your beautiful body."

He leaned forward and whispered in the girl's ear. "How does that sound, my poor, shabbily treated Isa?"

She rolled her eyes up to his, studying him. For a time her expression was skeptical, but as she worked his words through her simple head, her mouth corners lifted. They lifted still farther, and then she rose up onto her knees and threw her arms around the don's neck.

"*Muchas gracias, el patron!* Oh, *muchas gracias*! *Senor* Rincon is the finest tailor in all of northern Sonora . . . and so expensive!"

"Not expensive enough for you, my dear," the don said, placing his hands on the girl's own hands on his neck and smiling into her eyes. What was it about her doll-like face with her black eyes and eggshell whites that made him want to smack it?

She opened her mouth, but before she could say anything more, three hard knocks sounded on the stout oak door of the don's sleeping quarters. The don scowled when he heard his sister say in her low, reproving tone, "Alonzo. Open the door if you're decent!"

"*Mierda,*" the don groaned. "What have I done to deserve such a sad start to the day?"

He pecked the still-smiling girl on the forehead and then crawled gingerly down from the bed.

The knock came again—four of them, louder.

The don was looking around his sprawling, tile-floored room for his red silk robe with the fur-trimmed collar. "I heard you, Jacinta. I am trying to make myself decent so that I can come to the door!"

His harsh baritone echoed around the cave-like room with its heavy wooden furniture and brocade- or velvet-upholstered armchairs. Sun filtered through the windows, but there was a steel-like mountain chill in the air. He wished he'd instructed one of the maids to build a fire, though Jacinta privately made his quarters off-limits to the help when the don was "entertaining."

The bitter old crone . . .

When de Castillo found his robe on the long leather couch angled in front of the cold fireplace, he wrapped it around his shoulders, tied it at the waist, slipped his feet into a pair of fleece-lined slippers, and scuffed over to the door. He opened the door to find his sister, only a few years younger than he, standing in the hall, scowling at him.

"Yes, yes, what is it, Jacinta," the don said, wincing against another dull throb in his head. "You know you don't need my permission to have the houseboys whipped."

That was a joke. She was always having the houseboys whipped, and she never consulted the don about it.

"You look like hell."

"I feel like hell. And I was about to drift back to sleep when you so rudely knocked. Now what is it?"

The severe-featured Jacinta, her gray-brown hair pulled back into a large, prim bun atop her regal head, leaned a little to one side to peer over the don's shoulder into his room. When her eyes found the girl on the bed, she set her thin lips together, exhaled through her long, slender, bulb-tipped nose, and jerked her head and flared her nostrils condemningly.

"Scoundrel," she said, her long, slanted, coffee-brown eyes drawing up severely at the corners. She clenched her arthritic hands in front of her flat belly. "She is young enough to be your granddaughter. You will burn in hell, Alonzo. I promise you."

"Yes, but it will have been worth every minute," the don lied, giving his sister a jeering grin. "Now, what is it? Be quick, Jacinta—I had a long night, and I wish to catch a few more winks!"

Jacinta canted her head to one side, indicating three of the don's men standing at the far end of the hall lit by open, arched windows facing a flagstone-paved courtyard in which a stone fountain chuckled near a cracked statue of Mother Mary. The men were all shifting around uncomfortably, their high-crowned Sonora hats in their gloved hands. The guns on their hips and thonged on their thighs glistened in the saffron light washing over the *casa's* tile-roofed eastern wing.

The don frowned. "What is it?"

His *Segundo,* Ernesto Cruz, took one step toward the don, turning his hat in his hands. His mustaches dangled down the sides of his mouth and chin. "It is Franco, *Patron!*" He turned sideways and canted his head in the direction of the main yard. "He rides in! A half mile away . . ."

"Alone?"

"Only two of the *vaqueros* are with him. They must have seen him as he crossed the *hacienda*. They sent one man back to alert us. Franco is carrying a bullet. He rides very slowly."

The don felt his heart lurch in his chest. He scowled. "*Alone? Are you sure?* Of the six I sent out, only *he* returns?"

Cruz nodded darkly. "So it appears, Don de Castillo."

The don threw an arm up. "I'll meet you in the yard in five minutes!"

As he turned back to the open door of his room, he stopped. Jacinta was staring at him, amused lines crinkling up from her severely slanted eyes and radiating like spokes from the sides of her thin-lipped mouth.

"Six men and only one returns," the woman said in jeering disgust. "Now, what will you do, *mi hermano*? Send out an army?"

"Shut up and get away from me, crone!" The don bellowed.

He stomped back into his room and slammed the door.

CHAPTER 7

Don de Castillo was still strapping his silver-chased, pearl-gripped Colts around his waist as the high heels of his polished, black boots clacked on the flags of the *casa's* front patio. Orange and almond trees danced in the breeze around him, and there was the fragrant smell of mid-summer cactus blossoms.

As the don moved through the gate in the six-foot-high, vine-covered adobe wall that ringed the *casa,* he snapped the keeper thongs over both his fancy Colts and then adjusted the black felt, silver-trimmed *sombrero* that sat level on his head, his thin, wavy hair still wet from combing.

He stopped in the broad, dusty yard just outside the gate, and stared straight down a slight grade toward the barns and bunkhouses that lay a hundred yards from the *casa.* Sonora Creek angled through oaks and sycamores at the bottom of the grade, behind the outbuildings.

Three riders were just now moving between two of the large stock barns and passing the open blacksmith shop where the burly Rafael Loera was shaping a wheel rim on his anvil. Chickens of every size and color pecked in the dust around the blacksmith shop, Loera's old collie dog lying in the shade of the shop and thumping his tail with half-hearted menace at the feeding fowl.

The ringing clangs of Loera's hammer no longer penetrated as deeply into the don's tender brain. That was likely due in no small part to the three fingers of brandy he'd downed to quell

53

the barking of the previous evening's indiscretions.

He waited, staring incredulously at the three riders moving slowly toward him. Two were *vaqueros*—his range riders, the men he hired to tend his cattle—while the man riding between the two *vaqueros* was one of the don's *pistoleros*. A man with as many enemies and as much land and property, including two gold mines, as Don de Castillo needed many men by his side who knew their way around a six-shooter and a rifle.

Someone was always trying to steal from him, and neighboring landowners often tried to have him assassinated.

The man riding between the two *vaqueros,* de Castillo could see now as the trio drew within fifty yards of the casa, was Tio-Franco Loza. He could tell this despite that the man was riding with his head down. He was hatless, and his shaggy, dusty, dark-brown hair flopped down over his forehead.

He appeared to be wearing no shirt, only his longhandle top, suspenders, and bell-bottomed *charro* slacks. His gun belt hung down from his saddlehorn. As he and the other two men continued riding toward the don, Loza leaned far to one side. He appeared to be about to fall sideways from the beefy sorrel he was riding. The *vaquero* riding on that side leaned over, planted a hand on the *pistolero's* shoulder, and nudged him upright in his saddle.

The trio passed the *Segundo,* Ernesto Cruz, and eight or so other gun-hung pistoleros. And then as the three continued toward the don, Cruz and the other men on foot turned and followed the riders, staring skeptically up at Loza, who had obviously taken a bullet.

"Tio-Franco," the don said when the three riders had drawn to a halt before him. He walked up close beside Loza's horse. "What happened? Where are the others? Where is the man I sent you for?"

Loza lifted his head slightly, staring over the sorrel's head at de Castillo. His mustached, sun-blistered, pain-racked face was mottled floury white. His eyes bulged from their sockets, the whites liberally stitched with red. He was so basted in sweat that he looked as though he'd dunked his head in a stream.

"D-dead, Don de Castillo," the *pistolero* said in a pinched voice. "All dead. We . . . we lured him in . . . The Revenger . . . but it was six against one . . . and still he cut us down . . . one by one! I alone survived, got away to inform you. Please, Don . . . I'm hurt bad. Need . . . water . . . *doctor*!"

"Yes, Franco," the don said, placing a hand on the man's right thigh. He cast his gaze to the man's right side, where a large circle of blood shone above his hip. Some of the blood was dry and crusty. Some was fresh, glistening brightly in the morning sunlight. "We will get you water and a doctor. But"—the don shook his head, confounded by the turn of events—"I don't understand. Franco, you and Barreto and McDade . . . you were my best men. The most proficient shooters at Hacienda de la Francesca. How can you tell me this man . . . this one man . . . Sartain . . . beat you *all*?"

Franco must have realized his mistake. He stared at the don, and his eyes grew shrewd behind the hard glaze of his agony. He licked his lips, smiled sheepishly. "Did I say five against one? No. That was what I remembered. I have lost much blood, Don. Haven't eaten, had much water—lost my canteen—in two days.

"Sartain brought others. I only saw him, but there were others," the *pistolero* lied. "He's sneaky. Sneaky as a thief in the night, this man, The Revenger. He has quite the reputation in America! He and others—I don't know how many—shot us through the roadhouse windows while we waited for him to come and make a fair fight of it!"

"Ah, now I understand," said Don de Castillo. "The Revenger brought others and bushwhacked you. That's how it happened."

"*Si, Si!* It was not a fair fight."

"I heard he usually worked alone."

"That may be so, but this night he brought *many* others!"

"Thank god you escaped, Franco."

"*Si,* I alone survived. Lived to inform you, Don, that you might want to send more men"—he stretched his lips back painfully and gave a low wail—"if you decide to continue your efforts against this man . . . this *Revenger.* . . ."

"I will take that into consideration."

De Castillo looked away, pensive, thinking through his options. Finally, he turned to the *Segundo.* "Ernesto, I want you to pick five more men. Only five. Five should be enough."

The *Segundo* glanced at Loza, sinking lower in his saddle. "Are you sure only five?"

"*Si,* only five. And I want you to make it clear to them that any of those five who return with the head of Mike Sartain—I don't care if it is attached to his shoulders or not—will be paid one gold ingot from my mines. One ingot in addition to their regular salary! That's enough *pesos* for a whole year of drinking, gambling, and whoring in Juarez!"

"An entire ingot?" the *Segundo* said in a hushed tone, glancing around at the other men flanking him, all of whom had just snapped their eyes a little wider. "Are you sure, *patron*?"

"I am quite sure. Any of the five who survives and brings me the head of Mike Sartain, will be paid one gold ingot. If all five return, so be it. They will each be paid an ingot from the mines. In addition, they will be given two months off to enjoy themselves in Juarez!"

The men muttered amongst themselves, not sure they believed their ears.

"Don," wheezed Loza, his chin nearly resting on the pole of his horse. "*Por favor,* may I be helped down? I need water . . . and a doctor. *Por favor!*"

Ignoring the wounded rider, de Castillo cast a hard gaze at

the men gathered around the horse. "And let there be no mistake," he yelled. "Any man who fails in his attempt at bringing me the head of Mike Sartain better not ever show his face at Hacienda de la Francesca again. If he does . . ."

The don had pulled one of his fancy Colts. Now he raised the weapon, clicking the hammer back and aiming at the forehead of Tio-Franco Loza. The wounded *pistolero* snapped his bloodshot eyes wide in horror at the pistol being aimed at him, and had just opened his mouth to scream, when the don's Colt belched smoke and flames.

The bullet tore through Loza's forehead, blowing him straight back off his saddle. The gunman hit the yard in a bloody heap, quivering, dust billowing around him. His horse whinnied and sidled away, trailing its reins. The *Segundo* grabbed the reins and stared in shock at the dead man on the ground and the old don holding his smoking pistol.

"Any man who fails in his attempt at bringing me the head of Mike Sartain, either attached or unattached, and dares to touch his feet down on *hacienda* soil ever again, will be punished most severely."

De Castillo holstered his Colt, snapped the keeper thong over the hammer. *"Comprende?"*

The *Segundo* looked at the other men. He turned toward the bunkhouse. Several other gunhands had stepped out onto the brush-roofed front gallery and were staring gravely toward the don and the man sprawled bloody in the dirt beside the dancing sorrel.

"*Si,* Don de Castillo," Cruz said, staring down at Loza, whose tongue stuck out the side of his mouth and glassy eyes stared toward the rising morning sun. "*Si,* I think you have made it very clear." He turned to his boss, gave a reassuring nod, his mustaches buffeting in the dry wind. "I will choose five men. Five of the best." He dipped his chin and narrowed his dark eyes. "Rest assured, *patron*—you will soon have the head of Mike Sartain!"

De Castillo watched two men drag off the bleeding corpse of Tio-Franco Loza as the *Segundo* walked over to the bunkhouse gallery and barked out the names of five men, who then went running for the stables to saddle their horses.

When the *pistoleros* had disappeared, their dust sifting in the morning sunshine, a voice said behind the don: "Why five men when all you need is one, *Papa*?"

De Castillo wheeled, heart thumping. He balled his fists at his sides and glowered at the tall lean man standing before him—a man bearing the don's own familial features, including the broad, upturned nose and a birthmark under the right eye, above his sweeping black mustaches.

"What are you doing here?" the don grumbled, swelling his nostrils, the ever-present burn of anger stoking like a locomotive's boiler once more.

"This is my home, Papa," said Salvador de Castillo, the don's oldest and only living son, grinning his damnable grin. He tapped ashes from his fat stogie and then stuck the cigar between his mustached lips, blinking slowly and continuing to grin at his father.

He was dressed nearly all in black leather except for the silk shirt he wore under his brush jacket. His string tie was of red silk. He wore two black holsters positioned for the cross draw on his lean hips, the horn grips of his Remingtons angling toward each other across his lean belly. The grips were well worn, each one marked with many notches. The don thought he could see fresh blood crusted under his oldest son's fingernails, but that must have been his imagination.

"When I last ran you out of here, Salvador, it was for the last time."

Casually puffing the stogie, Salvador de Castillo grinned and shrugged and said, "I blew out a horse and I was hungry, Papa! Aunt Jacinta was kind enough to cook a nice breakfast for me." He glanced over his shoulder. Jacinta was standing under the tiled arbor fronting the *casa*, on the far side of the patio. She was too far away for the don to know for sure, but he thought her ugly mouth was set with her devilish, self-satisfied smile.

She would do anything to taunt him. They'd been rivals since childhood.

"Now, then," Salvador said. "As I was saying, Papa—why send five men when only one, if he's good enough, will do?" He broadened his smile, chocolate eyes flashing silver in the sunlight. "And you know as well as anyone I'm good enough, don't you, Papa?"

Salvador held the don's gaze for several seconds and then he stepped out from the opening in the adobe wall and, puffing the stogie, tapping ashes into the dirt, sauntered in his leisurely way toward the stables.

"You better have that ingot hauled in from the mines, Papa," Salvador said over his shoulder. "I'll be back soon with The Revenger's head, and I know how you don't like me hanging around the place!"

Salvador laughed before disappearing into a horse barn. A few minutes later he led a big, rangy Morgan steed out of the barn, stepped into the saddle, quirted the horse savagely, and galloped out of the yard to the north.

CHAPTER 8

Mike Sartain stopped his big stallion beside a cottonwood the wind was doing its best to strip and break as though over a giant, invisible knee. The wind had come up an hour earlier, and it was blowing heavy curtains of grit this way and that over the Arizona desert.

Holding his hat down over his eyes, Sartain squinted down over Boss's left stirrup at the stage road he'd been following. He slid his gaze along the shod hoof tracks he'd been following, as well, until he was looking at a single-track trail angling off the main trail.

"Hold on, Boss," Sartain said, wincing against the pain in his bullet-grazed thigh as he stepped down from the saddle. He dropped the buckskin's reins, crossed in front of the horse, and walked over to where the secondary trail angled off to the right of the main one.

The Cajun walked several yards up that secondary trail, an old horse trail, possibly an ancient Indian trail now being used by owlhoots and cow punchers, and dropped to one knee. He traced the outline of a shod hoof.

A *familiar* shod hoof.

Then he saw the indentations of several more shod hooves, and lifted his head to follow the trail with his gaze, squinting against the windblown grit. The trail rose up and over several rocky, cactus-studded hogbacks before disappearing from the Cajun's view.

Sartain ran a gloved hand across his unshaven right cheek. "Headin' for Mexico, just like I suspected," he muttered, his own voice nearly drowned by the rushing, moaning wind. "But where in Mexico?"

He rose and stared down the trail in frustration. Behind him, Boss whickered and shook his head, showing his own frustration with the wind and the dirt and sand blowing in his eyes.

Sartain cursed and walked back to the buckskin. He removed his canteen from his saddlehorn, dampened his neckerchief, and swabbed the stallion's eyes. Then he corked the canteen and slung it back over the horn. He glanced straight south along the stage trail. About a mile away, he could see the town of Sonora Gate spread out across red, rocky hills.

His quarry had avoided the little border settlement. Instead, he'd headed along this secondary trail that had likely taken him across the border into Old Mexico. He'd been in a damned hurry to get back to where he'd come from, which told Sartain he had a definite destination in mind.

With this wind having kicked up as violently as it had, Sartain had no choice but to abandon the trail for now. He'd pick it up again the next day, after the wind died.

He didn't like the delay. He wanted to catch up to the son of a bitch, find out who he was and why he'd wanted Sartain dead, and who, if anyone else, had put him up to the task.

And then Sartain would kill him.

That wouldn't bring Buffalo back, of course, but it would make the old reprobate rest a little easier in his grave. And it would make Sartain sleep a little better at night, though probably not by much for a while.

Sartain stared at the town barely visible through the veils of blowing dirt and sand. He'd visited Sonora Gate a few times in the past. They had a telegraph there, which was good, because he had a message to send. So his time in the rough-and-tumble border settlement wouldn't be a total waste of time.

He could rest his bullet-burned leg for a few hours, eat a steak, and swallow some whiskey. He'd be fit as a fiddle for the last leg of his vengeance trail . . .

Sartain stepped into the leather and urged the horse ahead. He didn't have to give Boss much of a nudge. The stallion probably already smelled the oats and fresh hay in the Sonora Gate Federal Livery & Feed Barn, and likely a couple of randy mares. He gave an eager snort and skipped into a jarring trot before settling into a ground-eating lope.

Five minutes later, Sartain slowed Boss back down to a trot and watched the mud brick shacks and stables of Sonora Gate's ragged outer edges jostle into view along both sides of the trail. Some of the shacks were only half visible against the rocky hillsides.

As he continued ahead to where the trail became the settlement's main street, he saw that the wind was having a detrimental effect on the town's business here at the heart of a midweek business day. There wasn't a soul on the street, and no horses were tied in front of the hitchracks fronting the town's two main saloons.

In fact, nothing at all moved along the street except Sartain himself, wind-jostled shingles hanging from chains from gallery eaves, and bouncing tumbleweeds. But then as he and Boss continued to clomp along the street, heading for the feed barn, Sartain saw that he'd been wrong.

The street was not totally deserted. Under the brush-roof of the gallery fronting the Sonora Gate Town Marshal's Office, a single figure dressed in rough trail gear sat in a rocking chair, slowly rocking. The figure slowly lifted the heels of his boots as he rocked—up and down, up and down.

Her boots, Sartain saw as he drew even with the marshal's office. Because just then the figure in the chair lifted the brim of her man's Stetson from her copper eyes, revealing a pretty female face framed in tawny hair that blew out around her shoulders in the wind. The wan light glinted off the five-pointed badge pinned to the young woman's brown leather vest.

Under the vest and badge, high, proud breasts jutted.

Sartain lifted his eyes from the girl's bosom to her face. She regarded him obliquely, still holding the brim of her hat up and preventing the wind from catching it. As the Cajun continued to clomp past the marshal's office on his big buckskin, Sartain quirked the corners of his mouth and pinched the brim of his sand-colored Stetson to the girl.

She gave no reply to the gesture but merely stared at the newcomer dully, maybe with a faint curiosity. A red neckerchief blew around her neck in the wind. She held a Winchester carbine across her thighs, clad in brush-scarred leather chaps. She'd stopped rocking when she'd spied Sartain, but now as he drifted on past her, she began shifting her weight again from the heels of her boots to the toes, gently rocking.

Sartain stabled his horse with a middle-aged black man, Hannibal Howe. He gave the man instructions on how to tend the horse while keeping the stallion from inflicting bodily injury on Howe's person, as Boss could get cranky when horny or when the wind kicked up or for any reason at all. Sartain then left Howe currying Boss, who was munching oats from a feed sack and twitching his ears at a couple of mares eyeing him from a nearby stable, and headed across the street to the Wells Fargo office, which had a telegraph.

He filled out a flimsy given him by the old man sitting in the cage eating a crumbly ham sandwich and regarding him suspiciously, head tilted to one side. The Wells Fargo agent was obviously trying to remember where he'd seen Sartain's countenance before. Sartain himself knew, because his image—or at least a vague likeness—was staring back at him from a wanted circular hanging from a nail on the wall behind the man, just left of his telegraph key and a window overlooking the main street.

The dodger was one Sartain had seen before, hanging in a similar office. It was offering one thousand dollars for the man known as The Revenger, wanted for a string of vigilante killings-for-hire, including a couple of lawmen, throughout the frontier.

Sartain grinned at the old telegrapher regarding him dubiously through the bars of the cage, as the Cajun penciled a couple of concise sentences on a pink telegraph flimsy:

JEFF ARE YOU ALL RIGHT STOP IS PHOENIX ALL RIGHT STOP REPLY SOON END STOP MIKE

Sartain instructed the telegrapher to hammer the missive off to Jeff Ubek at the Continental Hotel in New Orleans and to deliver any response to the Sonora Sun, where he intended to rent a room. He paid the man for the telegram.

As the oldster palmed the twenty-five cents, he spit crumbs from his mustache and said, "Hey, ain't you . . . ?"

Sartain tensed.

"Ain't you Matt Studebaker? Old Kent Studebaker's boy?"

Sartain's cobalt blues glittered a grin at the man through the bars of the shadowy cage. "Yep, that's just who I am."

He pinched his hat brim and then went back outside into the gusting wind that blew his longish hair around his ears and threatened to tear his hat off his head. He paused and looked around. The three-story, mud-brick, shake-shingled Sonora Sun Saloon and Pleasure Parlor sat a half a block away, on the other side of the street. Sartain's mouth watered at the thought of a few shots of Royal Oaks followed by a thick steak and a woman.

Those thoughts rattling around between his ears, holding his hat down taut on his blowing curls, he stepped down off the boardwalk and angled across the street. Dirt and ground horse-shit blew against him, stung his cheeks and eyes. The wind whipped his pinto vest out like batwings. A tumbleweed bounced off his tweed-clad knee, and then he trudged up the Sonoran Sun's broad wooden porch steps and looked over the carved oak batwings.

He had to blink several times before he could make out through the dim, dingy light within that the place was deserted. The wind licked in around his legs like invisible tongues, lapping at the dust thickly coating the saloon's floor puncheons, lifting it and blowing it around the chair legs and tables. The smell of tobacco smoke, old varnish, and liquor lured Sartain through the doors, and as he let them clatter heavily into place behind him, a tall, lean man stepped through a curtained doorway flanking the bar.

"Goddamn, is it windy enough for you, pard?" the man growled, thumbing a suspender over his left shoulder and then shambling along behind the bar, automatically twisting the upturned ends of his waxed mustache and sniffing.

"Just windy enough, *amigo*. Set me up with your best tangleleg, will ya?" Sartain tossed his hat onto the bar, leaning on his elbows and scrubbing his hands through his thick hair, dislodging a shovelful of dirt, sand, ground horseshit, and plant seeds, all of which ticked onto the bar top.

"Been out in it long, have ya?" the barman said, dubiously glancing at the stranger's leavings on his counter.

"Long enough to wanna get out of it."

"How's this?" The man, whose coal-black hair combed straight back from his high forehead was in stark contrast to the pastiness of his face and watery blue of his eyes, held up a bottle.

"Got any Royal Oaks?"

The man winced and shook his head.

"Sam Clay?"

"Kentucky bourbon?" The man thought about it, blinking.

"Might have." He replaced the bottle he held in his hand with another he had to rummage around for on a bottom shelf. "Here we go! A Sam Clay feller, are ya? Not to pry, but are you from Kentucky?"

Sartain shook his head. "Close, but no cigar. Same green hills though with some water between 'em. Lew-zee-anna," the Cajun said, giving his slow, petal-soft drawl its head and watching eagerly as the barman filled a shot glass.

The barman slid the drink toward Sartain and corked the bottle. "Don't get many gents in here thirsty for the expensive stuff."

Sartain held the amber liquid up in front of his face, grinned, wagged his head, and then threw back the entire shot. It burned pleasantly down in his throat and into his chest, spreading a warm glow, soft as the sun setting over the bayous, throughout his being.

"Fill her again and leave the bottle, will you, pard?" Sartain said. "And say, can you tell this poor wanderin' pilgrim where that trail on the north side of town leads? The one that angles away from that big cottonwood the wind is havin' its way with just now?"

"The one anglin' southwest through them rocky, rollin' hills?"

"That's the one."

"Mexico. Crosses the San Pedro about ten miles south of Sonora Gate."

"Any towns down thataway?"

"A couple villages," the barman said, playing with a waxed end of his mustache again. "One big *hacienda*. *Big* one in the Olvidado Mountains. *Forgotten* Mountains in English. An old Spanish land grant owned by the de Castillo family."

Sartain threw back half of his next shot and stared at the low ceiling, pensively scratching his chin. "De Castillo family . . ."

A woman's voice said loudly, "Hold it right there, Sartain!"

Sartain jerked around to see the young woman he'd seen sitting out in front of the town marshal's office standing between the open batwings. The dirty gray light from a window to her left winked off her badge and off the cocked Schofield repeater she held in her gloved left hand.

Chapter 9

"I am holdin' it, Claudia," Sartain said, raising his glass to the scowling, mixed-breed beauty standing between the batwings aiming her pistol at him. He tossed the shot back, sighed, and smacked his lips in satisfaction. "And there . . . I drank her down."

He canted his head toward the bottle. "Can I buy you one?"

"Stow it." She walked into the saloon, the batwings clattering into place behind her. She kept the barrel of the Schofield aimed at the Cajun's belly. Claudia Morales swaggered over to him, subtly swinging her hips, chaps flapping against her tapered thighs.

The hot blood of her south-of-the-border sultriness colored the nubs of her perfect cheeks. She raked a spur across the floor as she stopped about six feet away from Sartain and cocked one foot with her customary flourish.

"I really ought to arrest you, Mike."

Sartain studied her up and down. She was about five-feet-six-inches tall, high-busted, supple-hipped, and long-legged. Her eyes were the copper of newly minted pennies, and her hair was only a shade or so lighter, with slightly darker highlights.

Her breasts thrust toward him from behind her calico shirt and leather vest. The buttons of the shirt were straining, threatening to give.

"I'm up here, *pendejo.*"

Sartain slid his gaze up from the marshal of Sonora Gate's

deep, olive cleavage past her slender neck and across her rich lips and long, cool nose to her eyes that smoldered out from her smooth, tanned face that could have been carved by a master craftsman out of finest oak, depicting a heart-rendingly alluring *senorita* from the pages of ancient Spanish myths and legends.

A more perfect, intoxicating creature Sartain had rarely seen.

"Claudia, you're . . . all over," Sartain said, wagging his head in awe at the beauty before him, feeling a drum beating in his loins.

"As I was saying, I should arrest you."

"And go and spoil a good time?"

"What good time?"

"The one we could have later"—the Cajun grinned again, showing all his white teeth—"if you played your cards right and promised not to disrespect me in the mornin'."

The barman cleared his throat and shuffled off down the bar. "I'll leave you two to work it out." He glanced over his shoulder as he headed toward the curtained doorway. "Just please don't bust the place up." With that, he ducked through the doorway and drew the curtain closed behind him.

"Now, then," Sartain said, turning back to the girl holding the cocked pistol on him. "Where were we?"

"That price on your head keeps climbing," Claudia said, taking two more slow steps forward and pressing the barrel of her pistol against Sartain's belly. She looked down at the gun and then she stared into his eyes, her face only a foot away from his now, and added in a deep, sexy rasp, "And I could use a new dress for *Cinco de Mayo.*"

"How 'bout if I just buy you one?" Sartain closed his hand over the Schofield. She did not resist as he gently pried the pistol free of her grip. He held the hammer back with his thumb, squeezed the trigger, which gave a faint click, and then eased the hammer back down to the firing pin.

69

He slid the Schofield into the holster thonged low on her right thigh. And then he swept the girl up in his arms, held her against his chest, and brushed his nose across her cheek. "That way, you can save a bullet . . . and we can find a more creative a way of passin' this windy afternoon . . ."

She grabbed the bottle and two shot glasses off the counter as he turned and walked along the bar to the stairs. "What are you doing here, Mike?" she said as he began climbing, wincing a little at the burn in his thigh. He remembered that she rented a room on the second floor.

"I'm on the hunt, Claudia."

"When are you not, *pendejo*?"

"Such talk . . . after all we've meant to each other."

"You mean after the two times we curled each other's toes and you slipped away like a ghost in the night?" She lifted her head and pressed her silky lips to his cheek.

Sartain chuckled. "You know how I never wanna stay long enough to get boring."

He turned on the landing and continued up the last stretch of creaky wooden stairs. "Still keepin' a lid on this town, I see."

"It's not easy."

"Still got your deputies?"

Claudia had taken over the law-dogging duties in Sonora Gate three years ago when her father, Pedro Morales, had been ambushed out in the desert. She'd hired as deputies her uncle, Gustavo Morales, and a burly former cavalry sergeant from Fort Huachuca—a stocky gent with a thick Norwegian accent.

"They are dead," Claudia said coolly, nuzzling Sartain's ear, causing his blood to rise and his balbriggans to grow tight in the crotch. "Murdered in the desert—just like Papa."

Sartain stopped, dropped her feet to the floor, standing the town marshal of Sonora Gate up before him. "What happened?"

Claudia moved to a door on the right side of the dingy hall, threw it open. She strode inside, doffed her hat, and tossed it onto a dresser.

"Stock thieves," she said as Sartain moved into the room behind her. "Or maybe the men who've been robbing the stage coach from Tucson. Take your pick. I don't know. Who knows? It's the border, Mike."

The room was as dingy as the hall. She went to a window flanking the bed and drew the shade, allowing in the pasty yellow light. The wind was still blowing like a hundred warlocks stomping around the town on a mission to chill as much blood as possible. The dirt ticked against the glass panes of that window and the one Sartain drew the shade over on the other side of the brass headboard.

"Trouble country, they call this," the girl said, turning to the mirror over the dresser and lifting the heavy locks of her lustrous hair. She let the beautiful mass spill onto her shoulders and then swung around to face the Cajun. "I asked you a question. What brings you here?" She arched a brow and slid her lips slightly back from her teeth. "Me, perhaps?"

"A fella'd be a damn fool not return to . . ."

Sartain let his voice trail off. Beneath the moaning wind, hooves clomped in the street. He turned to stare out the window. Five horseback riders, all wearing *sombreros,* the brims basted against their foreheads, were trotting down the street from Sartain's left to his right. They were lean, dark-skinned men in calico and leather, with billowy, brightly colored bandanas.

Riding high-stepping horses with Arabian blood, not unlike the horses of the men who'd bushwhacked him and Buffalo, they were heavy with guns on their persons and jutting from their saddle scabbards. Sartain felt a not unpleasant scratching at the back of his neck as he watched the riders ride off down the street to his right, behind the shifting curtains of windblown sand and dirt.

One of the men's horses shied at a tumbleweed, and when he got the startled mount checked down, the rider galloped after the others, who'd turned down a side street to disappear behind the sprawling, white-washed adobe of the Santa Cruz Mercantile and Drug Emporium. Beyond the Emporium, in the direction in which the riders had disappeared, a church flaunted a sand-colored bell tower.

"Friends of yours?" Claudia's voice rasped in Sartain's ear.

He glanced at her. She stood close behind him, peering into the street from over his right shoulder.

"You recognize those Mescins?"

"*Si*," the girl said, nodding. "They are Don de Castillo's men. I recognize the brand of Hacienda de la Francesca on their horses. I've seen a few of them in town . . . too frequently, but at least they require me to keep my edge."

"Would that brand happen to be an 'H' and an 'F' in a circle?"

Claudia arched a brow. "I'm smelling trouble on you, Mike. Like sex on a cheap whore."

He canted his head toward where the riders had disappeared. "Pistoleers?"

Claudia nodded. "The don hires such men to protect his holdings . . . as well as his gold. He's a rich man. A vile man. It's his men, possibly one of those *hombres,* I suspect of my father's killing, as well the murders of my deputies."

"How so?"

"Don de Castillo doesn't care for the settlers on this side of the border, a large stretch of which at one time was part of his family's land grant. That stretch included Sonora Gate. He gives his men free rein over here."

Claudia paused.

"Mike?"

Again, Sartain turned to her. She studied him skeptically

from over his shoulder. "Please tell me you are not here to tangle with de Castillo."

Sartain gazed back at her, thinking about the five men who'd just ridden into town. Thinking about Buffalo McCluskey as well as Phoenix and Jeff Ubeck. He gave Claudia a thin, half-hearted smile and said, "I'm not here to tangle with de Castillo. But, just sayin' I was . . . just speculatin', mind you . . . where do you suppose those five are headed?"

Claudia turned her mouth corners down and sighed as she cast her gaze out the window, in the direction of the bell tower rising from a rocky hill on the town's far side. "That is the old Mexican part of town. They've gone there to stable their horses and to drink and visit the *putas* in the Mexican cantina owned by Senor Obregon. However . . ." She rolled her copper eyes toward the Cajun dubiously. ". . . they don't usually visit Sonora Gate this early in the week."

"I s'pect they'll be over here on this side of town in due time, then," Sartain said, unbuckling his pistol belt.

"I'd say we got an hour or so."

He grinned. "Best get to it, then."

Claudia's cheeks dimpled as she gazed up at him, her copper eyes sparking. "You like to keep it interesting, don't you, *amigo*?"

"Why the hell not?" Sartain said, coiling his shell belt around the front bedpost.

Claudia stepped back, staring up at him lustily from beneath her tawny brows and the brim of her tan Stetson, removing her own shell belt and holstered Schofields. Sartain unbuttoned his shirt. When the girl began unbuttoning her own, he shook his head.

"Let me do that." Lust was a wooden knot in his throat as he stepped toward her and began unfastening her shirt buttons.

Claudia lowered her hands and thrust her shoulders back, breasts out, as Sartain hungrily undid the buttons and then slid the sides of her shirt and vest back from the full mounds pushing out at him from behind a thin cotton chemise.

"Christ," Sartain muttered, cupping the pointed orbs in his hands.

He and Claudia were making slow, sensual love when Sartain heard beneath the bed's raucous clatter what he believed to be the squawk of a floorboard in the hall outside their door.

CHAPTER 10

The first squawk of a floorboard was followed closely by another.

Sartain looked down at Claudia. "You hear that?"

She peered around him toward the door and nodded.

Sartain glanced over his right shoulder. Beneath the door, a shadow moved. There was another faint squawk.

Claudia stretched her lips farther back from her white teeth and said, "What's the matter, Sartain—no follow-through?"

"Oh, hell!" He chuckled.

As though in another world entirely, he heard the doorknob turn ever so slightly. He glanced over his shoulder, saw the key in the lock. There was another squawk. This one louder.

Sartain glanced at Claudia. She was staring up at him, eyes bright, jaws hard. He rolled to the left while she rolled to the right. At the same time, there was a shotgun-like blast and in the periphery of his vision, Sartain saw the door burst wide.

Another shotgun-like blast as the door slammed against the dresser.

Sartain hit the floor and reached up to grab his big, pearl-gripped LeMat from the holster hanging from the bedpost. At the same time, he watched a burly man in a palm-leaf *sombrero* step just inside the room and stop the door's bounce back toward the frame with his left foot.

He bellowed in Spanish, "A present from Don de Castillo, love birds!" and there was another blast.

This blast was from the actual shotgun the man held in both

his black-gloved hands—a sawed-off, double-barreled gut-shredder that roared like an angry god, both barrels lapping crimson flames toward the bed on which Sartain and Claudia had been toiling two seconds before.

As the buckshot slammed into the bed, causing an instant cornhusk snowstorm, both Claudia and Sartain fired their pistols from either side of the bed, their bullets, three apiece, thumping into the shotgunner's chest. The man screamed and threw his shotgun in the air as he twisted around, for a second exposing a second man behind him.

Sartain and Claudia cut loose with a second barrage, and before the second bushwhacker could get his carbine leveled, he, too, was sent howling and stomping loudly back out of the room to bounce off the wall on the far side of the hall. He and his friend continued to stagger around, screaming and knocking into each other until their knees buckled and they piled up like two heavy sacks of cracked corn at the base of the wall smeared and flecked with the crimson of their blood.

Except for one of the dead men loosing a loud fart, silence fell over the saloon's second story.

As Sartain tripped the lever on his LeMat, engaging the sixteen-gauge shotgun shell residing in the short, stout barrel beneath the main one, a man's hatted head slid into the doorway, low on the right side. He shoved a pistol into the room. Sartain jerked his LeMat toward the third shooter as Claudia's Schofield barked to his left. The third bushwhacker triggered a round into the wall behind the town marshal a quarter-second before Claudia's round thunked into his right cheekbone, laying him out flat with the other two drygulchers.

Again, silence.

Claudia said coolly, quietly, "How many more *amigos* did you invite to the fandango, Mike?"

She was answered by the blast of another shotgun out in the

hall. A squash-sized hole appeared in the wall left of the door. Plaster and lath blew into the room. There was another blast, and another similar-sized hole appeared in the wall eight inches right of the first one.

Sartain aimed his LeMat just left of the two holes in the wall, and a little above, and triggered the shotgun shell. The LeMat thundered, flames lapping from the stout shotgun barrel, the sixteen-gauge buckshot tearing through the wall and into the hall, evoking a stunned yelp.

Sartain tossed the empty, smoking pistol onto the bed. He grabbed his Henry repeater and, forgetting that he was naked save for the bandage around his left thigh, yelled, "Hold your fire, Marshal!"

"Crazy Cajun!" the woman screamed behind him as Sartain ran through the door and across the hall, ramming his right shoulder into the wall and casting his gaze toward where the twin shotgun blasts had come. A short, stocky gent in deerskin *charro* slacks and green brush jacket over a white shirt was shambling toward the window at the far end of the hall.

He clutched his left arm with his right hand. A shotgun lay on the floor behind him.

Sartain shouted, "Turn around or take it between the shoulder blades, you drygulchin' son of a bitch!"

The drygulchin' son of a bitch swung around, screaming and raising a Remington revolver. Crouching against the wall, Sartain fired and levered the Henry.

Boom! Boom! Boom!

The empty cartridge casings clanked off the wall, dropped to the floor, and rolled.

Claudia screamed, "Mike, drop!"

Sartain dropped belly down on the musty floor runner, his empty cartridge casings warm against his thigh. Claudia's pistol barked three times, evoking a yell from the other end of the

77

hall, near the stairs.

Sartain looked behind him through wafting, gray powder smoke in time to see a man retreat down the dingy stairwell. His boots and spurs were thumping and changing loudly as he descended the steps.

Sartain heaved himself to his feet. Claudia was down on one knee in the open doorway of their room, the first two dead men piled up bloody before her. She was naked and lovely, wearing only her hat, breasts bulging beneath her arms. She held both her Schofields in her fists.

"Did you get him?" Sartain asked, holding his Henry up high across his bare chest.

"I thought I saw the *bastardo* flinch."

"My turn," Sartain growled.

He ran past Claudia, who stood and yelled behind him, "Mike, what did you do to make Don de Castillo so *angry*?"

"Your guess is as good as mine, *chiquita*!"

Sartain ran down to the first landing, stopped, crouched, and stared into the saloon hall, which was all misty blue shadows against the gray windows running along the front of the room on either side of the wind-jostling batwings. A shadow moved—a man raising his hatted head over a table about two-thirds of the way down the room.

Red flames lanced from a pistol barrel. The slug tore into the rail to Sartain's left.

The Cajun snapped up his Henry and fired three quick rounds at the spot where he'd seen the gun flash. The man's head sank down behind the table. There was the loud thud of a gun hitting the floor.

Sartain ejected his last spent cartridge casing, rammed a fresh one into the rifle's action, and waited.

The shadow moved again—jerking, halting movements. Sartain held fire as the shooter gained his feet heavily, turned, and began dragging the toes of his high-heeled boots toward the batwings. Chaps flapped against his thighs. Silver spurs flashed in the dull light.

The drygulcher didn't get far before his knees struck the floor with a boom. He knelt there, groaning and breathing hard, keeping his head up, back straight.

The Cajun descended the stairs and walked along the bar. He stood over the kneeling Mexican.

The man's round, pockmarked face was framed by thick, black mutton-chop whiskers. He wore a neatly trimmed mustache and goatee. He'd lost his hat, and his long, oily black hair tumbled loosely about his shoulders.

Blood stained his calico shirt in several places.

Sartain pressed the barrel of his Henry against the middle of the man's forehead. "Why does your boss want me dead?"

The Mexican rolled his rheumy eyes up at Sartain, pursed his lips, flared his nostrils, and shook his head.

"What about Phoenix?"

The Mexican tried to spit, but saliva mixed with blood merely dribbled down his chin.

"All right, then," Sartain said, holding the gun straight out from his right hip with one hand. "Go to hell."

Boom!

The back of the man's head splattered against the front of the bar.

Boots thudded at the back of the room. Sartain turned to see Claudia running down the stairs. She wore Sartain's long-handles stuffed into the tops of her boots. She had her Schofields in her hands but lowered them when she got to the bottom of the stairs.

She stared toward the dead man and the naked Sartain, his Henry still smoking. *"Dios mio,"* she said wistfully.

The curtain behind the bar ruffled. The barman poked his

head through it. He looked at Claudia and then at Sartain, and gave a pained expression. "I thought I told you two not to bust up the place!"

Forty-five minutes later, Sartain picked up the heels of the dead man lying at the far end of the hall, near the window he'd been heading for when the Cajun had punched his ticket, and began dragging him down the hall.

"Sorry, O'Brien," Sartain said to the barman, who was on his knees scrubbing one of the thick blood stains on the wall across from Claudia's room. "You can bill de Castillo for the cleanup and damages. From what I understand, he can afford it."

The barman only grunted and shook his head as, smoking a loosely rolled quirley, he continued scrubbing at the stain, causing soapy red water to run down the wall to the floor at his knees.

Sartain had dressed and retrieved all five of the killers' horses, which had been turned into a livery barn on the Mexican side of town. All five mounts wore the de Castillo brand burned into their withers. Four of the men had been tied belly down over their saddles. Sartain dragged the last man to the end of the hall and on down the stairs, the man's head making staccato, wooden cracking sounds as it bounced off each step in turn.

At the bottom, the Cajun stopped, straightened to ease the crick at the small of his back, and then dragged the man along in front of the bar and on out through the batwings. Claudia stood on the front gallery, the wind blowing her hair.

The gale had let up a little and seemed to be gradually diminishing.

"You know what this means, don't you?" Claudia asked, grunting as she helped Sartain lift the heavy dead man and half-carry, half-drag him to a waiting Arabian tied to the hitchrack fronting the saloon.

"That a man can't get a little privacy in your town?" the Cajun said as he and Claudia hefted the man up the side of the fidgeting Arabian.

"I am talking about your sending these men back to Hacienda de la Francesca," Claudia said, cleaning the blood off her gloves on the seat of the dead man's pants.

Sartain gave a last, loud grunt as he back-and-bellied the dead man over his saddle, legs hanging down the horse's left side, arms and head hanging down the right side. "Yeah, it means he can't accuse me of stealin' his horses."

Claudia waited until Sartain had used the dead man's lariat to secure his body to his saddle, and then said, "It means there will be more, *pendejo*. Many more." Claudia faced Sartain, boots spread, fists on her hips. "He won't rest until your bones are being cleaned by magpies."

"He hasn't seemed to be doin' a whole lot of restin', anyways." Sartain walked up to her and kissed her on the mouth. "Got a piece of notepaper and a pencil?"

She wrinkled the skin above the bridge of her nose at him. Then she dipped into an inside pocket of her vest and pulled out a small, pasteboard-backed notepad. From another pocket she produced a dull pencil stub.

Sartain jerked his chin and grunted. Claudia gave an ironic chuff and then turned around.

The Cajun placed the notepad against her back, touched the pencil stub to his tongue, and scrawled the briefest of notes: Two short words.

He tore the top leaf from the pad, returned the pad and the pencil to the marshal, wadded up the paper, and stuffed it inside of the last dead man's open mouth. He removed the man's neckerchief from around the man's neck and tied it over his head, forcing his mouth closed, and tightly knotted the cloth beneath the dead man's chin, so the note couldn't slip out.

"There—that oughta do it."

Sartain untied the five horses from the hitchrack, pointed them south, and then triggered his LeMat into the air over their heads. All five mounts lurched with a start and then lunged into hard gallops, their grisly cargoes jostling over their saddles.

"How far is de Castillo's *hacienda* from here?" Sartain asked Claudia as they stood side by side in the street, watching the horses gallop into the distance, shaking their heads against the smell of the dead men they were carrying.

"An hour's ride."

Sartain glanced at the sky. "They should be home for supper, then."

He turned to the marshal gazing at him darkly. "He killed Buffalo, Claudia." The Cajun felt his cheeks warm with barely bridled fury. "I'm gonna find out why. And then I'm gonna kill him."

CHAPTER 11

A low ridge stood to the south of the main house at Hacienda de la Francesca. The ridge overlooked a narrow valley cleaved down its middle by a flashing creek sheathed in oaks, sycamores, cottonwoods, and galleta grass.

There were tawny patches of corn and hay on both sides of the creek, and just now peasants in their traditional white cotton pajamas were scything the hay, the second cutting of the year, and tossing it into the back of two mule-drawn wagons.

The valley was sheltered from the wind, but up here, where the don stood, it rustled the shrubs and bunches of shaggy brown grass growing amongst the rocks and prickly pear. The wind had torn his hat off his head, and the *sombrero* now jostled down his back.

The don stared off into the valley. Such a beautiful valley. Long and curving and well watered, often teeming with deer, fox, elk, and even the occasional bear. Red-throated fish thrived in the creek.

The earthy blues and browns and greens shimmered in the lemony sunlight at this high altitude. Beyond the ridge on the other side of the valley were three more ridges and then the earth dropped to a long, sand-colored stretch of low, open desert with another, dark lump of a mountain range rising far, far beyond. That range seemed to hover in a blue-black cloud far above the ground.

Such a beautiful place.

The don's favorite place since he'd been a boy and his father had been *haciendado* of Hacienda de la Francesca. Back when life had seemed so simple, and his heart was still a live thing beating in his chest and not a dead thing merely spasming as it slowly—oh, too slowly!—petered away to stillness.

The don turned to the lone grave capping this beautiful ridge. One stout wooden marker fronting a mounded hill of pink gravel.

There was no cemetery up here. The cemetery of Hacienda de la Francesca, consisting of over a hundred graves, lay on a hill a quarter mile east of the main *casa*. That was reserved for family. A sacrosanct place encircled with a low adobe wall and bearing a shrine devoted to the memory of *Madre Maria* and her beloved *Jesus* and a stone crypt containing the remains of the great-great-grandfather of Don Castillo.

It also contained the grave of Castillo's youngest son, Pedro—the one of the don's three sons who most resembled the patron and who, if he had been allowed to live—would have taken over Hacienda de la Francesca upon the don's passing into eternity. Now, with his only living son banished from the *hacienda,* there was no one. The don's death would mean Jacinta would take over. That, in turn, would mean the beginning of the end for Hacienda de la Francesca.

The woman had no business savvy. She wanted only gold and power.

A gravely important matter, but not one that was currently on the don's mind.

He stepped to the grave, only a couple of months' old, and dropped to his knees. He stared down in sadness at the stout wooden cross of the grave that lay out here alone, for the most part unattended except by the don himself. No one else cared. Of course, the woman buried here could not have been buried with the family, for she had not yet become family.

She had been about to become family, but then . . . an indiscretion on her part as well as on the don's. And now she lay out here alone for all the centuries to come, beside that beautiful valley, under that arching Sonora sky.

"Why?" the don asked. "Oh, why did it have to end like this?"

Grief washed over him like a large ocean wave, swamping him, and he flung himself upon the cross. He held the cross to his chest, pressing his cheek to the top of it, grinding his teeth, pressing his fingers into the wood, openly sobbing.

His shoulders jerked so violently that his hat fell forward from his head and tumbled onto the ground. The don's thin hair blew in the wind. Tears dribbled down his cheeks to dampen his trimmed beard.

And still he sobbed.

When finally the sorrow passed—or at least the brunt of it; he knew he would carry the bulk of it around with him for the rest of his days—he pulled out a silk handkerchief and dabbed at his cheeks, his eyes. He replaced his hat, stood, sniffed, glanced down at the grave once more, and then turned and began walking down the hill toward the *casa* that sat like an enormous jewel in the valley to the west, not far below the ridge.

He took only three steps and stopped.

He stared straight ahead. His eyes grew as hard with anger as they had been soft with grief only a moment before. He hardened his jaws until his cheeks dimpled, and he flushed the red of a Sonora sunset.

Suddenly, clawing his right Colt's pistol from his tooled, black leather holster residing on his right thigh, he wheeled back to the grave. He cocked the fine piece, aimed, and fired, screaming, *"Puta* bitch! *Puta* bitch! *Puta bitch!"*

The gun roared six times before the hammer clicked on an empty chamber. The don stared through his wind-torn powder smoke at the cross. It was riddled by the six round, ragged-edged bullet holes and leaning precariously back and to one side.

"There you are now," the don snarled, holstering his pistol and snapping the keeper thong closed across the hammer. "How do you like it, *puta* bitch?"

His jaws set, he wheeled and continued on down the slope. But he'd taken only a half-dozen more steps before he stopped again.

Hooves drummed, and he saw riders galloping down the road beyond the *hacienda's* main compound. They were descending the last hill along the pale, curving trail from the north, the wind whipping their dust. A couple of the horses were buck-kicking curiously.

Don de Castillo lifted a hand to shade his eyes from the coppery sun as he stared toward the horses. They didn't appear to be carrying riders. From this distance it was hard to tell, but he thought it looked more like they had packs strapped over their saddles. Long packs hanging down over the flapping stirrups.

Quickly, one after another, the procession dipped down behind the *casa* and out of sight.

Apprehension poked at the back of the don's neck as he continued on down the ridge. When he was nearly to the bottom, he saw the horses galloping into the yard. They galloped over to the stable and barn area of the compound, a ways down the grade from the walled, sprawling, tile-roofed *casa*. A couple of *vaqueros* jogged from the mud-brick, L-shaped bunkhouse toward the horses, and then a stable boy dropped his pitchfork and went running, as well.

By the time the don had made his way through the trees and around the front of the *casa*, the *Segundo*, Ernesto Cruz, and several other *vaqueros*, were milling amongst the fidgeting, dusty, sweat-silvered horses, as well. The blacksmith's shaggy old dog was running around the mounts on his creaky hips, barking raspily, his tail in the air. Occasionally, the dog would run up to one of the horses and lift his snout toward the head of one of the men draped belly down across a saddle, sniffing.

The don had stopped when he'd seen that the saddled horses were carrying men. Likely, dead men. Likely the five men who had been riding the five horses when they'd pulled out of the *hacienda* earlier that morning, after being hand-picked by Ernesto Cruz himself.

"Oh, shit," the don said softly to himself.

A low ringing started in his ears.

The other men had grabbed the bridle reins of the horses and were holding them still. They'd all inspected the men sprawled across the saddles, and now Cruz stood in front of them, facing the don with a grim, haggard expression.

The don continued striding forward. His legs and back felt stiff, as though all his joints had been fouled with mortar. One of the horses bucked suddenly, whinnying, and for a moment the *vaquero* who'd lost the horse's reins grabbed them again and settled the Arabian back down.

De Castillo stared at the head of the man hanging down the near side of the horse that had just bucked, probably not caring too much for the smell of death clinging to its back. Something about the dead man interested the don, who strode stiffly past Cruz and over to the horse.

Cruz, who had not yet said anything, turned to follow the don. The don lifted the dead man's head by his thick, curly, dark-brown hair. The man's bandanna had been tied around his head, knotted tightly beneath his jaw. The man's cheeks bulged slightly.

Cruz glanced at the patron skeptically.

The don slipped the knot beneath the dead man's chin. The man's mouth opened. Something fell out from between his lips.

It landed on the ground between the toes of the don's polished black boots.

Cruz bent down to pick it up between two fingers. He opened it and tensed.

"What is it?" asked the don.

Cruz showed him the note on which two words had been scrawled in pencil:

"Hell's coming."

In the early evening, after the sun had died and the stars had opened up over Sonora Gate, Salvador de Castillo scratched a match to life atop a scarred wooden table. He touched the flame to one of the Cuban cigars he'd stolen from the old man's study at Hacienda de la Francesca.

As the eldest son of Alonzo de Castillo lit the scar, blowing the aromatic smoke out his mouth and nostrils, he sat back against the adobe wall in the shadowy cantina of Xavier Obregon, which was all that remained of an ancient Spanish settlement lining the dry creek known as Durango Wash. The wash was a quarter-mile or so from the western outskirts of Sonora Gate, whose dull, red lamps and torch lights shone to the north beyond the barrack-like, steepled church capping a rocky hill.

This night in Obregon's *cantina,* there were a dozen or so other customers, including the two men who sat at a square table to Castillo's right. These two were in the deep, silent, softly grunting throws of an arm-wrestling match. The stakes were high, which mildly amused Salvador. The five men sitting in a semi-circle around the two combatants—all Mexicans, as this was the old Mexican side of Sonora Gate—smiled lustily, greedily at the teetering, clenched fists of the two players.

Many *pesos* had been bet on the match. A bonus was the grisly fascination of the two scorpions held to the top of the table by rawhide strips strung through a hole on each side of the players' struggling arms. The end of each length of rawhide was tied to a leg beneath the table, securing each scorpion in place over each small hole.

The loser's hand would be smashed down atop one of the two waiting scorpions, both of whom had their dangerous tails raised in anger at their predicament, and would likely be painfully injected with the scorpions' toxic poison. So, the penalty for losing the match could very well be death, or, at the very least, an agonizing few days of painful recovery ahead for the loser.

Yes, the stakes were high. But then, the stakes were often high on this end of Sonora Gate. That's why Salvador was only mildly amused, despite his having bet two hundred *pesos* on one of the combatants.

At the moment, he was more interested in hearing word of the man known as The Revenger, and in the ass of one of Obregon's *cantina* girls—a full-hipped, well-endowed, brown-eyed blonde just now passing in front of Salvador's table, two steaming platters in her hands. Salvador stuck out his boot to hook the girl's skirt in an attempt to drag her over to him. He managed to hook the fancily embroidered and pleated cotton skirt, but it slipped on over the top of his boot as the girl sashayed away.

The blonde jerked her head toward Salvador, frowning incredulously, and then rolled her impertinent eyes as she continued to a table to the left of de Castillo's. She set the platters down on the table, whirled, and gave Salvador's table a wider berth as she passed.

Behind the counter consisting of three cottonwood planks resting over beer barrels, *Senor* Obregon himself was tending several steaming kettles and sputtering fry pans.

Salvador snorted a laugh as he finished lighting his cigar and tossed the match on the earthen floor. He blew out a long plume of cigar smoke, sipped from his stone mug of pulque—the agave-derived alcohol that Obregon brewed better than any other—and glanced once more at the arm wrestlers.

Both were facing each other, heads bowed as though in prayer, lips stretched back from their teeth. Their clenched fists were sticking straight up in the air between them. The scorpions turned angry circles on the table, inches from each combatant's right elbow, flicking their poisonous tails.

The bettors sat around the grunting fighters, leaning forward, none saying a thing, only anxiously picking their noses or raking their nails across their unshaven jaws.

All were smoking or working a tobacco cud.

Save for the bubbling and sputtering of Obregon's pots and pans, the place was so silent now on the lee side of the windstorm that Salvador could hear a couple of coyotes yammering in the near hills.

He hauled out his gold-chased pocket watch. Six-thirty. He'd sent his partner, Coyon, to look in on his father's five so-called assassins and the *gringo* known as The Revenger an hour ago. Salvador's own face was too well known on that side of town, and he didn't want to get the female marshal's panties in a twist. She'd banned him from the *gringo* part of town, after all.

Salvador would have put a bullet in her head by now, but he hadn't yet made love to her, and he very much wanted to do that . . . before he drilled her with a bullet . . .

He would show himself to The Revenger sooner or later, but first he wanted to savor the anticipation of their meeting, savor his father's anxiety.

He hooked the skirt once more and lifted his leg, driving the toe of his boot up high against the cloth. The brown-eyed blonde *cantina* girl gave a shrill yell as Salvador drew his knee up and back and pulled the girl unceremoniously onto his lap.

He bellowed a laugh as the girl fought him.

"I have work to do, you cow!" she screeched in Spanish.

"*Mi rubio* beauty, I am in love with you!" Salvador bellowed, sticking his cigar between his teeth and cupping the girl's full breasts in his hands.

He knew her to be half-Mexican; her father had been a German prospector who'd died when the girl was still an infant. Salvador, who had always had an eye for the young girls, had seen her from time to time, growing up in a little adobe with her mother and grandmother not far from here along the southern bank of Durango Wash.

Now she was a desert flower in full bloom. He wondered if her flower had ever been fertilized . . .

"*Por favor, Senor* de Castillo—I have work to do!"

"Xavier and the Indio can handle it," Salvador said, glancing at the plump Pima girl who also served drinks and food here at Obregon's *cantina*. "Can't you, Xavier?" he yelled at the short Mexican wearing a grubby green bandanna over his head, with a cornhusk cigarette smoldering between his thick, mustached lips.

Xavier glanced over his shoulder as he stirred some *carne asada*. "Salvador, *por favor,* uh? That one's not a *puta*. You want a girl? The *putas* are upstairs."

"I've had the *putas* upstairs," Salvador said, continuing to heft the girl's breasts through the lacy cotton of her low-cut blouse, holding her taut against him. "I want this little one tonight, I think. She's ripe, Xavier. Oh, brother, this one's ripe!"

"Salvador, her mother forbade me from whoring her. She said if she ever found her upstairs, she'd take her away. Hey, it's not easy getting good help these days—much less keeping it!"

"Don't worry—I will pay you well, *mi amigo*!" Salvador drew the straps of the girl's blouse down her arms. He closed his hand over the bare orbs and guffawed.

The girl screeched.

Xavier shook his head and shrugged a shoulder despondently. Salvador and the serving girl must have been too much of a distraction for one of the arm wrestlers, because just then there was the thud of a fist against wood and a shrill, agonized scream.

Chapter 12

When the money had been exchanged, the loser of the wrestling match was escorted mewling from the *cantina* by three of the winning gamblers and over to the home of an Apache medicine woman. Salvador had lost the bet, but he didn't mind.

He had the blonde on his lap, and he'd subdued her by setting his bowie knife on the table to his left, near her own left thigh, and threatening to use it if she did not become more friendly. His friend and sole confidant, Coyon, sidestepped through the small crowd that had gathered near the front of the *cantina* in the wake of the wrestling match, and shuffled over to where Salvador sat with his back against the wall, the suddenly subdued girl on his lap.

Coyon was short and broad with a fat belly and a hump on his back, drawing his head and shoulders down and forward. He was dressed much like Salvador, nearly all in leather except for a grimy red-and-black calico shirt and an even grimier bandanna knotted around his neck. He wore a long beard, and the left eye beneath the brim of his straw sombrero wandered up and outward, as if to view something on his temple.

Coyon slipped into the chair on the other side of the table from Salvador. The hunchback was staring lustily at the girl.

Salvador scowled at his partner, who once had worked on the *hacienda* as a stable boy, long before Salvador's exile from Hacienda de la Francesca. "Don't you know it is not nice to stare, Coyon? Were you raised by wolves? It took you long enough—what did you see? What did you find out?"

"Oh, very much, Salvador," said Coyon, grinning lustily as he pried his gaze off the blonde's opulent breasts filling his friend's hands. He chuckled; it sounded like a rooster's dying wails. "As you guessed, the don's men have returned to the *hacienda.*"

"What do you mean—*returned?*"

"Belly down across their saddles!" The hunchback lowered his head and laughed his wheezing laugh across the table.

Salvador stopped trifling with the girl as he stared blankly across the table at his friend. Then, when he realized what he'd heard, he grinned. And then the grin grew broader, and he laughed.

He continued laughing at the ceiling until he saw the hunchback pointing at his stone mug, sort of cowering and grinning like a dog asking its abusive master for a bone. Salvador yelled for a mug of pulque to be delivered to his friend, and when the half-breed Pima girl had brought the drink, and the hunchback drained half of it in a single draught, Salvador said, "Tell me—where is this Revenger bastard now, Coyon?"

"The Sonora Sun," Coyon said, raking the sleeve of his leather jacket across his mouth. "He was there with the princess."

"The princess" was what everyone called Claudia Morales, town marshal of Sonora Gate, though not to her face unless they wanted a bullet for their wit.

"Hmmmm."

Salvador nuzzled the blonde's neck. She stiffened against him, turned her head away from him. He rose from his chair, pulled the girl over his shoulder like a fifty-pound sack of grain, and placed his cold cigar between his teeth. He tossed the hunchback a few coins and said, "Enjoy yourself for the rest of the evening, Coyon. You deserve it."

The girl didn't fight too much as Salvador climbed the stairs with her hanging across his shoulder.

A half hour later, Salvador rolled off of Obregon's blonde on the lumpy bed in the *cantina's* second story. The girl was sweating and breathing hard, her blonde hair in her face.

"You're a pig!" she said in Spanish.

Salvador chuckled. He reached over onto the roughhewn table beside the bed and deposited an American half-eagle on her belly. She looked down at it, lower jaw hanging in shock.

"You still think so?"

The girl picked up the coin and held it up to the last of the twilight angling through a window. *"Mierda!"*

Salvador chuckled. "There will be another one waiting for you here."

The girl frowned, curious.

Salvador slid one of his Remington revolvers from its holster hanging from a near bedpost. He opened the loading gate, rolled the cylinder, and shook out a bullet. He flicked the loading gate closed and returned the Remington to its holster.

He rolled over and deposited the brass cartridge between the blonde's sweat-slick breasts.

"After you have delivered that to Sartain." Salvador winked. "If you're quick about it, I might even give you another roll!"

He pressed his fingers to his lips, shoulders jerking as he laughed. "Shhh! We mustn't tell Mama!"

Piñon pine and mesquite crackled in the sheet-iron stove beside where Sartain and Claudia hunkered over a chess game in the Sonora Sun's main drinking hall. The natural perfume of the wood helped cover the old whiskey fumes and fresh blood stench that permeated the place in the wake of Don de Castillo's second assassination attempt.

As though reading Sartain's mind, Claudia used a gloved

finger to nudge her rook ahead two squares and said, "Why, Mike?"

They were the only two in the Sonora Sun this night. The wind had kept Delbert O'Brien's usual customers away earlier, and the presence of the man whom Don de Castillo obviously wanted dead was keeping them away currently. No one wanted to catch a deadly case of inadvertent lead poisoning.

O'Brien stood behind the bar, morosely reading a newspaper. The burning wood crackled faintly in the stove and made soft sounds like bits of cloth blowing in a breeze. There were occasional, muffled thuds as burned chunks of wood dropped through the grate.

Sartain began to move a pawn, but then left the wooden piece where it was on the board and decided to advance a knight instead. "My only clues are two names. Two names from my past in New Orleans. Phoenix and Jeff Ubek. Old friends."

He advanced the knight and withdrew his hand.

Claudia looked up at him from beneath the brim of her hat. She had her hand on a rook. "Are you sure they are involved? Maybe the don only used their names to draw you into his trap."

"Maybe. But how would he know those names? No one who doesn't know me . . . doesn't know Phoenix and Jeff . . . knows those names, their connection to me." Sartain sipped from a glass half-filled with Sam Clay bourbon.

Claudia shook her head, puzzled.

"I'm sorry about Buffalo, Mike," she said, nudging the rook to protect one of her bishops. "I know you two were together a long ti—"

The marshal of Sonora Gate let her voice trail off as a figure appeared over the batwing doors at the front of the room. It was a short, female-shaped figure silhouetted against the night and a gentle, gray rain shower the wind had blown in.

Claudia dropped a hand to a Schofield on her thigh. Sartain had spied the movement on the porch first, and his right hand was already wrapped lightly around the pearl grips of his LeMat. The figure moved forward, parting the heavy batwings, and the girl strode into the room. She wore a blanket clutched tightly around her shoulders.

Sartain kept his hand on the LeMat's grips as the girl strode quickly to his and Claudia's table on the far side of the ticking stove from the doors. Her bare feet slapped wetly on the wooden floor.

The girl was a curvy blonde with sharp, desperate brown eyes. Her hair was wet and clung to the sides of her face. She slid her oblique gaze from Claudia to the man across from her and said in a soft, reedy voice, "Are you Sartain?"

Her voice was Spanish-accented.

The Cajun slowly dipped his chin, glanced suspiciously toward the batwings once more, wary of another ambush. Then he watched as the girl slid a hand out from inside the blanket she was holding around her and set a .44-caliber bullet on the table in front of Sartain.

The Cajun studied the bullet. When he looked up at the girl and started to ask her who had sent him the message, she'd already wheeled and was padding quickly toward the front of the saloon.

"Hey!" Claudia called.

"Let her go," Sartain said.

Claudia slid her chair back and rose. "I'll follow her. We'll get this settled once and for . . ."

"Claudia, let her go."

The marshal scowled down at the Cajun. "Why, *pendejo*?"

Sartain smiled and took another sip from his glass of Sam Clay. "All in good time."

Claudia gave a caustic chuff and stared toward the batwings

97

still shuddering in the wake of the girl's leaving. "Anyway, I know where she works. And I think I know who sent the bullet."

"This is your town—you gonna make me guess?"

Claudia slacked back into her chair. "I saw a hunchback named Coyon skulking around town earlier. He's very sneaky; thinks he's a shadow. Only he's a hunchbacked shadow. Rather conspicuous. As soft in the head as he is ugly. He is probably the only friend of Don de Castillo's oldest son, Salvador."

"Tell me about Salvador."

"His father disowned him, banished him from Hacienda de la Francesca years ago—after Salvador shot his younger brother, Pedro."

Claudia held up her own whiskey glass, took a small sip, and then curled her upper lip as she turned the glass between her index finger and thumb.

She said, "You see, Pedro caught Salvador in a stable at the *hacienda*. With Pedro's wife. Rumor has it that Pedro's wife had a mouthful of you can guess what. Pedro attacked Salvador with a pitchfork and got a bullet in the heart for his trouble. When Pedro's wife wouldn't stop screaming, Salvador shot her, too, orphaning his brother's two young children, who are now being raised by the don's spinster sister, Jacinta. They will likely turn out as wicked as Jacinta and her brother, the don."

"Now, see—that's why I never wanted to have kids. One pain in the ass after the other."

"So Salvador was banished. He is a brigand. He robs stagecoaches and gold shipments. Even some of his father's gold shipments. He enjoys being a thorn in his papa's side. Occasionally, he works with a gang. Mostly, he works alone. He is also an assassin. Has the run of northern Mejico."

Sartain picked up the .45 cartridge, held it up and down between his thumb and index finger. "If he hates his old man so much, why do you suppose he's after me? Habitual loyalty or some such?"

"I doubt it," Claudia said, shaking her hair back from her brown eyes. "My guess is his father has put a substantial bounty on your head, and . . ."

"And collecting the money from the father who exiled him would be just another, fairly sharp thorn in the old man's side."

"Miguel—sometimes, I swear, you are smarter than you look."

Sartain snorted. "You're just tryin' to flatter me back into your bed."

"I have to admit," the marshal of Sonora Gate said, throwing the last of her shot back and then leaning forward across the table. She glanced behind her at O'Brien and then said quietly so she wouldn't be heard above the rain, "You know how to treat a woman, Miguel Sartain. Around here a girl has to be careful."

"You think the gentlemen of Sonora Gate will think less of you for needing a good ash-hauling now and then?"

"No, that's not it," Claudia said. "Around here, men fall too easily in love with me. They follow me around like puppies. It gets embarrassing!"

The brown-eyed beauty gained her feet. "Come on. It's a short life and a rainy night. Let's go up and enjoy ourselves—on the new mattress O'Brien was kind enough to provide." She turned to the barman, who was drawing himself a beer. "O'Brien, fetch us a couple of burritos from Doña Flores's place. The Cajun will make it worth your while!"

She turned to Sartain, threw her head back, laughed lustily from her throat, and then hooked the Cajun's arm and led him toward the stairs.

CHAPTER 13

Sartain kissed Claudia's lips and then rolled off of her and dropped his feet to the floor.

He rose and walked over to the dresser and poured another drink from the bottle of Sam Clay. He could hear the softly drumming rain beyond the curtained windows flanking the bed. The quiet night, the slow lovemaking with the beguiling Claudia Morales, and the trouble that had brought him here had put the Cajun in a pensive mood.

He donned his hat, pulled on his longhandles, and grabbed his hide makings sack from his shirt pocket. He slacked into a ladderback chair by the window. He opened the window to let more of the quiet sounds of the rain in on the breeze that smelled of pine and cactus blossoms, then took a sip from his glass and placed it back on the windowsill.

Slowly, thoughtfully, he began building a smoke with the chopped tobacco and papers from the makings sack.

Claudia lay in the middle of the bed, eyes closed, smiling dreamily. Her hair was lovely, sprayed across the pillow. Finally, she rolled over like a cat, yawned, drew her knees up slightly, and looked at Sartain, her eyes soft and pleasant in the dull light of the single burning lamp.

Lightning flashed distantly through the window. Seconds later, thunder rumbled quietly. It sounded like the coupling of faraway train cars.

Sartain rolled the cigarette closed.

A Bullet for Sartain

"Tell me about her, Mike," Claudia said, one hand beneath her pillow, continuing to smile at him in a relaxed, dreamy, fulfilled way.

"Phoenix?"

"Sí."

Sartain pulled a stove match out of the makings sack, struck it on the windowsill, and touched the flame to the cigarette. When he had the quirley drawing, he plucked a tobacco crumb from his tongue, drew deep on the cigarette, and blew the smoke against the window and his bourbon glass.

"We grew up together in New Orleans. Street urchins. My ma died a whore's death, same as Phoenix's. Phoenix was taken in by her aunt, but her aunt was a whore too, so she was on the loose most of the time. Pretty girl. Hazel-eyed mulatto with wavy sorrel hair she wore to her waist. Skin the color of almonds dipped in honey. A headstrong girl, Phoenix. When she was six, she was going on sixteen. She had a deep, raspy laugh, and she loved to fish but she didn't eat fish. She preferred beef."

"I didn't know you grew up that way, Mike—on the streets," Claudia said, blinking slowly. She reached for his glass, took a sip of the Sam Clay, and then returned the glass to the window ledge. "But, then, I guess I really didn't know anything about you except that you were fast with a gun, enjoyed solving other people's problems, and were an *oh-soo-wonderful* lover."

She smiled, shifted her legs on the bed.

"I was raised in the French Quarter. Went to work when I was barely out of diapers, swampin' saloons and livery barns, sellin' newspapers, runnin' errands for businessmen, doin' odd jobs along the riverfront. Spoke Creole fluently."

"And Phoenix? How did she live?"

"By sellin' fish to the restaurants until she got old enough to work the line. She was only thirteen when she was recruited by the grandest parlor house in the Quarter. She married one of her customers, an older gent named Hoyt Abercrombie. Owned a shipping business. He died of a heartstroke, and not long after Phoenix had buried him she found out the man was not only broke but in debt up to the bald crown of his skull."

Sartain took another deep drag from the quirley, the sights, smells, sounds of the Quarter in those years swirling through his brain. The vision of Phoenix dressed up like a queen and being escorted by rich men to opera houses and cabarets when he, Sartain, was still sweeping the streets and cleaning spittoons at thirteen, fourteen years old, just before the war broke out and he lied about his age and joined the Confederacy.

"You loved her," Claudia said.

Sartain looked at her. "Yeah, I loved her. She loved me. But we were poor. Poor and tough. The streets of New Orleans brought us up hard. And practical. We talked of running away together when we were only ten years old, but two years later she was being courted by the wealthiest pimp in town. And then she went to work at the House on Royal Street, and the war broke out, and I headed east to fight in it."

"Heartbroken."

"How's that?"

"She broke your heart, didn't she?"

Staring at the end of his quirley, Sartain thought about that. He nodded slowly. "Yeah, I guess she did."

"Do you still love her?"

"I'll probably always love her. Don't we always love our childhood sweethearts?"

Claudia sipped his bourbon again. "When was the last time you saw her?"

"Last time I was in the Quarter. Three, four years ago now. She and a saloon owner named Jeff Ubek—he and I fought in the war—owned a cabaret together. Phoenix was singing and dancing, but she'd had enough of the line." Sartain sipped from the glass, replaced it on the window ledge, parted the curtains, and stared out into the misty night. "I think she was happy. About as happy as a person can be, growin' up like she did, goin' through everything she went through."

"And why didn't you marry her, Mike? When you saw her again?" Claudia stared at him as though peering right through him. "You wanted to, no?"

Sartain was a little taken aback by the directness of her words. And by the astuteness of her assumption.

Yes, he had wanted to marry Phoenix.

But he hadn't even brought it up to her, though she and Jeff Ubek were no more than business partners.

"Way too much water under the bridge," Sartain said lazily, sitting back in his chair and tilting his head from side to side, stretching his neck. "Way too much water under the bridge."

Claudia dropped her long, bare legs to the floor, rose, and knelt between the Cajun's knees. She draped her arms over his thighs and frowned curiously, tenderly up at him. "Is she here, Mike? Could she be with"—she made a bitter face, as though the man's name were a curse word she didn't like to use—"Don de Castillo at Hacienda de la Francesca? I've heard he travels to New Orleans once or twice a year to gamble and visit the bagnios. Maybe . . ."

She let her voice trail off.

Sartain had considered all possibilities, though none had made any sense to him.

He leaned forward and slid Claudia's hair back from her cheeks, exhaling smoke around the quirley between his lips. "Don't know that, darlin'. Don't know what Jeff's part in it is, either, though his name's been bandied about, as well. I do know this, though."

"What's that, Mike?"

"I'm gonna find out."

"Mike, you aren't . . . ?"

"Gonna pay a visit to Don de Castillo?" Sartain grinned. "Promised him, didn't I?"

"You dumb Cajun—do you know how many men he has? *Pistoleros?*"

"Sure, I do." Sartain took the last drag from his cigarette and flipped the stub through the window and out into the rainy night. "Eleven less than he did a week ago."

Claudia drew a deep breath and released it. "Please don't let your Cajun courage be the death of you, my friend."

The next day around twilight, Sartain scrambled up the side of a sandstone ridge.

He was breathing hard and sweating, for he'd walked nearly a mile from where he'd tied his horse near a run-out spring, amongst thick galleta grass, which Boss could fill his bottomless belly with.

The Cajun got down on hands and knees and crabbed to the top of the ridge, doffing his hat and setting it down beside him. He peered over the ridge crest to the south, where the *casa* of Hacienda de la Francesca lay in a broad valley quickly pooling with purple shadows.

From here, Sartain could make out the sprawling structure's red tile roofs and pale adobe walls amongst the trees and shrubs of its courtyards and patios. Lambent light emanated from parts of it, as though to hold back the coming darkness of this high mountain valley. Between the high, rounded peaks rimming the valley, the smoke of cook fires hung in a thin, gauzy web. Sartain figured he was a half-mile away from the main house, but he could catch intermittent whiffs of roasting meat and beans on the occasional, fleeting breezes, and they made his stomach rumble.

He'd eaten a large steak burrito with seasoned rice and a

plate of tortillas and frijoles before leaving Sonora Gate a couple of hours earlier, after another healthy romp with Claudia, but it had been a long ride out here. He'd traveled cross-country, avoiding the main trails as well as de Castillo's range riders, and the walk from where he'd left his horse to this ridge had been long and hard over treacherous terrain in the fast-fading light, and with the bullet-burned thigh that still grieved him.

He'd wanted to make his approach to the *casa* as inconspicuous as possible. Claudia had assured him that the don would have many men patrolling the range within a mile of the main house and that, in light of Sartain's message to de Castillo, the *casa* itself would be under heavy guard.

Of course, Sartain had known it would be. That was all right with him. He enjoyed a challenge. He also enjoyed the fact that the don was likely sweating, if only a little.

He'd be sweating more soon . . .

Sartain could see no guards from here. He picked out a route through the dark humps of the bluffs and low hills, then donned his hat and scrambled back down the ridge to the gravelly bottom of the arroyo he'd been following.

He hefted his Henry in his hands and continued walking nearly silently in the doeskin moccasins a young Sioux woman had sewn him a couple of winters ago on the northern plains near Bismarck. Tonight, to make himself as indistinguishable a night shadow as possible, he wore a navy-blue wool shirt and dark denims with a black bandanna knotted around his neck.

A rock tumbled down the side of the narrow, seven-foot-deep canyon that Sartain was threading. The Cajun stopped suddenly, raising the barrel of his Henry and tightening his kid-gloved index finger across the trigger.

He stared up the right side of the canyon, heart thudding.

A figure moved. He could make out the round head with triangle-shaped, tufted ears. A long tail flicked upward. Two eyes glowed yellow at him. They seemed to pulsate, turn red. The lower jaw dropped, and a guttural growl sounded from deep in the bobcat's throat. A keening, angry whine.

A few more rocks spilled down the side of the ridge, and then the cat, the size of two large house cats, pulled its head back away from the ridge, flicked its tail once more, and was gone.

Sartain drew a calming breath. He'd thought he'd been targeted for a mountain lion's supper. The bobcat was probably off to catch something a little more its size—a rattlesnake or kangaroo rat, say. The Cajun continued on down the wash.

For most of his tramp through the rolling, rocky, cactus-spiked terrain, he could not see the *casa*. Occasionally he climbed to higher ground to get his bearings before tramping on.

Twice he'd had to stop and hunker down behind a boulder or a shrub, for de Castillo had indeed sent out pickets. Fortunately, the Cajun had heard them or spotted their shadows before they'd seen him, and when they'd passed, he'd continued on until taking a knee in a stand of pecan trees about twenty yards away from the six-foot-high adobe wall ringing the don's sprawling, multi-level *casa*.

The night had closed over Hacienda de la Francesca. Stars sparkled in the velvety sky. There was only a slight lilac smudge between the far western peaks, marking where the sun had dropped an hour ago. Coyotes yammered in the hills on one side of the *casa* while a lone wolf howled on the other. Probably from a bunkhouse came the faint strains of a mandolin.

The *casa* itself was quiet. At least to Sartain's ears. Now, he had to find a way over or through the wall without being spotted.

He moved out from behind a pecan tree and started moving at a crouch toward the wall. Boots crunched gravel somewhere ahead and on his left. The sounds were growing steadily louder.

Someone was moving toward Sartain, who whirled and high-tailed it back to the pecan on the balls of his moccasins and crouched behind the tree once more.

A figure rounded the corner of the adobe wall on Sartain's left. The man was a vague shadow, but his crunching boot thuds and spur chings were loud in the quiet night. A big man in a *serape*, gray slacks, and black *sombrero*, a billowy red neckerchief flopping on his chest. He had a carbine cradled in his arms.

As he approached Sartain's position, the man slowed steadily until, when he was to the place where Sartain had turned around and retreated, he stopped altogether. A silhouette against the pale adobe wall, he stood staring toward Sartain, who jerked his head back behind the pecan, gritting his teeth and squeezing the Henry in his hands.

There was a long silence. And then the man's voice sounded crisp and clear as he said in Spanish, "Hey, you—*amigo.* I know you're there. Show yourself or I'll start shooting!"

CHAPTER 14

Sartain remained hunkered on one knee, pressing his cheek and shoulder against the pecan. He'd doffed his hat and hooked it on his other knee.

A dull ringing sounded in his ears. He cursed his carelessness. He'd come so far. If he had to shoot and run away like a damned tinhorn, he was going to be mighty piss-burned at his fool self. Unless . . .

He reached behind and wrapped his right hand around the horn handle of his Green River knife.

"Hey, *amigo*," the man standing between the pecan and the adobe wall said again. Then, more softly, less certainly: "Someone there?"

Sartain began to slide the knife from its black leather sheath and parted his lips to draw a calming breath. He released both the breath and the knife when he heard the man's boots begin crunching sand and gravel again, gradually growing quieter. Sartain looked around the tree to see the big, broad-shouldered figure walking away along the wall, to Sartain's right.

The man turned the wall's far corner and disappeared.

Again, silence.

"Whew!" Sartain whispered softly, his heart slowing.

He moved out from behind the tree and hot-footed to the wall. He walked along the wall in the same direction as the big Mexican. When he rounded the rear corner, he saw the man striding off along the wall on his left, breeze-ruffled mesquites

108

and orange trees waving on his right.

An opening in the wall lay about thirty yards beyond Sartain. Keeping his left shoulder nearly brushing the wall, he moved to the gap and swung through the gateless opening and into a courtyard. On the other side of the courtyard lay a gallery running along the building's wall. Sartain made for it, weaving around transplanted trees and shrubs, until his moccasins tapped softly on the stone tiles of the brush-roofed gallery floor.

There were several large, arched windows in the wall of the *casa*. Many were lit. Sartain could smell coal oil, candle wax, piñon smoke, and the belly-nibbling aroma of roasting meat.

As he made his way along the gallery, he moved swiftly past a window opening onto a large kitchen and dining room area, which was tended by two plump Mexican women standing just then with their backs to the window. They were chopping food on a long preparation table, chattering in Spanish peppered with Pima.

Just beyond, a corridor opened off the gallery, running through what appeared the heart of the *casa*. Sartain had no idea how he was going to find Don de Castillo. He figured he had some time, as it was still early.

He had all night to find the man, learn why de Castillo wanted Sartain dead, what Phoenix and Jeff had to with it, and then kill the man by inserting his Green River knife into his belly, just below the man's breastbone, and shoving it up and into his black heart.

He turned into the dark corridor and found himself under a roof. A short flight of steps took him to another level of the *casa*, and then he was walking down a dim hall between two adobe walls and with no longer any roof over his head.

He stopped. He'd heard something behind him. The sounds grew louder—the clacking of shoes. A quick, determined tread. A soft, jovial whistling rose with the clacking, and Sartain darted into a dark doorway and stood in the shadows, waiting, listening to the clacking shoes and the happy whistling growing louder. He could smell the aromatic smoke of a fine cigar.

Sartain's pulse throbbed hopefully in both temples.

The don himself?

Could the Cajun be that lucky?

He waited. The sounds and the cigar's aroma intensified until a short, stocky figure strode past the opening hiding the big Cajun. Sartain stepped out quickly and pressed the point of his knife against the man's back, stopping him instantly. The man threw up his hands and gave a surprised, shallow groan.

In near-fluent Spanish, Sartain said, "If you call out, I'll poke this pig sticker through your spine and into your heart. You'll be dead before you hit the floor." Sartain licked his upper lip and added in the same low, menacing tone, *"Comprende?"*

"Sí."

"Drop your arms. Turn around slow."

The man did as he'd been told. Sartain found himself looking at a short, thick man with coal-black hair pomaded to one side. He was maybe Sartain's own age, early thirties, but he had the dapper look of a dandy. He was well dressed in a short, broadcloth waistcoat, gaudy red tie, silk shirt, black belt, and Spanish-style dress slacks.

His polished black shoes glistened in the darkness.

He wasn't old enough to be Alonzo de Castillo. Perhaps one of his sons.

"Who are you?" Sartain asked, holding the knife against the man's soft belly.

"Dios," the short, thick man said, eyes flashing fearfully. He looked at the rifle in Sartain's left hand, at the knife in his right hand, then returned his gaze to the Cajun, who stood a full head taller. He knew who'd jumped him.

Sartain said with a quiet edge, "Once more—who are you?"

110

"I am Carlos Areces," the man said quickly, hoarsely. "The don's bookkeeper."

"Where is the don now?"

The thick little man thought about that. Then he said, "Probably in his quarters. His young lady just got back from San Luis with a new dress." His voice sounded ever so faintly sheepish at the admission.

"Take me to his room."

"You're going to kill him, aren't you?"

"Wanna join him?"

"No!" The bookkeeper's eyes nearly bulged from their sockets. In the darkness, Sartain could see his face turn a full shade lighter.

"Then show me. Avoid the populated parts of the house. If we run into anyone, we're gonna hide until they're gone, *comprende*? If anyone sees us, I'm holding you personally responsible." He paused for emphasis. *"Comprende?"*

"Si, si. Oh, dear god!"

"Which way?" Sartain said, keeping his voice low and level.

The bookkeeper lifted his chin and glanced behind Sartain, who then turned and, keeping his knife pointed at the thick man's bulging belly resting on broad, womanish hips, gave the chubby bookkeeper room to step around him. Then the Cajun followed the little man through two more corridors, up and down some stairs, and out into a dark, breezy courtyard. There was the sound of water splashing in a fountain. Sartain believed they were now on the southwestern end of the *casa*.

The little man had done a good job. He and Sartain had run into no one.

They came to a tall, deeply recessed window, heavy wooden shutters thrown back, red velvet drapes pushed aside. The bookkeeper stopped in the dark gallery before the window, turned to Sartain, and canted his head toward the window through which flickering red firelight emanated.

Odd, quiet sounds drifted out the open window, as well.

Sartain gestured the little man back around him. He prodded him a ways back down the gallery and then he rapped the butt of his rifle against the back of the little man's head. The book-keeper grunted and his knees buckled. Sartain sheathed his knife, grabbed the chubby man by the back of his collar, and eased him down against the wall of the *casa*. The little man turned his head and slumped to one side.

He was out. He'd waken with a headache, but Sartain knew how to put a man out without seriously injuring or killing him. Most of the time, anyway . . .

Sartain doffed his hat and stepped up to the window. He slid a look into the room.

It was large and well appointed with heavy wooden and leather furniture and trophy heads on the walls. A canopied bed abutted the far wall, in a shrine-like recessed area roughly twenty feet to Sartain's right. An elegant, balding old man stood at the end of the bed, facing the outer wall.

The old man, who had a carefully trimmed beard and mustache, had his eyes closed, head tipped back slightly. There were many rings on his knotted, brown fingers. He wore only a purple silk robe. The robe was open. His chest was bony and pale, grizzled gray hair bristling between the pouch-like lumps of his breasts. His belly bulged over bony hips. A dark-haired girl in a gaudy, frilly, peach-colored dress—obviously new and trimmed with white lace—knelt on the floor in front of the old man.

The dress had been pulled down to her waist, baring her fragile, brown shoulders and slender back to Sartain. Her hair was immaculately coifed beneath a peach-colored *mantilla*. A string of pearls ringed her brown neck.

The old man grunted, placed a beringed hand on the back of

the girl's head.

Sartain's guts writhed. He curled his upper lip distastefully as he pulled his head back away from the window and donned his hat. He stood there on the dark gallery, listening to the breeze and the splashing of the fountain, until he heard the don moan and gasp.

Suddenly, the don cursed the girl as though deeply unsatisfied, then loudly ordered her from the room in such fast, heated Spanish that Sartain couldn't make out everything he was saying.

The girl apologized, cowering. Her new dress rustled. Bare feet slapped on the tiles. There was the click of a door opening, the soft thud of it closing.

Sartain looked into the room again.

The don was moving away from him. He'd closed his robe and was looking down, moving his arms as though tying the robe about his waist.

He stopped before a cherry cabinet backing a long, leather couch that fronted a fireplace on the room's far end. The flames of the fire leaped and crackled, occasionally popping and spitting sparks into the room. The flames were reflected off the room's thick, well-decorated walls.

Sartain lifted one leg over the window ledge, and then the other. He strode quietly toward the don, who was pouring liquor from a cut glass decanter into a green goblet. The don must have heard or smelled the sweat on him, because suddenly he dropped both the goblet and the decanter with a crash. His right hand shot to a drawer. He'd just got the drawer open when Sartain slammed his rifle butt hard between the man's shoulder blades.

The don fell forward across the cabinet, dropping the silver-plated pistol he'd tried to pull out of the drawer. De Castillo gave a guttural groan against the pain in his back. Sartain rammed the butt down hard against the man's back once more and then tapped it against the back of the man's head.

That stunned the don into silence as he continued to flail across the top of the cabinet. Sartain pulled him off the cabinet, threw him to the floor where he went sprawling. The Cajun rammed the butt of the Henry into the man's crotch, and that caused the old man to jackknife, clutching his groin.

His warty face was a mask of agony.

As he stared up at Sartain, he hardened his jaws and then opened his mouth as if to scream. The Cajun snapped the butt of his rifle against his shoulder and aimed at the don's open, gold-filled mouth. Sartain grinned, threateningly.

"You wanna die now? Go ahead and scream."

The don closed his mouth, wincing and groaning against the fiery pain in his loins.

"You'll kill me anyway."

"True. That's why I'm here. But I'll do it fast as opposed to slow. If you scream now, I'll blow your stinkin' oysters off. And then I'll blow your knees out. And if I still have time, I'll cut off the end of your nose and leave you here to die slow, screamin'."

Sartain shook his head slowly, grinning savagely, remembering Buffalo hanging from that tree in the rainstorm. "And there won't be a damn thing anyone will be able to do for you, you old pervert."

De Castillo made another face as another bayonet of pain stabbed his crotch. "And . . . what do I have to do . . . for this quick death?"

"Tell me why you want me dead. And what do you know about Phoenix Catipulso and Jeff Ubeck?"

CHAPTER 15

"Pour me a drink," the don said, writhing on the floor, clutching his battered balls.

Sartain glanced at the pistol the old man had dropped. He kicked it against the wall. Then he backed up to the liquor cabinet, opened another decanter, and poured what appeared to be brandy into the same, stout goblet the don had been about to fill when he'd been so deservedly interrupted.

Sartain handed the man the glass. De Castillo took it, threw back half, winced again, and lowered the glass to his left thigh. He still had one hand over his tender balls.

He narrowed one eye as he stared up at Sartain. "You'll never get out of here alive—you know that."

"All that matters is I settle a score for a friend of mine your first set of hunters killed."

"Ah, yes. Revenge is your profession." The don looked grimly down at his glass. "Perhaps I underestimated my quarry."

"You wanted it to be easy, eh? Have me killed—*bushwhacked*—and you'd feel better." Sartain negligently aimed the Henry at the man's right temple. "Why?"

The don stared at the Henry's barrel, studying it. Only it wasn't the rifle he was seeing in his mind's eye. He slid his gaze up the barrel and past the scrolled receiver to the cobalt-blue eyes of the dark-haired man aiming the weapon.

He flared his nostrils, ground his teeth, and raked out, "Phoenix."

"What's she got to do with it?"

"She loved you."

Sartain blinked, said nothing. His hard stare belied his incredulity. But he could feel his heartbeat gradually increasing. His hands began to sweat inside his gloves.

"She loved you," the don repeated in that same angry tone, his eyelids fluttering over his rock-hard eyes as he continued to stare right through Sartain. "More than me."

"Where is she?"

"On the southern ridge." The don waited a few seconds, and then his lips stretched in a smile, revealing his expensive teeth. The smile faded quickly, and the man's lips began to tremble.

"In New Orleans, I asked her to marry me. She accepted. I brought her here to Hacienda de la Francesca. A priest was traveling from Mexico City to marry us. But during the days that we waited, I could see that something was troubling my lovely Phoenix. She grew darker and darker, quieter and quieter, until finally, after I'd prodded her desperately, needing to know what thoughts *so* haunted her, she told me that she couldn't marry me after all."

Tears dribbled down the don's pasty cheeks and into the mustache that hid his upper lip. He brushed them away with one hand, took a desperate sip of his brandy, and then continued to glare through wet eyes at Sartain. "She loved another."

The Henry shook in Sartain's hands.

Phoenix . . .

"She hadn't realized how much," the don croaked out. "Until after I asked for her hand. Her love, her devotion."

The room pitched around Sartain. He took one step back, spread his feet, resetting himself. He could hear a shrill scream, as if from far away, from the bottom of a deep well.

"What . . . what did you do?" he rasped, gritting his teeth as he aimed down the Henry's shaking barrel.

The don's eyes widened. The lids were fluttering. His face acquired a weird sensation, as though he was both laughing and crying at the same time. "She summoned a man to fetch her. He came. His name was Ubeck."

"Jeff Ubeck," Sartain heard himself say. He could barely hear anything above the pounding of his heart in his head, the rushing of the blood in his veins.

"I was so heartbroken that I ran down their carriage as they left the *hacienda*. My men and I. We ran them off the road and into a canyon. Phoenix was still alive but badly broken. Ubeck was dead. I kissed my lovely Phoenix once more . . . and then I shot her in the head as she lay sobbing in my arms."

Tears rolled down the don's cheeks, soaking his goatee. He was sobbing openly now, shoulders quaking. He tipped his head back as he screamed, "I shot my lovely Phoenix over and over and over again . . . *goddamn you, Sartain!*"

The man bawled, raked in a breath, and glared at the Cajun once more, his face flushed and swollen as he shouted, pointing his brandy glass, "And I wanted you dead, as well! I wanted you dead, as well, *you son of a bitch who took her away from me before I even had her!*"

Sartain suddenly heard, beneath the don's racking sobs and the screaming in his own ears, running footsteps approaching from outside the room's door and from the patio by which he himself had entered the don's quarters.

Sartain swung toward the door as it burst open. A beefy, bearded man in a striped *serape* bolted into the room, eyes wide beneath the brim of his straw *sombrero.*

He fired the carbine in his hands a half-second after Sartain fired the Henry. Sartain's bullet punched dust from the middle of the man's billowing *serape* at the same time it punched the *hombre* back into the hall, wincing, his own slug screeching over Sartain's left shoulder and burying itself in a wall.

117

A man shouted behind the Cajun. Boots pounded, and spurs jangled wildly.

Sensing the presence of others entering the room through the open window, Sartain turned full around and threw himself over the liquor cabinet and the sofa on the other side of it. As he hit the floor, two belching rifles momentarily drowned out the loud, racking wails of the don. The bullets plunked into the liquor cabinet and couch.

One spanged off the hearth, sparking.

Sartain rolled toward the fireplace, rolled off a shoulder and hip, and lurched to a crouch, the Henry crashing and lapping flames toward the two men now standing just off the foot of the don's bed. One stood before the other, but as Sartain's bullets punched through each man in turn, they did a bizarre death dance together, one man triggering his rifle into his partner's right knee. They flew back, screaming, losing their hats and rifles, blood splashing the floor behind them, before piling up in twisted heaps near the window through which they'd entered.

Another gun barked. It was the hollow pop of a pistol. The bullet burned across Sartain's upper left arm. He slid his gaze to the left. The don was aiming his smoking pistol at him, lips pulled back from gritted teeth.

He shouted a Spanish curse as he thumbed back the hammer of the pistol once more but did not get the revolver leveled again before Sartain's Henry thundered. The don screamed as Sartain's bullet took the man through his right arm. The bullet hammered him around, his back to Sartain. The Cajun aimed carefully and shot the wailing man through the back of his left arm.

Blood splashed out the ragged hole on the other side of the man's arm.

"You crazy bastard!" Sartain ground out, cocking and firing the rifle again, shooting the man through his left knee.

The don was on the floor, flopping around, bleeding and wailing.

"Finish me, you bastard!" he shouted in Spanish. "You promised you'd finish me!"

Sartain triggered another round through the man's other knee, and then he shot him in the balls. As he ejected the last, smoking cartridge, which clanked off the hearth behind the Cajun, he said through a snarl, "I lied. You don't deserve a fast death. You die long and hard, *Don!*"

More boots hammered in the hall.

Sartain whipped around, fired three shots through the open door, evoking shouts and barked epithets, and then he jumped over the coach and onto the liquor cabinet. He leaped over the don's writhing body, the man having grown silent and pale now in his unendurable agony, and hit the floor running. He leaped through the window as rifles roared behind him, the bullets hammering the walls and window shutters, making the curtains dance.

Sartain landed on the stone tiles of the outer gallery, stepped to his right, and pressed his back against the adobe wall, looking around him. Two shadowy figures moved toward him from his left.

A gun flashed.

The bullet burned across the nub of the Cajun's left cheek.

He leveled the Henry from his right hip. The rifle leaped and roared in his hands. The shadow moving toward him screamed and dropped, and then Sartain took off running across the courtyard, heading for the dark mouth of a corridor on the other side. Behind him, rifles barked and men shouted shrilly, furiously in Spanish.

Bullets screamed around and over Sartain, one sparking off the stone fountain, another grinding into a gallery roof support post. They tore into the gravel around his hammering moccasins and then into flagstones as he gained the opposite gallery. They thudded into the adobe wall on either side of the corridor mouth as he threw himself into it, half losing his balance.

He dropped to one knee and with the same motion heaved himself up and continued sprinting, scissoring his arms and legs.

He wasn't sure how he got out of the *casa* until he was out of it. He wasn't sure how he got through the wall, either—or over it—until he was beyond it and running through trees and climbing a rocky hill. Half-consciously, he headed north as much as he could, avoiding men and cracking rifles, remembering beneath the hammering in his head and the screaming in his ears that he'd come from that direction.

"Phoenix," he heard himself muttering, wheezing, sobbing as he ran into the hills beyond the *casa,* his bullet-torn left arm and the graze on his cheek feeling only warm and numb. "Oh, Christ . . . *Phoenix!*"

He wasn't sure how far he'd run and walked and then run again, before weakness and nausea overcame him. The ground came up to slam his knees hard. Cactus thorns bit into his right knee. He vomited, crawled ahead. Behind him, men screamed and continued to trigger rifles and pistols, but absently the Cajun opined that they'd lost his trail.

They couldn't track a man wearing moccasins in the dark.

Sartain needed to get off the *hacienda* tonight, under cover of darkness. He needed to find Boss and ride. And he would have done just that. Only weakness and sickness washed over him like a wave of warm, black tar. Try as he might, he could not regain his feet.

Vaguely, he noticed a dark, shallow chasm between two rock- and cactus-spiked hills to his left. He flopped onto the ground, rolled, and let the dark mouth of the wash engulf him. And then everything was dark and silent for a long time.

His arm began to ache and throb, but it was nothing akin to the sorrow that hammered his soul.

"Phoenix," he cried as he slept his pain-racked sleep, blood leaking from his arm. "Oh, Phoenix!"

Cold was a rough blanket around him. The ground was an even colder stone beneath him—an uneven stone pinching him, poking him. When warmth lay for a long time on his cheek, growing warmer to the point of discomfort, he opened his eyes.

The sun burned into his skull.

He could feel a lance penetrating his left arm. He turned to look at it. No lance was there. He knew a moment's surprise. His black neckerchief was wrapped around the arm, north of the elbow where the throbbing was the most severe. Automatically, before passing out the night before, he must have had sense enough to wrap the wound, knowing that he'd likely bleed to death if he didn't.

He looked around. He lay in a crease between low hills. His Henry lay across his thighs. His hat lay to his left. The wash was only about twice his body's width. On both sides, a tan-colored slope of rocks, Spanish bayonet, prickly pear, and catclaw climbed away from him.

A voice sounded to his left. A distant voice speaking Spanish. Sartain couldn't make out what the man was saying. Then a horse whinnied, and a second man said something also in Spanish.

Sartain placed his hands on his rifle. He lifted his head and winced as pain shot through him. He ached all over. His neck and shoulders were as stiff as the ground beneath him. His arm ached and burned and throbbed.

He grunted and cursed as he hauled himself to a sitting position. Quickly, he checked the rifle. Empty. Not a single shell left in the tube. He couldn't remember having fired sixteen rounds, but he must have.

He filled the tube from his cartridge belt and then checked the LeMat. It was fully loaded.

He wrestled himself to a standing position, all of his joints crying out. But after a minute of hard breathing, he realized he wasn't hurt as badly as he'd thought he was. Mainly stiff and sore, and then, of course, there was the bullet wound, but he thought the slug had gone all the way through, missing the bone.

If it hadn't, he'd still be flat on his back.

He donned his hat, shouldered the Henry, and walked up the slope, following a faint game or cow path. Near the top, he dropped to his knees, doffed his hat, and lifted a look over the bluff's rocky crest.

Immediately, he dropped his chin, bringing his head back down beneath the brow of the bluff. Three riders were riding toward him—actually, two were riding, one man was leading his horse by its reins and picking out Sartain's trail amongst the rocks. Sartain had merely glimpsed the man leading the horse, but the *hombre* had looked dark enough to have some Indian blood.

Maybe Pima or Apache, both especially good trackers.

He'd found the Cajun's trail.

On all fours and staring at the ground, Sartain smiled grimly. *Come on, you bastards,* he thought. *I haven't exacted enough revenge yet.* Not for Phoenix or Jeff or Buffalo McCluskey.

If you're fool enough to follow me, with your boss either dead or close to it, you're fool enough to die foolish deaths.

The men's voices grew louder, as did the clacking of their horses' shod hooves. Occasionally, one of the horses blew. When the men and horses were close enough that the Cajun could hear the men breathing, hear the spurs of the walking men ringing, he walked calmly up to the top of the hill.

He stared down the other side.

The two riders saw him first. They both sucked sharp breaths and made faces. The man on foot was too busy inspecting the sign on the ground. When his two compatriots stopped their horses, he glanced at them and then followed their gazes to the crest of the bluff they were climbing.

He cursed and stepped back, tripping over a rock then pushing off his horse to regain his footing—a short, squat, fat-faced *mestizo* in a ratty brown *poncho*. He wore a brace of pistols on his hips, the *serape* tucked behind the wooden handles.

"Oh, shit," he said again in Spanish.

Sartain's lips formed an icy smile, showing the edges of his teeth. He kept the Henry on his shoulder.

"Is de Castillo still alive?" he asked in Spanish.

One of the riders—the man to Sartain's left—said, "So far."

Sartain nodded his grim satisfaction.

He challenged the three with his eyes and by flexing his fingers around the Henry resting on his left shoulder.

The one who'd told him the don was still kicking drew first, and thus he was the first to die as Sartain's pistol belched smoke and flames and flung him from his saddle.

The other rider was next to roll off the back of his horse, triggering his own pistol into the ground and starting all the horses to fiddlefooting. Sartain's next shot missed the *mestizo* by a hair's breadth, as one of the startled horses behind the squat man plowed into him, sent him rolling amongst the rocks.

As the half-breed lifted his pistol from the ground, Sartain's LeMat spoke once more, drilling a neat round hole through the middle of the tracker's forehead.

Sartain managed to run down one of the three horses. He got his bearings and then rode off in search of Boss.

CHAPTER 16

Claudia Morales rolled the quirley closed as she walked to the open door of her office.

She leaned a shoulder against the doorframe and poked the quirley into her mouth, sliding her gaze along the main street in the same direction she'd been sliding it for the past two days— south. She worked the quirley back and forth between her lips, moistening it with her tongue, sealing it, and then struck a lucifer to life on the doorframe.

She touched the flame to the end of the quirley and drew the smoke into her lungs. She released it through her nose, withdrew the cylinder to inspect the coal, and then cast her gaze once more to the south where the main street became a pale ribbon of trail rising and falling through the desert, toward far mountains that jutted in soft gray against the light-green sky of dusk.

Still nothing. No sign of him for the past two days.

He should have been back by now. Really, he should have been back that morning. If he'd accomplished his task the previous night and had left the *hacienda* alive.

If . . .

Claudia gave a soft snort. A right capable man, Sartain. But could he take on twenty armed men, maybe more if you threw in the don's *peons,* and make it back alive? *Twenty armed men on their own turf?*

She should have gone with him. But he was on a personal errand. It didn't officially involve her. She was the town marshal of Sonora Gate. If her jurisdiction didn't extend beyond the limits of town, it certainly didn't stretch across the San Pedro and into Old Mexico. She had no dog in Sartain's fight except Sartain himself.

Not that she wouldn't have loved to see Don de Castillo dead.

She should have removed her town marshal's badge, saddled a horse, and gone with him. He hadn't wanted her to. In fact, he'd forbade her, saying it was his fight, which it was. His fight alone. Still, she should have trailed him and at least holed up on this side of the border to help him shed any of the don's men who came after him.

But that again was supposing he would even make it off the hacienda alive . . .

She didn't know what he meant to her, if anything besides their passionate couplings, but he did mean something, though she wasn't in the business of getting involved with vigilantes. Even handsome, passionate vigilantes who knew their way around a woman's body . . .

"Forget it," Claudia told herself in Spanish, exhaling another cigarette plume over the office's front gallery and into the soft, gray-green light of dusk. "It's not your business to save fools from themselves."

Still, she stared along the pale ribbon of trail growing dimmer and dimmer the farther the sun sank behind the western mountains. She widened her eyes with interest when she saw something bobbing along the trail. It was a hatted head. And then she saw a horse's head. A horse and rider riding on out of the dusky desert toward the outskirts of Sonora Gate . . .

Claudia stared hard, forgetting her quirley, but then she saw that it was only Owen Gallantly, the lanky, simple-minded, middle-aged son of an old desert rat, Pete Gallantly, whose diggings lay a couple of miles from town. Pete often sent Owen to town after the workday was done for a bottle or two of cheap tequila and maybe a couple of burritos from Doña Flores's place, if Pete didn't feel like cooking.

Watching Owen canter into town on his beefy, cream mule, Claudia flicked her half-smoked quirley into the street, and then swung around and strode purposefully into the office. She passed her cluttered desk, took her Winchester down from the gun rack, and strode back through the door. She drew the door closed, locked it, and then clopped down the gallery steps, stopping abruptly in the street and sliding her gaze back south.

No.

There was no point now. If she'd been going to help him, she should have ridden out earlier. Now it was too late. Now, if he was alive, he was likely badly wounded and lying out in the desert somewhere. She'd never be able to find him. Even if she did happen to find him, he'd be dead by the time she reached him.

Besides, he meant nothing to her. For the love of all the saints in heaven, sister, he was a wanted man! A fugitive from justice! If you had any self-respect you'd have locked him up and sent for a deputy United States marshal to haul his vigilante ass up to Prescott!

Instead, you make love with him and now you're worried because he might have ridden into Mexico to kill a man for whatever reason, and ended up dead himself!

Cristo!

Claudia returned the Winchester to the gun rack. She ran the chain through the three rifles she kept in the rack, locked the padlock, pocketed the key, and left the office, locking the door behind her and then pocketing that key, as well.

She hadn't eaten all day, but that was about to be remedied. She pulled her hat brim down low, took a quick swing through town, making sure there was no trouble, and then, deeming that all the laws were being obeyed even on the Mexican end of Sonora Gate this weekday night, she headed over to Doña Flores's place for tacos and menudo. She took her time, eating and reading an old Tucson newspaper some drummer had left behind, and then she had a couple of shots of tequila over at the Sonora Sun.

There were only a few customers in the place—one mestizo goat herder and his little brown and white dog wearing a red bandanna, and three sullen saddle tramps no doubt riding the grubline. She doubted the pilgrims would be much trouble, as sun-blistered and saddle-sore as they appeared, but she waited until they'd finished their game of red dog and had shuffled off to find a pile of straw to bed down in before she headed upstairs to her room.

"Any sign of Sartain?" Delbert O'Brien asked behind her as he swabbed the table vacated by the three pilgrims.

Slowly climbing the stairs, Claudia glanced over her shoulder at the barman. "Was that his name?"

And then she gave a caustic chuff, ignoring the hollow feeling in her belly despite her recent supper, and continued to the saloon's second story. Normally, Claudia was more careful about opening her door and entering her room. Being a law woman of a border town had earned her a fair share of enemies, any one of whom could lie behind her door in bushwhack. All they really needed was a skeleton key.

But this night, despite her determination to forget Sartain, she was deeply distracted, so when she'd entered her room, she didn't bother to look around before closing the door and lighting one of the lamps. Just as she touched a match to the lantern's wick, however, she smelled man sweat and leather and sour alcohol, and she knew instantly that she'd made a grave mistake.

127

A deep, Spanish-accented voice sounded inordinately loud in the silent room when it said, "Welcome home, Marshal Morales." Claudia gasped and dropped the lantern's glass mantle, which shattered on the floor.

As she jerked around, she reached for one of her Schofields but stayed the movement when she heard two gun hammers click, one after the other. Someone whistled softly, almost inaudibly, between his teeth.

The whistler lay sprawled on her bed, on his side, facing her. Grinning at her. Salvador de Castillo's legs were crossed at his ankles, and his *sombrero* hung from the front post of Claudia's bed. In his right hand, he held a Remington revolver, its butt resting on the edge of the bed.

The barrel was aimed at her belly.

A thick shadow moved out from behind a chest of drawers near the closed door. It was a hunched, bizarrely menacing figure with a hunched back. Coyon grinned, and his teeth were a hideous, crooked, tobacco- and food-encrusted mess beneath his long, hooked hawk's nose. The brim of his ragged *sombrero* half-hid his eyes, the pupil of his wandering left eye glistening demonically in the lamplight.

Claudia kept her right hand on the handle of her right Schofield, leaving the pistol in its holster. Her chest rose and fell sharply as she snarled out, "What in the *hell* are you two bastards doing in my room?"

"Waiting for the most beautiful law woman in all of America. Possibly in all of Mejico, too." Salvador closed his fingers together, touched them to his lips, making a kissing sound, and flung his open hand out to indicate Claudia. "Wouldn't you say, Coyon?"

"Oh, yes," the hunchback said, his good eye resting hungrily on Claudia's sharply rising and falling breasts. "I would say so, *amigo.* Hee-hee-hee!"

128

"Answer my question, *pendejo!*"

"Shut up," Salvador said mildly, his grin in place. "I'll do the question-asking around here. After all, we got the drop on you, *senorita*. Tsk-tsk. So careless. That isn't like you."

"Diddle yourself, *pendejo!* Answer my question, or I'll—!"

Salvador raised his pistol, aiming the barrel at her right tit, and narrowed one eye. Claudia thought she saw his finger tighten over the trigger. Fear washed through her. She wasn't accustomed to the feeling, and it caught her by surprise. It also left a bad taste in her mouth. It mixed in as much fury as fear, so that her heart was pounding savagely in her temples.

"Keep your voice down," Salvador warned. "You want to wake up the whole town?"

"Does O'Brien know you're here?"

"We came up the back way, *senorita*," said Coyon in his soft, phlegmy voice, keeping his own Remington aimed at Claudia. He opened his other hand to reveal a skeleton key. He snickered.

"To answer your question, Marshal," Salvador said, resting the side of his head on the heel of his free hand, "we were wondering where your friend is. Sartain." He grinned widely, his dark eyes flashing beneath a cowlick of his dark-brown hair. "Did he get scared and run off after receiving my message? That would be too bad. I was waiting to make his anticipation build, and then when I finally made my move, he is nowhere to be found!"

Claudia laughed, only half faking the humor. "You think Mike Sartain is afraid of you, you vermin? Hah! That is a good one!"

That turned both men's seedy grins into indignant scowls. Coyon looked at his friend uncertainly.

Salvador said with soft menace, "You have a sharp tongue. Tell me where Sartain is, or I will put your tongue to better use. Your tongue and your entire mouth."

The seedy smile returned.

"Go to hell!"

"Yes, something like that. Where is Sartain?"

"None of your stinking business, *pendejo*!"

Claudia wasn't sure why she didn't want to tell Salvador where Mike had gone. She doubted that Sartain was alive. But something inside her would not give an inch when crowded by the likes of Salvador de Castillo, whom she had banned from Sonora Gate over a year ago.

A man wearing a badge might have had a little room to play with. But a female wearing a badge needed to command respect at all quarters. She could not give an inch, even if it cost her her life.

Or worse.

Salvador blinked slowly. The grin was gone now. "Unbuckle your pistol belt and let it fall to the floor."

Claudia stared at the man hard. Rage was a living thing inside her. She wanted to pull her pistols and start shooting. Maybe he'd drill her from five feet away, but maybe she wouldn't die before she drilled him.

Maybe . . .

That wasn't good enough. She'd do as he said for now, wait for a chance to kill the bastard.

She drew a heavy breath as she moved her hands to the buckle of her cartridge belt. She unbuckled it, untied the thongs from around her thighs, let the rig drop to the floor. She wondered if O'Brien had heard the thud on the wooden floor. She hoped not. She didn't want him to come to her aid. The apron was no match for de Castillo. No one would die on her account.

At least, not anyone not currently in her room.

"Now, take off your shirt," de Castillo said.

Claudia's shoulders tensed. Her guts slithered around like

130

snakes in her belly. She told the bastard before her to do something impossible to himself. He laughed at that too loudly. She jerked a look at the door, hoping O'Brien didn't come. If he thought something was wrong, he'd likely grab the Greener he kept under the bar and run upstairs. Him being a man, he'd feel he had to.

And he'd be killed for his trouble.

"I said," de Castillo repeated, louder this time, with even more menace, "kindly remove your shirt, Marshal Morales."

Claudia cleared the knot from her throat. "You're right. He headed north."

"Huh?"

"Sartain headed north." Claudia slapped her thighs. "You're right. He'd heard your reputation, and he didn't want to tangle with you, Salvador. Congratulations. Now why don't you and your dog scurry on back to your cave?"

Coyon curled his upper lip at that.

"Make her do it," the hunchback grunted. "Make her take her shirt off!"

"We're past Sartain now, my lovely marshal." De Castillo waved the gun in his hand. "Now the subject is your shirt. Remove it, please."

"No."

"I am not going to ask you again!"

Coyon laughed, excited. He laughed too loudly and stomped his heavy foot on the floor. Alarm bells tolled in Claudia's ears. O'Brien had a wife, a daughter. He had a whore working for him. She was likely asleep just down the hall, as she hadn't been feeling well for weeks. Likely pregnant, though O'Brien hadn't said. The town doctor came and went. Claudia didn't want anyone else endangered here.

She began unbuttoning her shirt.

CHAPTER 17

"Mother Mary from Nazareth—look at those," said Salvador in a voice pitched with awe as Claudia lifted her chemise over her head and tossed it to the floor with her guns.

Her hair spilled down her shoulders. The air through the open windows had cooled, and Claudia felt its effect. Salvador's eyes were where she'd expected they'd be. So were Coyon's. Claudia gazed at Salvador's cocked gun, her heart thudding as she wondered how she could get her hands on it.

Just then, Salvador tapped his thumb on the cocked hammer of his walnut-butted Remington. Whistling softly, he dropped his legs to the floor, keeping his eyes on the law woman's chest rising and falling behind the thin screen of her hair.

"Coyon, have you ever seen such a beautiful woman?"

Coyon seemed to have lost his voice. He only made a wet, guttural sound deep in his chest. His gun was slowly wilting, the barrel slanting toward the floor.

Claudia returned her eyes to Salvador's gun, which he kept cocked and leveled at her belly as he rose from the bed and walked to her. He pressed the cold, round maw of the Remington against Claudia's belly. He closed his left hand to her right breast. It was cold and prickly with calluses.

"Pig!" Claudia snarled and spat in his face.

Her saliva dripped down his cheek. Salvador didn't seem to mind. In fact he dipped a finger in it, touched the finger to his tongue. Then he wrapped that hand around the back of her neck and violently snapped her head toward his, closing his mouth over hers.

His mustaches raked her lips as he stuck his tongue in her mouth. It felt wet and leathery and tasted sharply of bacanora.

Claudia struggled against him, unable to breathe. She closed her left hand over his pistol and tried to snatch it from his grip while angling the barrel away from her.

No doing. Her strength was no match for his. The ploy enraged him. Pulling the gun away from her, he stepped back and smacked her hard across the face with the back of his hand.

The blow turned her sideways. Claudia had to clutch at the edge of the dresser to keep from falling. The next thing she knew, he was grunting savagely as he grabbed her by one arm, twisted her around, causing the room to spin around her, and threw her onto the bed.

She bounced once, and then he was on top of her, the gun he'd held on her now in its holster, and they were bouncing together. She tried to fight him, kick him, but her brains were scrambled from the vicious backhand. Behind him, standing at the end of the bed, Coyon was snickering behind his hand.

Salvador climbed up Claudia's body, got her arms under his knees. Pain racked her.

She gritted her teeth and was about to call him a pig again, but she'd just started to scream the word when someone pounded on the door.

"What the hell's going on in there?"

It was the saloon owner, O'Brien.

Claudia's heart turned a somersault. She lifted her head and shouted, "Delbert, go away!"

The doorknob twisted. The door started to open. Coyon stood in front of it, pressing his back against it, laughing. Atop Claudia, Salvador slid his right Colt from its holster and thumbed the hammer back. He jerked his head sharply to one side, and Coyon scrambled away from the door.

"No!" Claudia screamed.

Salvador twisted around to aim his Colt straight out from his shoulder at the door.

Pop! Pop! Pop!

The bullets chewed ragged holes in a nearly straight line across the door's top panel. From the hall came a loud groan. Then there was the thump of someone hitting the floor.

"Bastard!" Claudia screamed, lifting her head and shoulders from the bed and glaring her mindless rage at the grim-faced, mustached man straddling her, keeping her arms pinned to both sides.

Then the hand holding the gun flew down toward her head. As the back of his hand hammered against her right cheekbone, she knew a brief, sharp pain and the brightness of fireworks behind her retinas before everything went black. When she woke, he was stretched out on top of her, lapping her with his rough, wet tongue.

She looked around. They'd tied her wrists and ankles to bedposts with strips torn from a sheet. Coyon was no longer in the room.

There was only Salvador, and he was sprawled naked on top of her. His clothes and boots and hat and gun belt lay on the floor to her left. He was a heavy, hot, hairy weight on top of her.

She looked at her right wrist—tied securely to the corresponding bedpost. She looked at her other wrist—tied to the opposite bedpost. She arched her back, funneled all of her strength into those two wrists, and, with a great, agonized, enraged wail, jerked her arms hard, trying to free herself.

To no avail.

All she did was cause the dull pain in her head to grow sharp and to throb in both temples and ears. Salvador lifted his mustached lips from her right bosom. He smiled wetly, his brown eyes rheumy from drink and lust.

"Are you hungry, Marshal Morales?" he asked her. "I've sent Coyon out for some of Doña Flores's burritos. I thought we would have us a good time in private and then, when Coyon returns, fill our empty bellies. Our passion will probably make us very hungry, no?"

Again, Claudia spat in his face.

Salvador didn't mind this time, either.

He merely smiled in his seedy, dreamy way, and then he walked two fingers down her chest, through the valley between her breasts, and across her rising and falling belly.

He poked the tip of one finger into her belly button, chuckling as he gazed into her eyes.

Claudia arched her back and mewled like a leg-trapped mountain lion.

Sartain drew sharply back on Boss's reins.

A half-moon was on the rise, limning this narrow, winding secondary street of Sonora Gate in sparkling pearl.

Sartain was about halfway through town, having come in from the west end, the Mexican side. Now as he sat out front of a small adobe hut whose sashed windows were wanly lit and from whose stone chimney gray smoke curled skyward, he slid his right hand to the LeMat holstered on his thigh.

The door of the little café had just opened and a stooped figure was ambling out, spurs chinging loudly on the boardwalk fronting the place. The man closed the door and stepped into the street, breathing hard, as though he'd run a great distance.

He seemed to be limping, hunched low and to one side—an odd-looking figure in a frayed straw *sombrero* and striped *serape*. Two pistols on his hips flashed in the moonlight. He hadn't seen Sartain sitting there in the shadows fronting the café, whose wooden shingle announced simply DOÑA FLORES, and he nearly smacked into Boss's head. The horse whickered and tossed his head to one side while the odd-looking, thickly built, hunched figure stepped back with a startled grunt.

He lifted his head toward Sartain and lowered one hand from the bundle he was carrying against his chest to the handles of one of his pistols. Sartain already had the LeMat out. Aiming the big gun across his saddle pommel, he clicked the heavy hammer back.

"I wouldn't do that if I were you."

The thick little man's eyes flashed in the moonlight as he shunted them toward the big popper aimed at his head. One eye seemed to wander, showing a lot of white. He took another, incredulous step back, muttered something in Spanish, and wrapped both hands around the bundle, which smelled like seasoned meat and beans.

The wafting aroma was making Sartain's stomach bellow.

The strange little man brushed a wrist across his mouth, adjusted the *sombrero* on his head, swung around, and began walking down the street in the same direction Sartain was headed. The little man walked with a pronounced limp, dragging one boot and causing dust to plume in the moonlight.

When he was about twenty yards away, he glanced back at Sartain, like a dog who'd been hazed out of a chicken coop, and quickened his shuffling, ambling step.

Claudia had told Sartain about a hunchback.

What was his name?

Coyon?

Amidst his trials and tribulations and hard-won victory out at Hacienda de la Francesca, Sartain had forgotten about the don's son, Salvador, who fancied himself a killer. But now the younger de Castillo's name bounced around in the Cajun's head as, his suspicions tolling bells in his ears, he watched the hunchback dwindle into the distance, becoming a murky shadow as the man entered the intersection of this secondary street and the main one, which ran from north to south through the heart of Sonora Gate.

What was he doing over there?

And did his heading in that direction mean that his *amigo,* Salvador, was there, too?

Why would Salvador be over there? Sartain remembered Claudia telling him that she'd banned the younger de Castillo from town.

When the shadowy, pearlescent night had swallowed the hunchback, Sartain touched his moccasin heels to Boss's flanks. The horse was tired. Sartain had traced a slow, circuitous route back to town, not wanting the don's riders to follow him here and make trouble for Claudia. When he was sure none were on his backtrail, and after he'd rested up and tended his wounded arm, he'd headed on in.

Boss was tired and hungry, as was Sartain.

But first, the hunchback . . .

The horse knew when to step lightly. It did so now as Sartain directed the buckskin along the hunchback's scuffed tracks in the finely churned dirt of the side street.

When horse and rider gained the intersection, Sartain looked ahead and to his left. He thought he saw a shadow move in front of the Sonora Sun Saloon & Pleasure Parlor. Then he heard the clomp of a boot followed by the dragging scrape of another boot. The shadow jostled atop the porch, and then there was the raspy scrape of a door being opened and closed.

The movement fanned the flames of Sartain's suspicion. It was nearly two o'clock in the morning. He knew that Delbert O'Brien locked the saloon at midnight and went to bed in his shack out in back of the watering hole. The only light on in the two-story, mud-brick affair was in the second story.

In Claudia's room.

Sartain slid his Henry from its boot and, in one easy motion despite the grief his left arm was giving him, he swung his right boot over the saddlehorn, slipped his other foot free of its stirrup, and dropped straight down to the ground. He released the buckskin's reins and quietly racked a live round into the Henry's breech, off-cocking the hammer.

"Stay, boy," the Cajun said softly as he began following the hunchback's tracks across the street and to his left.

Behind him, the horse blew and shook his head testily.

Sartain kept an eye on the window over the shake-shingled roof of the Sonora Sun's front gallery, as he approached the gallery's front steps. Claudia's curtains were drawn over both windows that he knew framed her bed. No shadows moved. He could hear no voices, either, though the night was as quiet as an empty opera house.

Apprehension was a pack rat building a nest in the Cajun's consciousness. He cast one more cautious glance at Claudia's window and then mounted the steps, moving slowly because even in his moccasins the rotting wood squawked beneath his weight. When he'd crossed the gallery, he opened one of the batwings and fingered the latch of the inside door.

Locked.

His heart thudded in frustration.

The hunchback had gone inside and locked the door behind him. And was no doubt headed for Claudia's room . . .

Sartain slipped back across the gallery and down the steps. Running, he rounded the saloon's front corner and went sprinting along the side toward the rear. He froze when a woman's muffled scream from inside the saloon sliced across the night.

"Mike! Mike—they're coming, Mike!"

A man's Spanish accented voice shouted angrily, "Shut up, *puta* bitch!"

Three quick, muffled rifle shots froze the blood in the Cajun's veins.

"Claudia!" Sartain shouted at the top of his lungs.

CHAPTER 18

The Cajun flung himself around the saloon's rear corner, where a rickety-looking staircase rose to a second-story door.

He bolted up the stairs, the steps creaking and cracking beneath his moccasins. The railing swayed and threatened to fall away beneath his right hand. He barely noticed. His heart was thudding, blood sizzling in his veins as the echoes of the three rifle shots continued to bounce around inside his head.

Claudia . . .

He kicked the door open, leaned the rifle against the wall, and unsheathed the LeMat. He cocked the pistol and ran down the hall lit by a single candle lamp bracketed to the wainscoting on his left. The candle was burned down to a nub, its light watery and uncertain. Shadows shunted.

Ahead, a crouched figure moved. Sartain stopped, extended the LeMat. He kept moving when he saw Delbert O'Brien down on all fours and dribbling blood as he crawled toward a long-barreled shotgun lying just beyond him.

"Stay down!" Sartain said.

The wounded barman glanced over his shoulder at Sartain.

The Cajun did not pause in front of Claudia's bullet-pocked door. He cocked his leg and rammed his right, moccasined heel against the door, just beneath the knob. The door slammed open with a thunderous boom, and Sartain stepped inside, extending the LeMat straight out from his right shoulder.

He tracked the gun from left to right and back again. The

140

room, lit by a single lamp on the dresser to his right, was empty except for Claudia, lying naked and spread-eagle on the bed, wrists and ankles tied to the frame. Her face was cut and swollen, but she appeared otherwise unharmed.

Bullets had torn into the new mattress on each side of her. Bits of corn husk lay everywhere. The shots hadn't struck the woman. They'd likely been intended misses. Apparently, not even Salvador de Castillo could kill such a splendid beauty.

Salvador . . .

He didn't appear to be here. No one appeared to be here except Claudia, who continued to struggle and to speak through a gag in her mouth.

Sartain strode quickly to the bed, sliding his Green River knife from its sheath. He flicked the blade through the cotton strips binding her ankles to the bottom of the frame. He crouched over Claudia, who stared up at him through swollen eyes, and cut her left wrist free, then the right one. She pulled the wad of sheeting out of her mouth and screamed, *"Under the bed!"*

She flung her arms around Sartain. The Cajun threw himself straight backward, the woman in his arms. At the same time, the muffled blasts of a pistol sounded once, twice, three times. More corn husks geysered straight up out of the bed through the fresh bullet holes in the mattress where Claudia had been lying one second before.

Ribald laughter accompanied the blasts.

Sartain fell back against the dresser, threw Claudia to his left, and raised the LeMat. He hammered three shots through the already-shredded mattress. A scream sounded beneath the crashes of the heavy pistol.

Sartain tripped the lever, engaging the shotgun barrel, and fired once more. The concussion filled the room as the sixteen-gauge buckshot punched a fist-sized hole in the dead center of the mattress.

In the silence that followed, there was a gurgling grunt.

And the click of a door latch on the other side of the hall.

Claudia rasped, "Coyon!"

The hunchback's round, mustached face with one wandering eye peered through the two-foot crack between the door and the frame. A wide-eyed young woman, her belly bulging out behind her thin cotton nightgown, stood in front of the hunchback, who peered over her left shoulder. His short arms were wrapped around the girl from behind, and in each hand was a cocked pistol.

The hunchback grinned, showing a mess of crooked, grime-encrusted teeth. The girl, taller than Coyon, was sobbing, tears dribbling down her pale cheeks.

"Help me!" she screamed as Coyon, grinning, leveled both his pistols on Sartain . . .

. . . who leveled his own LeMat and sent a bullet hurling an inch over the girl's left shoulder and turning the hunchback's unmoored eye to jelly before it punched on out the back of his head to clink into a wall hanging behind him.

Coyon's lower jaw fell. His guns fell straight down to the girl's sides. He dropped back out of sight behind the pregnant whore. There was the solid thump of the hunchback hitting the floor.

The girl dropped to her knees with a weary sigh and turned to glance behind her at the dead Coyon. Then she turned to Sartain and buried her face in her hands, crying.

Claudia glanced at Sartain, tossed her hair back from her bruised face, and nodded. "Nice shooting, *amigo.*"

"Hope I wasn't interrupting anything."

"Nothing important."

Sartain wrapped the woman's calico shirt over her shoulders. Clutching the shirt closed across her breasts, the otherwise naked marshal of Sonora Gate rose to her feet and walked into the hall to comfort the crying whore.

Sartain moved to the foot of the bed. He reached down and pulled Salvador's naked, bloody body out into the room. He turned the man over onto his back. Salvador had been hit in the chest and both shoulders, and part of his face was still under the bed.

Still, his chest rose and fell.

His remaining eye found Sartain. It seemed to beg for help.

Sartain answered the plea with the one remaining .44 round from his LeMat.

"Say hey to your old man for me," said the Cajun.

★ ★ ★ ★ ★

REVENGER #2
DEATH AND THE SALOON GIRL

★ ★ ★ ★ ★

CHAPTER 1

Mike Sartain, the Revenger, reined his big buckskin to a halt on the trail he'd been following for the past two days, and squinted his cobalt-blue eyes against the howling wind and blowing nettles.

Before him lay a town that didn't appear much more than a handful of shabby, mud brick and wood frame buildings doing their humble best to keep from being overrun by the high-desert sage, cedars, piñons, rocks, cactus, and jouncing tumble-weeds.

The Wells Fargo office and San Juan Valley Stage Company building sat on the trace's left side, about halfway down the street. It was by far the largest building in the settlement, and its signs were the brightest, the rest having been badly faded by the sun and blasted to gray splinters by the wind that often howled either over the San Juan Range to the west or the San-gre de Cristos to the northeast.

Sartain knew about the wind in these parts. When he wasn't hunting men who needed killing, he often holed up in an old mountain prospector's shack in the nearby Sawatch Range. It was one of several "hidey holes" The Revenger maintained on the frontier and to which he repaired when he was tired of hunting and being hunted.

The big buckskin shook its head and blew, shifted its weight beneath Sartain.

The big, blue-eyed man clad in denims and a pinto vest

leaned forward and ran his left hand down the stallion's long, sleek neck. "I see it, Boss." His right hand slid to the big, silver-chased, pearl-gripped LeMat residing in a holster thonged to his right thigh and released the keeper thong from over the hammer.

What both horse and rider had seen was the man who'd been standing under a porch awning on the street's right side, across from a mercantile. The man had just turned away from the awning support post he'd been leaning against, his brown hat tipped against the wind, and disappeared down an alley mouth. He'd moved with his chin dipped as though to hide his face beneath his hat, and his shoulders were furtively hunched.

If he'd had a tail, he would have tucked it between his legs, like a wildcat slipping into cover.

Just before he'd ducked into the alley on the far side of Logan's Tonsorial Parlor, he'd cast a quick, over-shoulder glance toward Sartain, ringing warning bells not only in The Revenger's ears but obviously in Boss's ears, as well. The buckskin and Sartain had ridden the vengeance trail for some time now, and they themselves had been hunted for long enough that they were most often in perfect harmony with one another.

"Yeah, I see him," Sartain said, giving the horse's neck another pat and quickly scanning the rest of the street, looking for more trouble signs.

Where there was one man gunning for Sartain, there were usually two or more, for The Revenger's reputation generally preceded him.

But the street, save for the occasional bouncing tumbleweed and a ranch supply wagon sitting in front of the mercantile, was deserted. The wind was obviously keeping everyone indoors. There weren't even any saddle horses on the street before either of the town's two saloons.

Sartain reached into the inside pocket of his pinto vest, where his pearl-gripped, over-and-under derringer resided, and pulled out a small piece of notepaper, which he let the wind unfold. His eyes scanned the two short lines scrawled in pencil by a crude female hand:

Mr. Sartain, please come to the Belle of the Ball Saloon in Silverthorne, Colorado Teritory. Pleese do hurry! An inosent girl needs your help bad!

It was signed simply and without ornament, *"Belle Hendricks, Belle of the Ball Saloon."*

"Belle of the Ball," Sartain said, stuffing the note, which someone had slipped under the door of his hotel room in Alamosa, where he'd gone to cool his heels, drinking and gambling, after his last hunt. A young widow from a small ranch had wanted him to kill the crooked deputy sheriff who'd hanged her husband at the behest of a rich rancher and, discovering how cold-blooded and cowardly the deputy was, Sartain had had no qualms about honoring the woman's wishes.

He'd killed the man and left him to the coyotes and the wild cats. He'd left the rancher living in fear of a visit from The Revenger, which Sartain might just give the man one of these days. After the man had pissed down his leg for a good, long time . . .

Sartain touched spurs to his buckskin's flanks and said in his slow, Cajun-accented drawl beneath the wind, "All right, Boss, let's pay us a visit to the Belle of the Ball, shall we? See what's got Miss Belle's drawers in such a twist . . . Keep your eyes and ears skinned, though, *amigo.* I didn't like the looks of that lurkin' *hombre* any more than you did."

The horse gave an uneasy snort and started forward. Sartain held Boss to a walk, holding the reins up high against his chest in his left hand, leaving the right one free for the LeMat. He scoured every nook and cranny of the dusty, windblown street on both sides of which shingle chains squawked in the howling wind, and Boss started every now and then at windblown trash and tumbleweeds bounding out of alley mouths.

The Revenger's cobalt blues scoured the rooftops, as well, wary of a rifleman possibly snaking a Winchester around from behind a false facade.

He pulled up to the Belle of the Ball, which sat across from the Wells Fargo office on the right-hand side of the street. It was a two-story mud brick building with a large, wooden facade jutting over its roofed front gallery. The sign over the facade was dark red with "Belle of the Ball" painted over it in large, ornate green letters, every letter of which was so badly faded it was hard to make out against the silver-weathered red.

An *olla* and a tin dipper swung from a rope beneath the gallery's roof, and two wicker rocking chairs rocked as though fidgety ghosts were rocking them.

Both hitch racks fronting the place were empty.

Sartain rode around to the building's north side and found another hitch rack, to which he tied Boss out of the wind. He loosened the horse's girth and slipped the bit from his teeth so the mount could drink freely from the half-filled stock trough.

He slapped his sand-colored Stetson against his thigh and ran a gloved hand through his thick mop of dark-brown curls. Setting the hat, adorned with a snakeskin, *concho*-studded band back atop his head, letting the chin thong swing free against his chest, he walked around to the saloon's front and mounted the porch steps.

He crossed the porch slowly, sort of kicking his heels out with his usual, southern-bred flair, ringing his spurs, thumbs hooked behind his cartridge belt. He might have appeared to a passerby just another carefree, raggedy-heeled cowpuncher happy to pass the time drinking whiskey and playing faro on this windy afternoon, but he was watching everything around him and keenly listening, his senses sharp from the several years he'd spent staying just ahead of the law.

His lips quirked a good-natured smile as he pushed through the wind-jostled batwings, and then he took one long step to his left, putting his back to the wall, not wanting to be backlit too long in case someone inside had decided he needed a pill he couldn't digest.

Moving from washed-out, stormy sunlight to the dinginess of the saloon, his eyes took a moment to adjust. But only a moment. He blinked once, twice, and then they were all laid out before him—four men standing in a row along the bar to his right, and two more men sitting at a round table about halfway down the deep room flanked by a wooden, red-carpeted staircase that rose to a balcony running around three sides of the main drinking hall.

None of the men was moving quickly or holding a weapon, and those were the two things Sartain always looked for first. What he saw next was the pretty girl—she was too young to be called a woman, even a young one—standing behind the bar in a black and burgundy corset and bustier. Young, yes, but not so young than she didn't fill the corset so well that Sartain didn't have to gently remind himself not to lose focus.

Now, with a second look, he didn't like the way the four men were standing at the bar with uniform gaps between them of about six feet. As though they were synchronized players on an opera stage, they all turned slowly toward Sartain at the same time, resting their left elbows on the edge of the bar and letting their right hands dangle down over their holstered pistols.

They all wore their revolvers low, in the manner of men accustomed to using them not just for shooting coyotes. All four men had already unsnapped the leather keeper thongs from over their gun hammers. They all gazed at The Revenger with lips quirked in either faint smirks or with shrewd cunning.

One of the two sitting at the table halfway down the room and about ten feet out from the bar was the man who'd been holding up the awning support post earlier. Sartain recognized him by his brown Stetson and unshaven jaws. Now he sat with his boots atop the table, arms crossed on his chest, a delighted grin flashing his large, pale-white teeth, the edges of which were crusted with chewing tobacco, some of which he just now turned his head to spit onto the scarred, dusty floor beneath him with a liquid plop.

"Use the damn sandbox," the well-set-up girl in the corset and bustier said tightly, keeping her brown-eyed gaze on Sartain. She'd hardly moved her lips. "That's what it's for."

"Uh . . . sorry, Belle," said the man in the brown hat, also keeping his gaze riveted on Sartain.

The Revenger broadened his smile, pinched the brim of his own hat to the room, and turned to the girl. "Belle of the Ball . . . ?"

"That's right," the girl said, in nearly the same toneless voice she'd used when addressing the man who'd spit on her floor. "You The Revenger?"

"I am indeed. Your note sounded"—he raked his gaze across the hard faces of the men along the bar and across the two at the table—"urgent."

"Oh, it was. Very urgent." The girl took one step back, her large, dark-brown eyes flashing excitedly, her pretty, heart-shaped face flushing as she snapped a look at the other men before her. "This here's The Revenger, boys. Told you he'd come!"

As the man standing farthest away stepped out away from the bar to stand just left of the table at which the other two sat, the man nearest Sartain said, "Friend, you got a two-thousand-dollar government bounty on your head."

He was a duster-clad, stocky gent with a ginger beard and

close-set gray eyes, a dusty red neckerchief billowing down his broad, lumpy chest.

Sartain shot a quick glance at the girl. She smiled so brightly he thought she was going to clap her hands and laugh and jump up and down, proud of herself for having lured the Revenger into a whipsaw.

CHAPTER 2

Sartain sighed as he looked at the men standing gun-ready before him, in a ragged semi-circle across the right half of the room, and slowly let his gaze settle on the girl still standing behind the bar. He could see the back of her head and her bare, slender shoulders in the mirror behind her. "Reckon I should have checked out the ole Belle of the Ball before I rode into town. Your note just sounded so . . . desperate."

"What do you think, boys?" the girl said, nervously cutting her eyes around the room. "Do you think you can take him? Remember, there's two thousand dollars on his head. Ya'll can split it six ways and just give me a hundred for lurin' him in." She spoke with a faint Texas accent.

"That's not a small bait o' money." Sartain put some steel into his voice, though his eyes still crinkled at their corners with a faint, affable smile. "You sure you fellas can afford it?"

He recognized a couple of them. Bounty hunters. They likely all were.

The one he knew to be Clayton Demry, the second man from the door standing now with his back to the bar, said, "Them federal boys gonna be pleased as punch to see your head in a gunnysack . . . finally."

"They would be at that, Clay."

"Let's cut the chinnin', shall we?" This from the man in the brown hat, who'd gained his feet, as had the man he'd been sitting with at the table—a yellow-haired *hombre* named Lancaster,

154

if Sartain remembered right. Lancaster had been a deputy U.S. marshal himself before he'd turned in his badge to start collecting bounties for a living. Bounty men earned more than lawmen.

"Yeah," said the stocky gent nearest Sartain. "Let's stop with the lollygaggin'. Me—I got a drink to finish." He smiled.

Sartain let his right hand hang down over his holstered LeMat. His right index finger tingled, as it often did in this situation. It was an anxious twitch that he tried to keep in only the finger while the rest of him remained calm, his face implacable, his heartbeat slow.

Not that he was overconfident. Six against one were steep odds, and he was not the fastest gun in the west. In fact, he'd never faced six at one time in close quarters. Chances were, he'd kill three of these men within five seconds.

The fourth would get him.

Oh, well. It was what he deserved for getting careless. But the girl's note really had seemed desperate, and Mike Sartain was a sucker for desperate women.

He glanced at her once more. Her wide eyes were rolling anxiously around the room, her lips slightly parted, her lovely corset rising and falling sharply as she breathed. In the mirror over her right shoulder, the third of the four men standing with their backs to the bar jerked his right elbow up.

Sartain's LeMat was in his fist, blasting.

The third man howled and fired his Peacemaker into the floor. Next, The Revenger shot the man standing to the third man's right—both shots coming so fast and furious that the second shot sounded like an echo of the first—and then he bounded left, lofted himself into the air as the bounty hunters' guns thundered and bullets shredded the batwings and the front wall and window.

Shattering glass screeched, exposing the room to the moaning wind.

Sartain fired the LeMat again as he flew through the air, evoking a shrill curse as Lancaster doubled over and staggered backward. The Revenger slammed his left shoulder on the side of a table, upending the table, which, as Sartain and it dropped together, flew up to become a wooden shield.

As Sartain hit the floor, two bullets slammed through the shield from the other side, spraying slivers and carving a hot line across the outside of his right shoulder, tearing his shirtsleeve. Wincing against the burn, he bounded to his heels, lifted his head and smoking LeMat above the table. He winced again as a bullet tore the table's edge, spraying more slivers. He shot Clayton Demry before jerking the big horse pistol slightly left and hurling the last man standing at the bar over the top of the bar and into several shelves of bottles behind it.

More glass shattered.

In the corner of his left eye, he saw the man in the brown hat standing about ten feet away, near where the man had been lounging in his chair. He was screaming wildly at the tops of his lungs as he flung lead at Sartain. As bullets screeched and thudded around him and blew out more window glass, The Revenger hurled himself back to his right and rolled up onto his left hip and shoulder in front of the swinging batwings, extending the LeMat toward the brown-hatted gent.

The hammer of the man's Russian .44 clinked on an empty chamber.

He flung the revolver aside and reached for another one holstered over his belly, his wide, white-ringed eyes blazing beneath the wide brim of his hat. He hadn't got the belly gun even half pulled before Sartain flipped the LeMat's lever, engaging the shotgun shell, and squeezed the trigger.

The thunder caused the room to leap as though from an

earth tremor. Dust sifted from the ceiling. The heavy piece's recoil caused The Revenger's wrist to ache.

The brown-hatted man's hat flew off his head as the .12-caliber wad of buckshot shredded his chest, lifted him two feet in the air, and hurled him straight back over a table and into a piano, which gave an indignant, raucous belch as the man bounced off its side and piled up at its base. Rising, twirling the LeMat on his finger, and dropping it back into its holster, Sartain drew his derringer from inside his vest with his other hand and clicked both hammers back.

Only one of the six bounty hunters was moving.

Clayton Demry crawled down along the bar toward the back of the room, groaning, panting, and leaving a smeared blood trail behind him. As he reached a dead man, he stopped, picked up the dead man's cocked Colt, and twisted around toward Sartain, who raised the derringer and popped a pill through the dead center of Demry's forehead.

Demry fired the Colt into the ceiling as he rolled over onto his back, shaking his head and jerking before gradually growing still.

Sartain glanced around the room, gauzy with webbing powder smoke and rife with the coppery smell of fresh blood.

Where was the girl?

As if in response to his silent question, she lifted her eyes above the bar. They were even wider than before. She looked around until her shocked gaze landed on Sartain then flicked to the cocked derringer he held in his hand, aimed at her.

"Holy shit," she said, lifting her head still farther until she was standing up straight, smiling, showing all her fine, white teeth between ruby lips. "You're really him, ain't ya? The Revenger." She leaned forward to peer over the bar at the dead men lying at the base of it and shook her head in awe. "Yep, you're him, all right." She smiled. "Thanks for comin', Mr. Sartain."

Sartain studied her critically. "You got a fine way of makin' sure a man is who he says he is."

"When Northcutt said he seen you in Alamosa—"

"That'd be me," a man's voice said from behind Sartain.

The Revenger wheeled on a heel, leveling the derringer at the gray-bearded face hovering just above the batwings from the other side.

The old man drew his head down behind the doors, yowling, "Now, don't go acuttin' loose with that pocket popper, mister! This wasn't my idea. I told her it was you I seen in Alamosa, sure enough, but Belle done thinks I'm so damn old I can't see straight, or leastways, knows what I'm lookin' at when I'm lookin' at it!"

"Get in here!"

The oldster bulled through the doors like a bull through a chute, keeping his head down and holding his hands in front of his face as though to shield himself from a bullet. He sidled away from Sartain, crowing, "It's her fault! It's Belle's fault! If'n you're gonna shoot somebody—I mean, add to the pile of dead you done already piled up—shoot *Belle!*"

"Oh, shut up, Northcutt, and put your hands down!" Belle scolded the old man from behind the bar. "Mr. Sartain, this is my swamper and sometime piano player, Raymond Northcutt. He was once a deputy sheriff. My father's deputy sheriff. Worked for my pa—back when he could see straight, that was, and knew what he was lookin' at when he was lookin' at it."

She grabbed one of the few intact bottles from a shelf along the back-bar mirror, glanced down at the dead man who'd been blown over the bar and was likely lying at her feet, and wagged her head.

She sighed, plucked two glasses off a pyramid atop the bar's near end, and walked out from behind the bar to stand before Sartain in all her half-dressed glory—tall for a girl, and pretty as a speckled pup. Willowy and full-busted. All of seventeen, The Revenger judged, trying to keep his eyes off her overflowing corset while reminding himself that she'd sicced six seasoned bounty hunters on him.

If not for a few fast moves and a good bit of luck, he'd be lying where the six bounty men were, mingling his bodily fluids with the cow dung, tobacco, and sawdust that fairly carpeted the place.

"Where's my glass?" Northcutt asked, indignant. His bearded face was as dark and wrinkled as a walnut, and his canvas trousers and calico shirt, over which he wore a ragged deerskin vest, hung on his spindly frame as though from a badly stunted tree. "I fetched him here, made two trips to Alamosa in the past week, and now you treat me like dirt!"

"Get your own glass and take it outside," the girl said, staring brashly up at Sartain, who stood only a few inches taller. "The Revenger and I have business to discuss. Oh, and take Mr. Sartain's horse over to the Occidental and make sure he's tended properly—curried and given plenty of hay and oats. Best keep that stallion away from the mares."

Her cheeks dimpled as her eyes flicked to Sartain's broad chest and the dark hair curling out from the open top of his shirt, beneath the collar and knotted red neckerchief. "I saw that stallion when he rode in, and I bet he could do some damage in a barn full of fillies . . . left to his own devices."

"Ah, ya ungrateful pup," the oldster groused, stomping around behind the bar. "I'm gonna tell your pa—if he's still kickin'—about how you been treatin' me since he's been gone, and he'll bend you over his knee. I'd do it myself if I was a few years younger and could catch ya. Let me see here . . . where's the Tennessee? Oh, there it is!"

He cackled, bending stiffly forward to lift a bottle from under the bar, cradling the bourbon like a beloved infant in one arm and patting the fancy label as though it were the baby's belly. "Worked myself up a powerful thirst, with all that ridin' around the country on old Millicent. Do believe I'm deservin' of the Belle of the Ball's best."

"Millicent is his mule," the girl informed Sartain, turning her mouth corners down.

Northcutt ambled out from behind the bar and headed for the batwings. "Don't worry—I won't dirty up a glass."

"Good," the girl said impatiently. "Could you be gone now?"

Still standing before the girl, his mind spinning over the killings and this cool, smiling, scantily clad seductress acting as though it were all just a melodrama performed by some traveling theatrical show, The Revenger said sharply, "Old man, you leave my horse where he is."

Northcutt shrugged. "All right—if you say so." He glanced at the dead men heaped around the room and then looked at the girl. "What about all that fresh beef? You leave these bodies here, they'll attract coyotes, and those coyotes will soon be after Mrs. Patrick's cats, and you know who she'll be complainin' to. Me, since I'm the last lawman in town!"

"Some lawman," the girl said through a low, caustic snort, keeping her bold eyes on Sartain. "Send a couple of the Occidental's hostlers over later with a wagon. They can load 'em up and take what's in their pockets for payment. Have 'em bury 'em up in that Potter's Field, backside of Boot Hill." She wrinkled her nose as she glanced at the dead men sprawled near her pretty red high-heeled shoes. "Worthless trash. Bounty hunters, my ass!"

"That ass of yours needs a good paddlin'," the old man grouched, digging the cork out of the bottle with a small pocketknife.

"Are you still here?"

"I'm goin'! I'm goin'!" Northcutt stopped between the batwings and glanced peevishly over his shoulder, suspiciously scrutinizing Sartain before sliding his castigating eyes to Belle. "You mind your p's and q's now, girl. Your pa done ordered me to see to your honor while he was away!"

"My honor—*hah*!" The girl laughed.

"And how many times I gotta tell ya—you shouldn't go around dressed like that, with them titties of yours spillin' out all over the place. Mr. Sartain's liable to mistake you for a percentage gal. It ain't decent to dress like that, if'n you're not a whore."

She placed her hands on her hips and pivoted toward the old man, giving him a good look at her wares and coquettishly fluttering her eyelids.

"Sure, go ahead," Northcutt intoned, his dark face turning darker as a flush rose high on his craggy cheeks. "Give an old man a heart-stroke!"

Northcutt indulged in one more sheepish glance at the girl's bosom and then grumbled and cursed and continued on out through the batwings and into the wind, which was blowing waves of dust and dried leaves and the smell of horse shit through the saloon's broken front window.

"Didn't think he'd ever leave," Belle said, raising the two goblets up close to The Revenger's chin. "Shall we?"

He grabbed her wrist and said through gritted teeth, "What the hell is your game, girl? And, if you ain't a whore, how come you're dressed like one?"

"What—this old thing?" She laughed and twisted her hand out of Sartain's grip. "Can't blame a girl for wantin' to look pretty. Besides, wearin' it instead of my old Mother Hubbard seems to bring in higher tips." Belle turned, swinging first her shoulders and then her hips, and smiled at The Revenger over her bare left shoulder. She walked around to the far side of a near table, kicked out a chair, and sat down. "Now you stop lookin' like a mean ole bear. Come on over here and have a drink with me, and I'll tell you all about my game."

CHAPTER 3

Sartain had never before met such a brazen, arrogant young hussy.

He kicked a chair out and instead of sitting down on it, propped one boot onto it and leaned against his knee, drilling the devilish, long-legged beauty with a seriously castigating scowl. "Do you realize you just got six men killed? Six! And I could have been one of 'em. So you'll have to forgive me if I seem just a little reluctant to smoke the peace pipe with you, miss."

"I ain't askin' you to smoke the peace pipe," she said, pouting. "Just have a little drink's all." She smiled again winningly, looking up at him from beneath her auburn brows.

She popped the cork on the bottle, filled one glass, and slid it across the table. She filled the other glass and set the bottle aside. "I've been wantin' to meet you for a long, long time, Mr. Sartain," she said, sitting back in her chair. "Been readin' about you in the papers for quite some time now. The *Revenger!*" She lifted her shot glass in salute. "To your fine shootin' here today!"

She sipped and then held the glass down by her jaw, turning it slowly between her long, delicate fingers.

Sartain just stared at her, not knowing what to make of her. She stared back at him, chin lowered with fake demureness, chewing her lower lip and turning the glass slowly in her hand.

Finally, despite himself, Sartain gave a dry chuff and sat down in the chair.

"This is a first," he said.

"The first for what?"

"The first for me sittin' down and havin' a drink with someone who damn near killed me."

"I saw the whole thing, and I don't think it was even close."

"It's always close." Sartain threw back half the shot.

"Now I know you're the man for the job," she said, throwing back a good half of her own drink, making a face and wiping her lips with the back of her wrist. "Powerful stuff!" She smiled, eyes boring into his. "Just like you, Mr. Sartain."

Sartain scowled again, though his judgment of the girl was losing its edge. You couldn't help admiring a girl this saucy and unflagging in the face of what she'd just seen. In the face of what she'd just caused, even.

"This was a test of some kind?"

"You don't expect me to believe what all the newspapers write about you, do you? My pa, the sheriff, says ten percent of them yarns sits within shoutin' distance of the truth while the other ninety percent is off on a fishin' trip."

"Smart man, the sheriff. Where is he, anyway? Off on a fishin' trip?"

The girl looked down, the cloud of a somber mood passing over her face. "He's why I summoned you here, Mr. Sartain."

"The sheriff is why you called me into this ambush?"

"Oh, it weren't nothin' of the sort! Well . . . maybe it was within shoutin' distance." She threw back the last of her whiskey, gave a sheepish snort, almost choking, and wiped her mouth and nose.

Glancing around, she said, "They was all regulars. I'm gonna miss their business, but . . . they came in last week huntin' stage robbers that headed south toward Mexico. I told 'em that Northcutt said you was in Alamosa and that I had an idea about how to get you here, so's they could collect the bounty and give me somethin' to see, like what the newspaper scribblers scribble about, and they could give me what they saw fit for the work of sendin' Northcutt with the note.

"You see, Mr. Sartain, the job I have for you concerns my beloved father, and I really needed to know if you were the right man for the job . . . despite what them yarn-spinners are always spewin' ink about. I only have so much money, and I need to know I'm spendin' it on the right man."

Sartain glanced at the dead men sprawled around them. "And you didn't think any of those men was the right man?"

Before the girl could respond, Sartain heard sniffing sounds and the scratching of toenails around the batwings. Both he and the girl turned to see a brown and yellow mutt sniffing around under the doors, mewling and looking sheepishly in toward where the fresh meat was starting to molder.

The girl said, "You go on home, Titus. That ain't food for you. Them varmints'll make you sick. Go, now!"

The dog gave a frustrated yip, turned, tucked its tail between its legs, and bounded reluctantly down the porch steps and out of sight.

The wind continued to blow dust and grit through the broken window and under the batwings. Sartain could smell the tang of an approaching storm.

"That's one hell of a way to land a job, Miss Belle," he said, helping himself to another glass of whiskey and giving a wry chuckle. He supposed the shooting had been half his own fault. The girl obviously didn't know better, and he should have checked the situation out more thoroughly. He'd take it as a lesson learned.

Besides, the world minus six bounty hunters was a better place. In fact, now he wished there'd been a few more here today . . .

"To answer your question, Mr. Sartain, I think it's rather

obvious that none of these fellas here"—she jerked her head toward the human beef aging on the floor—"was the right man."

She held him with a smugly serious expression.

"*Touché*," he said, chuckling and taking another sip of the whiskey. "All right, Miss Belle, tell me about your pa. Tell me about the sheriff."

She was staring straight at him, a pensive cast to her large, brown eyes and a flush in her cheeks. "If you'll forgive me for sayin' so, Mr. Sartain, you sure are one good-lookin' man. The newspapers—they were within shoutin' distance of that, at least."

It was The Revenger's turn to blush.

"Oh, sorry." Belle looked away, sheepish. "It's just I was born and raised out here in this canker on the devil's ass, and most of the men through here are . . . well . . . like them on the floor. Anyway, the sheriff."

"Yes, the sheriff."

Topping off Sartain's glass and refilling her own, Belle said, "He went missin' last month, Pa did. It was when he and his chief deputy, Jasper Garvey, was haulin' a strongbox of gold bars down from the Painted Lady mine up in the Sangre de Cristos. He and Jasper hauled the gold down once every two months for the Painted Lady Minin' Company run by the Englishman, Mr. Maragon. Last month my pa and Jasper Garvey was due to have the gold down to the Wells Fargo office at noon on a Monday, which is when the weekly stage to Alba-kurk pulls through, and they never showed. Ain't been seen since. Neither hide nor hair."

"What do you think happened, Miss Belle?"

Belle hardened her jaws and leaned forward, pressing her bosom against the edge of the table until both those sweet, pale orbs bulged up like two mounds of freshly churned butter, showing all but her nipples. "Here's what I think happened."

She scrunched up her eyes and an angry flush replaced the

previous one of embarrassment. "I think Jasper Garvey done hooked up with his outlaw brother's gang, and"—a sheen of tears brightened in her eyes, and she had to swallow and shake her head before continuing—"most likely killed my pa, Sheriff Stephen Hendricks, and run off to Mexico with the gold!"

"What makes you think that?"

"Because Jasper Garvey, who my father made chief deputy out of the goodness of his heart, and because he wanted to give Jasper, who once let his wolf run with his no-good firebrand of a brother, a second chance. Pa wanted to give Jasper the opportunity to prove he could be a good man, and I think Jasper tried for the two years he wore his badge, but then . . . but then I seen a change come over Jasper. He'd stop by here for drinks on his nights off. He was startin' to drink more than usual, and he was gettin' ornerier and ornerier. Him and me used to kid around—you know, he'd sort of jokingly ask me to marry him an' such, though there was no way in hell I'd ever marry a man like Jasper Garvey, but—"

"Why not?"

"Why, because his pa was Harvey Garvey, a known outlaw in these parts since before the War Between the States. I'd never let a man like that sow his foul seed in my womb . . . and . . . and suckle the result of such an unsavory union. Gosh, no! Me—I'm gonna marry an upright man someday, and he's going to have that blue blood in his veins, and my boys will be doctors and lawyers, too, and my girls . . . well, the wives of doctors and lawyers and . . . and . . . scholars, like the ones they have back east. That's where my ma was from, and though I do dearly love my pa, he comes from a poor strain of farmers from the Dakota Territory while Ma was the daughter of an attorney in Council Bluffs, Iowa."

Sartain didn't bother to ask the girl where she thought she'd run into a blue-blooded man out here on the backside of nowhere.

"Anyway," Belle continued, "Jasper and I used to joke around like that, but once he got mad, he grabbed my arm until it hurt, and he said somethin' like, 'I've had enough of your teasin', Miss Belle—how 'bout if we go upstairs and get serious?' "

The girl's mouth and eyes widened in shock and exasperation. "As if I ever would do such a thing! With the ilk of Jasper Garvey!" She sipped her whiskey and made another face. "He was quick to make a joke out of it when he saw I was not one bit compliant with his goatish urges, and I was too embarrassed to tell Pa. But that's when I started to realize that Jasper's true character was startin' to surface again."

"All right, so much for you and Jasper Garvey livin' happily ever after," Sartain said. "Do you have any other reason to believe Jasper turned on your father? Don't you think common owlhoots, like the ones the bounty hunters were after, could have attacked the gold shipment?"

She hiked a shoulder and ran the tip of her index finger around the rim of her glass. "Of course that's a possibility. But I think otherwise." She raised her eyes to Sartain's. "That's what I would like you to find out for me, Mr. Sartain. And if I'm proven right and Jasper Garvey did indeed kill my father and make off with the gold with his brother and his brother's no-account ruffians, I'd like you to run 'em all down and kill 'em!"

Suddenly, her lips trembled and her eyes filled with tears.

Sobbing, she said, "I only have a little bit of money, which I've been savin' from tips, but I'll give you anything you want if you'll help me learn the fate of my father and deal your brand of justice to anyone who might have brought him to harm!"

She reached across the table and squeezed The Revenger's wrist.

"To hell with my honor, Mr. Sartain. I offer you anything at all—myself included!"

CHAPTER 4

"If you know anything about me—anything at all, Miss Belle—then you know that I don't require payment of any kind."

She sniffed, wiped tears from her cheeks with her hands, and looked mildly confused and disappointed. "You . . . don't?"

"Nope. If I think a person has a legitimate reason to seek revenge for some misdeed and cannot otherwise exact that revenge for him- or herself, I'll set to it. No payment necessary. Even . . . uh . . . of the kind you've so generously offered."

"Oh . . . well . . . please don't think me a charlatan, Mr. Sartain."

"Mike."

"Mike it is." She sniffed again, smiled, still collecting herself. "I don't make a habit of offering such a thing. I just . . . well, I just really want to know what happened to my father. I want justice served, and I thought, well, if that's the only way I can get it . . ."

"It's not."

"Well, at least let me offer you a room. I rent half a dozen rooms upstairs, but yours of course will be free. And I'd like to cover the charge for quartering your horse, as well."

"That's not necessary," Sartain said, finishing his whiskey, setting his empty glass down on the table, and rising from his chair. He jerked his shoulders at what sounded like a shotgun blast that rocked the saloon and rattled the glass pyramid atop the bar. "I'll stable him myself and, judging by how close that thunder was, I'd best get him under a roof pronto. The room will be fine. I'll get started on your father's trail first thing in the morning."

He pinched his hat brim to the girl and started to turn away but turned back when she said, "I'll have Northcutt cook you a steak with all the trimmings. He does all the cooking here at the Belle of the Ball, and while I can't say he's any good, no one I know has so far died from his concoctions. He makes a darn good peach pie—I can vouch for that myself, and the cream's fresh from Mr. Burlinson's cow in the pasture just behind the Belle."

"Makes me hungry just thinkin' about it." Sartain pinched his hat again, started to turn toward the batwings once, but turned back when she added:

"The beds are right comfortable. I'll give you the room next to mine. That's the best bed in the whole place!"

"Much obliged, Miss Belle."

"Oh—how do you like your steak?!"

"Still kickin'."

"Still kickin'—that's just how I like mine!"

He was about to push through the batwings when she called once again: "Can I fix you a nice hot bath, Mike? I got the stove stoked in the kitchen, in preparation for supper, so it'd be no trouble at all to fix you a hot bath. I laid in a store of Dr. Mulligan's Fine Soap and salts straight from the Great Salt Lake on my last run to Albakurk!"

She ran her hands down her arms, squirming around in her chair. "They make a body feel fine all over . . ."

"That'd be delightful," Sartain said, "as long as I'm not putting you to any trouble, Miss Belle."

"Please, skip the Miss and just call me Belle. And it's no trouble at all, Mike." She smiled charmingly as she rose from her chair, adjusting her corset and causing a warm stiletto of desire to tear through him. "The Occidental's up one block and north one more. It's the only building in town that's been painted in the last five years. You can't miss it. I'll have your bath ready by the time you get back . . . Mike."

Sartain pinched his hat brim once more, swung around, and headed for his horse.

Hours later, after tending his horse, soaking in a hot bath, and enjoying that steak "with all the trimmings," Sartain found himself alone in his room with Belle Higgins.

"You like that?" he asked the girl in his slow, Cajun drawl, beneath the intermittent rumbles of thunder from a fragrant summer storm that was pelting rain against the window and gurgling down the roof and off the overhang onto the street below, where it was forming large puddles.

Groaning, Belle said, "God, where . . . where on earth . . . did . . . you . . . ever learn to . . . do such things to a girl?"

"I grew up an orphan in New Orleans . . . the French Quarter."

"Oh," she said, though he doubted she understood the implications. She just wanted him to keep doing what he'd been doing to her for the past half hour, ever since she'd knocked on his door with the pretense of offering him an extra quilt.

He'd taken the quilt, because the night was deliciously cool, but she'd been flirting with him all night long while he'd played poker with a couple of cowhands holing up from the storm and who were now snugged into their beds just down the hall.

A man could take only so much toying from a girl like that. Just after he'd finally got himself to sleep an hour after she'd closed up shop for the night, and Northcutt had slinked off to his cabin near the livery barn, Belle had knocked on his door holding the quilt. In fact, the quilt had been all she'd been wearing.

In fact, she hadn't been wearing a stitch, which he fully re-alized after he'd taken the quilt.

Suffice it to say, a man can take only so much. Sartain took the quilt and the girl along with it.

"What are you . . . why are you stopping?" Belle asked now, breathless.

"Gonna leave it right there for now." He stepped off the end of the bed, stomped over to the dresser for his hide makings sack, and sat down in an upholstered armchair near the half-open window. The cool, damp air felt soothing against his sweat-damp skin. "Sometimes, the best part of love-makin', dear Belle, is patience . . . anticipation."

She sighed, stretching her legs out full on the bed and grinding her head in frustration against her pillow. "Oh, Lordy!"

He lifted a whiskey bottle from a small table on his right, took a drink, swishing the whiskey around in his mouth, savoring the taste of the good bourbon. He swallowed, sighed, and set the bottle back down on the table.

"Patience," he said, troughing a wheat paper between the first and second fingers of his left hand and deftly dribbling chopped tobacco into the crease.

Slowly, enjoying the relaxed feeling that lovemaking always gave him, having learned to enjoy and savor it from the whores back in the French Quarter, the tender, lovely, salty doxies of varied races who'd been his mother as well as his first lover, he leisurely built the smoke, lit it, and slacked back in the chair, crossed his ankles, and just as leisurely smoked it.

Outside, the rain eased, made a peaceful sound as it ticked against the window and gurgled off the roof overhang. The thunder was drifting away, the rumbling growing fainter, more and more peaceful.

Occasionally, out the window over his left shoulder, Sartain could see the lightning flashing in the southwestern distance, beyond the silhouetted facades on the opposite side of the street. The rumbles of the diminishing thunder were the only sounds for several minutes, until the girl stirred on the bed, lifting her head from her pillow and rising to a sitting position, her hair tumbling in a beautiful dark mess around her head.

Her breasts were rich, round, and full, shaded by the flickering umber lamplight. They jostled as she crawled down to the bottom of the bed, slipped to the floor, and knelt before him.

"What a wonderful evening . . . with the rain and all," she whispered.

Sartain blew out the smoke he'd just taken into his lungs.

She raised her head and placed her hand on his knees. "Tell me, Mike, how did you come to do what you do?"

For a long time, he didn't respond. He just sat with his head resting against the back of the deep chair, staring at nothing across the room.

"That's all right if you don't want to tell me," Belle said, kissing him tenderly.

"It was years ago, now," Sartain said. "Five . . . six . . . I came home from the War, became a galvanized Yankee—"

"What's a galvanized Yankee?"

"Since I'd been a Grayback, fought on the side of the Confederacy during the War of Northern Aggression, I had to swear allegiance to the Federal army . . . in order to join the frontier cavalry, you understand. It's called becomin' 'galvanized' to the federal ways."

He shrugged a shoulder. "I had nowhere to go after the war, and knew really only one thing—fightin'—so I decided the cavalry would be the best place for me. Besides, I'd never been any farther west than New Orleans. So I swore allegiance, got stationed at Fort Huachuca in the Arizona Territory . . ."

His gut tightened with the dread of those cloying memories. An odd sensation to feel the agony of his past while a girl entertained him. Belle's tongue, her sweet lips, and gentle hands took some of the teeth out of the horror that, despite the pain, was good to remember from time to time. Good to remind himself why he was here, doing what he was doing . . .

He swallowed, licked his lips, ground his heels into the floor as Belle slid her head forward.

"My patrol was ambushed one afternoon. Chiricahuas. They—"

Belle looked up at him again. "What's 'Chiricahuas'?"

"Apaches. A nasty bunch, though who could blame them? We were—are—the interlopers in their ancestral territory. Anyway, the entire patrol was ambushed, wiped out . . . save myself. I was badly wounded. Somehow, when the squaws were sent in to finish off the wounded soldiers, they didn't find me lying in the brush and rocks. I must have been shaded or somethin' . . . I don't know. An old prospector and his granddaughter . . . Jewel . . . found me and nursed me back to health."

"Jewel," Belle said.

"Yeah," Sartain said, wincing at the pain of the memories as well as Belle's sweet manipulations. "Jewel . . ."

"Was she your girl?"

"Yeah. She came to be my girl. Became . . . well, she got in the family way."

"Oh," Belle said, her tone growing ominous, as though sensing the dark way that the tale would turn.

"I'd gone out hunting one afternoon. On the way back I spied five bluebellies—federal soldiers—riding fast. Viewed 'em through my spyglass. They were whoopin' and hollerin' like Apaches on the warpath. Later, when I got back to the camp, I discovered why those five renegade bluecoats had been stompin' with their tails up. They'd plundered the old prospector's cache of gold. Killed the old man. Killed Jewel . . . after they'd raped her. Each one of 'em, most like."

The Revenger tried to swallow down the hard knot in his throat, felt the warm wetness of tears rolling down his cheeks. "One after another . . ."

Sartain squeezed his eyes closed against the bloody images, tried to concentrate instead on Belle's sweet and gentle manipulations. She seemed to sense the comfort he was needing. The girl had a deft touch. She was a natural master at giving a man pleasure. Some women were born with such skills. Despite the darkness of Sartain's thoughts, his blood rose to a crescendo.

Belle grunted.

"And then I hunted them all down—all five—and killed them bloody," The Revenger said tightly, clenching his fists against the memories as well as the lovemaking.

Belle rose and moved to the washbasin. When she'd returned with a damp cloth, she said, "I'm sorry, Mike."

"You were wonderful," Sartain wheezed, easing back into the chair.

"No. I mean about . . . about . . . Jewel."

As she dropped to her knees and extended the damp cloth toward him, he spied movement out the window over his left shoulder. He turned, blinking against the darkness and the ambient light flashing silver in the puddles pocking the street. A horse stood in the middle of the street.

As the short hairs bristled along the back of his neck, Sartain blinked again, trying to focus.

A hatted figure in a rain slicker stood on the other side of the horse, near the horse's off rear hip. The man was extending something over the top of the saddle toward the Belle of the Ball.

Sartain's heart hiccupped. He'd just turned toward Belle, yelling, *"Get down!"* when he glimpsed the rifle's orange flash. He heaved himself up out of the chair, shoving Belle to the floor and landing on top of her, hearing the soft tinkle of breaking glass followed closely by the rifle's roar.

CHAPTER 5

"Good Lord—what's happening?" Belle cried beneath Sartain, her voice muffled by his chest.

"You stay right there, Belle!"

Outside, a horse whinnied shrilly. He could hear someone cursing.

Sartain crawled over to where his Henry repeater was leaning against the wall. He grabbed the sixteen-shooter and, crouching, ran back over to the window. He edged a look around the frame.

The shooter was no longer aiming the rifle toward the Belle of the Ball, but was trying to check his horse down. The animal had apparently started bucking at the man's rifle report. Sartain could see only the horse and the shooter's silhouette, but he could see them just the same—the man's shadow sidestepping this way and that in the street while jerking on the horse's reins.

The horse's dark eyes flashed with fear.

Sartain pumped a round into the chamber and extended the Henry toward the street. He pressed his cheek up to the rifle's rear stock and aimed low, intending to only wing the son of a bitch. He couldn't slap the hell out of a dead man, nor find out why he'd drilled a pill through Belle's window. Just as Sartain squeezed the Henry's trigger, the man cursed again and was nearly jerked off his feet by his angry, scared, buck-kicking mount.

Sartain's bullet plumed dust as it hammered into the street

where the bushwhacker had been a half-second before. Then the horse half-dragged the gent into the deep, black shadows on the opposite side of the street.

Sartain cursed. Belle looked up at him from where she lay belly down, naked, on the floor, squirming like a landed fish. Her eyes were wide and round with fear. "Who is it, Mike? Who fired a shot in here?"

"I don't know, darlin', but I'm going to find out!" He tossed his rifle onto the bed and began pulling on his summer underwear. "You just stay down there, in case he starts hurling lead again!"

She looked so frightened and vulnerable down there that he took her in his arms, squeezed her reassuringly, and pressed his lips to her temple.

"Don't worry—I'll get him!"

He grabbed his rifle and ran to the door while she cried behind him, "Do be careful, Mike!"

Sartain was a careful man. He'd already scouted the place thoroughly and knew there was a rear door to the outside from the second story. He ran to it, raking one hand against the wall as a guide down the dark hall, and then threw the door's locking bolt, ran out onto the landing, and quickly descended the steps to the shadowy backyard that dripped now after the rain.

He made for the saloon's rear corner, stopped, pressing a shoulder against the building's back wall, and threw a look toward the main street.

He couldn't see anything but ambient, lilac-blue light and heavy shadows, starlight beyond a clearing sky reflecting silvery on the wet rooftops. But he could hear a voice raised in anger. It was coming from down a cross street, somewhere on the other side of the town's main drag.

Sartain pushed away from the building and bolted around the corner, sprinting toward the front. The saloon was on his left. Another, smaller, adobe brick structure—a furniture store, if he remembered—was on his right. He kicked a couple of tin cans and other sundry trash, and then he dashed out into the street just as a horse-and-rider-shaped shadow hurled itself out of the heavy shadows of the cross street, swung hard left, and galloped away down the main drag, heading for the settlement's ragged outskirts.

"Hold it there or take it in the back, you son of a bitch!" Sartain shouted.

The silhouetted rider merely crouched lower in his saddle and whipped his rein ends against his mount's right hip.

The Henry leaped and roared three times in Sartain's hands. He sprinted forty or fifty yards forward and loosed another barrage, the rifle's reports echoing over the dark town, the heavy, humid air somewhat muffling them.

A dog started barking somewhere in the distant darkness.

Sartain stared ahead through his own wafting powder smoke, the tang of cordite in his nostrils. Horse and ambusher had been swallowed by the night. He could hear the distant clomps of the horse's galloping hooves. They dwindled quickly into the distance until there was nothing but the dripping silence.

Somewhere, a man said angrily as though to someone else, "Listen to all that shootin' out there! This town is goin' to hell in a damned hand basket!" And then there was the thud of a window being slammed shut.

Sartain cursed and lowered the smoking repeater to his side. He gave a sigh, scrubbed moisture from his forehead with his forearm, then drew his hat down taut on his head, turned, and tromped on back down the soggy street, his boots making splashing, sucking sounds as they ground into the mud.

As he approached the Belle of the Ball, he saw movement on the second story. His window had been raised higher, and Belle poked her head out.

"Mike?" the girl said softly but loudly enough to be heard in the heavy quiet that had descended after the shooting.

"Yeah?"

"Them two fellas you was playin' poker with earlier?"

"Yeah?"

"They pulled out of their room just after you left." Belle turned her head this way and that, looking around suspiciously. "They must be out here somewhere."

There was an orange flash at the saloon's left front corner. Sartain flinched as the bullet screeched passed his head so close that he felt the warm curl of air just off his right ear.

Crouching and pivoting while raising the Henry, Sartain fired two quick shocks, evoking a groan. There was another orange flash from the saloon's opposite corner, but Sartain had instinctively thrown himself forward, landing on his shoulder and rolling. That shot, too, missed its mark to thud into a building on the street's opposite side.

Sartain rolled up on his right hip and shoulder, lifting the Henry from the mud, and fired two more rounds and then a third when he saw the bushwhacker's staggering shadow separate from the saloon wall. The man threw up his arms and collapsed just after Sartain had heard the shooter's rifle drop in the mud.

The man lay on his back, kicking. Quickly, the kicking ceased and the shooter lay still.

Sartain aimed his rifle from his hip at the first man he'd shot, who also lay still, and walked over to the second man—a tall *hombre* with a thick, black mustache. Earlier, when they'd been playing five-card stud, he'd said his name was Clements. Now he was merely Clements's bloody ghost.

Sartain walked over to the second man, whose chest was rising and falling behind his checked vest and white shirt. Unlike Sartain, and just like Clements, he was fully dressed, his empty holster tied down on his right thigh clad in brown wool trousers with hide-patched knees.

He'd said his name was Brown. Billy Brown. A young man with a blonde fringe of mustache mantling his pink upper lip that had a small, corded notch scar, as though he'd been poked with a blade. A short-barreled, five-shot Smith and Wesson "Baby Russian" revolver, .38 caliber, lay in a tuft of wet bunch grass just off his right shoulder.

An old-model Remington .44 conversion revolver lay near his left hand. He was sliding his hand toward it, inch by painful inch, until Sartain stepped on the hand.

Billy Brown groaned and arched his back, grinding the back of his head and the heels of his boots into the wet ground.

"Oh, you're hurting me, you nasty devil! You're *hurting* me!"

"Devil, huh?" Sartain said, keeping his boot pressed down on the kid's palm. "You bushwhacked me, remember?"

"Oh, you nasty devil—I'm dyin' here! You blew my guts out!" With his free hand, he was trying to keep his intestines from slithering out through the gaping hole in his belly.

"Why'd you do it, dumbass?"

"Go to hell, you! I'm—!"

"Yeah, I know—you're dyin' here." Sartain hunkered down and stared into the kid's pain-pinched eyes, glassy with fast-approaching death. "*Why* are you dying, kid?"

"That . . . that little bitch upstairs!" the kid grunted out, still grinding his heels painfully into the soggy ground. "She knows . . . she knows where the loot's at . . . from the mine. Don't let her kid ya!"

Sartain frowned. He kept his voice low as he said, "You think Belle knows where the gold is?"

"Sure as shit. Her and Jasper Garvey . . . they done . . . slipped an extra . . . jack . . . into the *deck*!" He winced, squeezed his eyes closed. "Oh, Lord, you killed me!" The kid sobbed, convulsed. "I'm comin' Momma!"

"Hold on," Sartain said, pinching the kid's chin and shaking his head. "Who was that bastard with the horse?"

The kid fell slack against the ground. His head rolled to one side, and he gazed up at Sartain, glassy-eyed. He gave a soft fart, made a gurgling sound in his throat, and that was it. He was dancing with his mother, if his mother was dancing the devil's two-step amongst the butane vapors, that was.

"He dead?"

Sartain jerked at Belle's voice. She was standing a few feet away, just off the corner of the saloon. She had a blanket wrapped around her shoulders. That appeared all she was wearing. Her feet were bare. Her hair tumbled messily across her shoulders.

Billy Brown's disembodied voice said: " 'She knows where the loot's at from the mine . . . don't let her kid ya!' "

"He dead, Mike?" she repeated, coming up and prodding the kid's shoulder with one bare toe.

"Yeah," Sartain said.

"The other one . . . ?"

"Dead, too."

Sartain straightened, looking down at the slack, staring form of Billy Brown and then shuttling his gaze to Belle Higgins. She returned his look, hiked a shoulder beneath the blanket. "Any idea why they was gunnin' for you, too, Mike?"

Sartain shook his head. He wondered if she'd heard what Billy had said. If not, he wasn't going to tell her. "No. None at all."

He swung around to stare off into the murky western distance, where the rider had disappeared into the night. "He must've been in with these two. More bounty hunters, maybe." But they didn't need to be bona fide man-hunters. More than a few times, men who'd merely crossed trails by happenstance with The Revenger had tried to kill him for the bounty on his head.

Maybe that's who these men were. And they'd brought in a third man—the man on the horse—to back their play.

Still, Billy Brown's dying words kept bouncing around inside Sartain's head: " *'Her and Jasper Garvey slipped an extra jack into the deck!'* "

"We'd best go in, Mike. Come on. I'll have Northcutt tend to these two in the mornin'." Belle tugged on his arm and stretched her lips in a lusty smile. "Look at you—you're covered in mud. I think we'd best get you back soakin' in a nice hot bathtub!"

"Yeah," Sartain said. "Yeah, I suppose I'd best have me another bath."

Pensively, chill fingers of apprehension dancing along his spine, he let her lead him back around the side of the saloon toward the rear.

"Her and Jasper Garvey done slipped an extra jack into the deck!"

CHAPTER 6

Sartain woke feeling as though he'd had only an hour of sleep. Which he supposed was about right.

After a bath, which he'd taken in lukewarm water because he hadn't wanted Belle to waste the stove wood to heat it, nor had he wanted to wait for it, he'd slept lightly and fitfully.

The Revenger's mind was foggy and troubled by the intriguing words Billy Brown had uttered on his deathbed, so to speak. But by the time he'd finally drifted off for a short slumber, he'd pretty much dismissed the whole notion that Belle could be in cahoots with Jasper Garvey.

If so, why would she send The Revenger out after the deputy sheriff? It made no sense for her to sic a killer on her accomplice. Billy Brown might have believed what he'd said—possibly only because Belle and Garvey were known to horse around in the Belle of the Ball together—and he and his friends might have decided to try and catch the two together with the strongbox of gold bars from the mine.

But Billy Brown hadn't looked like the sharpest tool in the shed. Nor had he acted like it. He'd most likely been dead wrong about the Belle-and-Garvey conspiracy.

In the wash of dull, gray light pushing through the room's sole window, Sartain glanced at Belle. She lay on her belly, head turned away from him, the sheet and quilt exposing her left buttock and the pale downward curve of her left breast beneath her arm. He leaned down, pressed his lips to the small of her

185

back, then drew the sheet and quilt up and over her. The air was damp and cool.

The girl groaned, moved her legs, and then drifted back to sleep once more. Exhausted.

The Revenger gave a wry chuckle. He moved to the window and looked out. The sun didn't appear to be up yet, but it was hard to tell with the scalloped, gunmetal clouds arching in relief across the sky. It was a soggy, moody, post-storm morning. Northcutt was squatting over the body of Billy Brown. The old man looked up toward Sartain's window, spat to one side, and shook his head.

Sartain shrugged.

On the other side of the street from the old man, at the mouth of a break between the Wells Fargo office and a small laundry, a coyote stood, ears and tail raised, as though waiting for the old man to leave him to a breakfast of Billy Brown and Billy's unlucky cohort.

While Belle snored softly into her pillow, Sartain dressed, stepped into his boots, donned his hat, draped his saddlebags over his left arm, picked up his Henry repeater, and went out. He gently closed and latched the door behind him.

"You wear that girl out?" Northcutt asked him downstairs in the main drinking hall, where the oldster sat over a steaming stone mug of coffee at a table near the bar. Beyond him and the batwings, the sky was turning a lighter shade of gray.

"Looks like it." Sartain set his gear on a table near the old man and then walked over to the bar, where a large, speckled black coffee pot sat on a thick, leather potholder. Steam skeined from its spout to unravel in the misty morning air still soggy from the storm. "Leastways, *I* could have used another hour or two in the old mattress sack."

He leaned back on his hips, stretching, and grabbed one of several coffee mugs lined up beside the pot, and dumped some smoking mud, black as tar, into it.

"Well, good, I'm glad you wore her out," the old man groused. "That girl's been so damn owly of late, I half-feared she was gonna toss a butterfly loop over my head, tie me to the cookin' range back there, and have her way!" He laughed and lifted his mug to his bearded mouth, blowing ripples on the coffee's surface.

Sartain brought his coffee back to the old man's table and sat down across from him.

Northcutt hauled a small, canvas tobacco pouch out of his pocket. "Headin' out?"

"Just as soon as I swill this and saddle my horse."

Northcutt withdrew rolling papers from the sack, but when he tipped the sack over the paper troughed in his fingers, only a few grains of chopped tobacco came out. Sartain tossed his own sack down beside the old man's smoking mug.

"Obliged." Northcutt set to work building his smoke. "Some handy shootin' you did last night. You keep shootin' all our regular customers, Belle's gonna have to board the place up."

"There was a third one."

"Wouldn't doubt it."

Sartain sipped his coffee and took back his tobacco pouch. Sitting back in his chair, he started building a quirley of his own. "You know who that third bastard might be?"

"Got no idea."

"I know one was Billy Brown. Leastways, that's who he said he was. The other one—"

"The other one was Calvin Clements. The two rode together. Sometimes with a third man named Reeves, sometimes with a fourth one named Iverson. I've seen five of 'em ride through here a time or two. Don't believe I was ever told the fifth one's name, or if I did I can't recall it. Old age ain't purty, Mr. Sartain."

He twisted his cigarette closed and rolled it between his lips, sealing it. "They were all cowhands workin' at various ranches—sometimes only two or three together at the same brand. Sometimes all five. One or two was always drawin' his time and gettin' hazed onto the grubline trail—fired for one reason or another—so they wasn't always all runnin' in the same pack together, or workin' for the same spread. But they had history in that they was all soldiers together, stationed up at the Tawny Buttes outpost north of here. I think Billy Brown grew up in this country. Clements might have, too."

The graybeard fired a match to life on his cracked, yellow thumbnail and held it up in front of his quirley. "Any idea why they ambushed you? At least, I'm assumin' that's why that coyote out there is lickin' his chops. They tried gunnin' you, same as the others. My, you're fillin' up the cemetery faster'n the Utes and Southern Cheyenne did back in the day!"

Sartain set his elbows on the table and touched a flame to his own cigarette, blowing smoke out his nostrils and waving out the lucifer. "I got no idea why they were so intent on dressin' me in a wooden overcoat, Mr. Northcutt."

"Call me Dad. Most folks around here do. And since you've become such fast and close friends with Belle and all . . ."

"All right—Dad. I will share a secret with you, though, if you promise not to share it with Belle."

"Secrets already? Say, you two oughta get hitched!" Dad wheezed a laugh and then choked on cigarette smoke. When he stopped convulsing, his face bright as a freshly cooked brick, he said, "All right." He twisted his fingers beside his mouth, locking his lips.

"Just before he died, Billy Brown told me that Belle and Japer Garvey were in on the robbery together."

The old man said, "He did, did he?"

"You don't seem shocked."

"Well . . ." The old man drew on his quirley and looked away, blowing smoke toward the far side of the room from the bar. "Pshaw! Everybody's got a theory. That don't sound like Belle. At least . . . I don't think it does. Come to think of it, she and ole Jasper were mighty . . ." He scowled and shook his head. "Ah, nuts! No, sir, I don't believe it. Folks think all kinds of things when somethin' like this happens. Nothin' like stolen gold to start the yarn spinners agildin' their lilies!"

"You don't seem to think it's totally impossible."

"Well, hell—Belle's a headstrong kid. And she's been trapped here in this little flea on a gnat's ass of a wide spot in the trail for most of her life. But—ah, hell, I don't believe that! There's all kind of rumors goin' around, and they started about five seconds after it started gettin' odd that the sheriff and Garvey weren't pullin' into town with the strongbox."

"What were the other rumors?" Sartain asked, blowing smoke and lifting his half-empty mug to his lips.

"Well, hell—folks started thinkin' maybe both the sheriff and Garvey took off with the gold. Neither one of 'em is a rich man. Some folks—namely, them who had no fondness for the sheriff, started thinkin' out loud that maybe he killed Garvey and headed for Mexico."

Northcutt glanced past Sartain, throwing a cautionary look at the stairs. Lowering his voice, he continued. "They think maybe the sheriff is waitin' down there for his daughter, who will join him after a reasonable amount of time has passed, and it doesn't look too odd that she's sellin' the saloon."

"Uh-huh," Sartain said, nodding as he pondered the possibility. "But if that were so, why would she bring me in, almost kill me to test my skills, and then put me on the scent of her old man?"

"Right," Northcutt said. "I didn't say I thought any of these rumors made sense. I'm just tellin' you what's been goin' around town and the whole damn county."

"Any more theories?"

"Aside from Belle's theory, which is also shared by others, you mean? Well, sure—they mighta been cut down by road agents. And, if you ask me, that's most likely what happened. Could have been bushwhacked by the same gang them bounty hunters was after before you made it so they wouldn't be after anything anymore. At least, not on this side of the sod."

"I assume someone has ridden into the mountains to investigate."

"Sure, sure. I did myself. Gotta admit, my trackin' skills ain't what they used to be. Once upon a time I could track a nekked Apache over a caprock under cover of darkness, but the peepers have dimmed a might. I rode both trails, didn't see hide nor hair. Though, like I said, that don't really mean much."

"Has anyone else investigated?"

"Oh, I'm sure the mine owner, Maragon, sent someone out to investigate. I was here when he sent a courier down to the Wells Fargo office to wire the Pinkertons, askin' them for help. The Pinkerton rode through here last week, asked a few questions, and headed on up the mountains. Didn't seem like the capable sort to me. Ain't seen the federal marshals Maragon asked for. Likely won't tell next year." Northcutt chuckled, sipped his coffee again, and licked his mustache. "Now, Belle's a smart girl. Too smart for her own good sometimes. She wouldn't call in a man like you unless she really wanted you to find her father and the gold, or at least find out what happened. To him and Garvey and the gold. No, sir."

Sartain pondered the puzzle. Coming up with only more questions, he asked Northcutt for directions to the mine.

"There's two trails—Weaver's Meadow Trail and the Old Ute Trail," the oldster said, tapping ash from his cigarette onto the floor. "Higgins always went up into the mountains via one trail and came down the other. He never told me—or anyone, as far as I know—which trail he'd be taking whichaway. It was his way of lessening his chances of getting held up. So I don't know which way he went into the mountains and which way he started down. Doubt he told anyone up at the mine, either. The sheriff was the cautious sort."

Northcutt went on to draw both trails to the mine with his fingers on the table, and laid out the landmarks that Sartain should look for. He told The Revenger it was a good four-day trip, two days climbing, another day and a half coming back down.

"Another cup of coffee?" he asked, stubbing his cigarette out on the table. Judging by the scars, it wasn't the first quirley mashed out on the age-silvered boards. "Stove should be hot enough by now. I can cook you some breakfast. How's ham and eggs sound? I just brought the eggs in from the Burlinson coop. Still warm from the hens' behinds!"

"That does sound good," Sartain said, finishing his coffee. "But maybe next time, on my way back through town. I'm burnin' daylight, Mr. Northcutt."

"Dad!"

"I mean, Dad."

"That gold's been gone nearly two months now. Same with the sheriff and Garvey. You got time for a bite o' my vittles— which ain't too shabby, I might add, despite what Belle might say about 'em. She musta taken some juice out of ya last night. You look a little yellow around the gills. A near-virgin in heat will do that to a feller. Just glad it was you and not me. If it was me, I'd likely be gettin' fitted for a wooden overcoat about now. Food will put some lead back in your gun."

The old man rose, winking and cackling. "If'n you get my drift?"

Sartain thought the man was probably right. He did feel a

little hollowed out and bone-tired. His gun needed some lead. Another cup of coffee and some belly padding might be just what the doctor ordered. And what his trip into the Sangre de Cristos required.

"All right, Dad, you done twisted my arm," Sartain said, and got up to refill his mug at the coffee pot.

CHAPTER 7

An hour later, a grub sack that Dad had packed for him hanging from his saddlehorn, Sartain put Boss onto the trail that led northeast out of Silverthorne. The two-track wagon trail wound through sage and wheat-colored bunchgrass over tabletop-flat country for about three miles. Then it began to climb—first over low hogbacks and then twisting up through the creases between crumbling buttes.

The country quickly grew more and more rugged. Prettier, too.

The bunchgrass and sage gave way to cedar and piñon stippling the shelving rock formations and pitch-roofed mesas. A creek meandered along the ever-climbing and twisting and turning trail for short stretches before swerving away and then swinging back to it for a few more twists and turns before dropping down into a canyon obscured by pines and taller, greener grass and ferns.

The air was rich with the tang of pine resin and the verdant richness of forest duff. Now as Sartain continued to climb, the cool air drying his sweaty shirt and vest and burning like a hot iron against the back of his neck, the sounds were birds chirping—nuthatches, magpies, and robins—and squirrels chittering noisily from pine boughs. Occasionally he heard the low roar of a falls echoing up from the canyon.

He kept a close eye on the trail, looking for any sign of a holdup or shooting. Two months' worth of wind and rain would have erased hoof prints, but there still might be a cartridge casing or two, or maybe some blood staining a shrub.

Around noon, he swung off the trail and into the deep, sun-dappled pine forest, and drew Boss to a halt near another, narrower creek rippling down from the higher reaches, its bed studded with mossy rocks and lined with boulders, deep grass, and ferns. Dark trout pools cut into the banks; one such pool, under an escarpment of black granite, had toppled a large aspen. The aspen's dead branches would make a hot fire.

A prime place for lunch.

He unsaddled and hobbled Boss in grass near the creek, rubbed the horse down, and gave him some grain. Then he dug a small fire pit, ringed it with stones, and snapped off some of the dead aspen branches. When he'd gathered tinder comprised of bark, dried pine needles, and cones, he built a fire and brewed coffee.

Dad had made him some ham and egg sandwiches on crusty wheat bread, and he ate one of these with some cheese he'd bought in Alamosa, washing it down with the hot, black coffee. Finished with the main meal, he ate peaches from an airtight tin with his fingers, and washed the sugary dessert down with another cup of coffee.

He wanted to head on up the trail, but he found the previous night's lack of sleep weighing heavy on his shoulders, tugging on his eyelids. The lulling music of the creek dropping down the slope and over the shelving rocks in its bed, the warm sun shining down through the forest canopy, and the rich fragrance of the woods only further convinced him that he needed a nap.

He lay down in the soft grass, rested his head against the wool underside of his saddle, and tugged his hat brim down over his eyes.

He intertwined his hands on his belly, and the piping of the robins and the warm, fragrant breeze caressing his face soon had him snoring. He wasn't sure how much time had passed when he woke with a jerk.

Something had reached into his unconscious and pulled him out of his slumber. It was a sixth sense keen to possible trouble that his years of hunting and being hunted had developed and honed.

He looked around, blinking, shrugging off the sleep that had ensconced him. Boss stood near the water, tail arched, ears twitching, staring into the pines on the far side of the six-foot-wide creek. Sartain followed Boss's gaze. Something was moving in the forest about fifty, maybe sixty yards away. There was a splash of red moving there, maybe some yellow and tan.

A person, most likely. Possibly someone trying to sneak up on him.

Sartain shucked his Henry from his saddle sheath, walked over, and ran a soothing hand down Boss's neck. "Easy, boy. You stay here and stay quiet. I'm gonna check it out."

The horse gave a quiet snort of understanding and lowered his snout toward the grass once more, but Boss's ears kept twitching, and he kept his eyes on the forest beyond the creek.

Sartain moved upstream, which was also upslope, about fifty feet, and then crossed the creek on a short stretch of beaver dam composed of a fallen aspen and intricately woven aspen and fir branches. On the creek's opposite side, he crouched as he traced a zigzagging path through the trees, using the pine boles for cover as he moved as quietly as possible toward the movement in the forest beyond and slightly downhill from him now.

He topped a rise, dropped into a shallow ravine threaded by a spring-fed rivulet, and climbed three-quarters up the opposite ridge. Doffing his hat, he crawled the rest of the way and edged a slow, cautious look over the ridge crest littered with old leaves and pine needles. Shadbark and ferns screened him from view of the person in the next shallow ravine.

Sartain had no problem discerning that the person was a woman. A pretty blonde woman, at that. She'd opened her man's plaid wool shirt and, kneeling beside the little stream that trickled through the ravine, as well, facing in The Revenger's direction, she was cupping water to her pale breasts. She'd pulled an undershirt up to her neck.

In spite of the Revenger's recent tussle with Belle the night before, his throat constricted at the surreal vision of this young woman—a blonde with thick hair the color of the summer sun pulled behind her head in a loose, French braid—taking her ablutions in the fragrant forest with birds chirping all around, and a crow cawing somewhere in the distance. The sun slanting through the pines shone like diamonds the same color as the woman's hair on the surface of the chuckling brook.

She was leaning far forward over the water. Her porcelain-pale, cherry-tipped bosoms jostled and swayed as she cupped water to each one in turn, slowly massaging the refreshing liquid into each. Sartain regaled himself for not pulling his head back and giving the woman some privacy, but what man could in such a situation?

He'd slip away in a second, and she'd never know he'd been here . . .

When she was finished bathing, she lowered her head to the water and drank, slurping audibly. For some reason, those sounds further warmed the blood coursing through Sartain's loins.

A mule brayed loudly. Sartain jerked with a start.

He'd been too enamored of the woman to have done more than merely notice and vaguely register the short, cream mule standing beyond the woman, partly screened by shrubs and trees. The woman did more than merely notice and vaguely register Sartain, however.

She'd snapped her head up quickly with a gasp, and as her eyes darted up the slope and locked with Sartain's through the brush that had inadequately screened him, she gave a clipped cry. She pushed to her feet with one hand while pressing her other arm across her chest. Wheeling, she ran over to the mule, which was outfitted with a wooden pack frame and canvas panniers.

A rifle was also strapped to it, and this she quickly shucked from its scabbard.

His face burning with shame, Sartain had left his rifle on the ground and risen to stand now with both his hands in the air. "Miss, I do apologize. I didn't mean to intrude. My horse just warned me that . . . hold on, miss—I'm tryin' to explain!"

But she was listening to none of it. Instead, she loudly pumped a cartridge into her old Spencer's chamber and, jaws hard, cheeks flushed with fury, and eyes narrowed, she raised the carbine to her shoulder. The rifle belched, stabbing smoke and fire, the slug tearing up dirt and leaves at The Revenger's boots.

"Miss, I assure you I meant no harm!"

But now she was pumping another round into the chamber and, to avoid getting himself deservedly drilled by the understandably piss-burned woman, he wheeled and flung himself back down the slope. The woman's bullet snapped the brush near where he'd been standing a quarter-second before. Sartain landed hard on his right hip and shoulder, rolled, and then crawled back up to retrieve his rifle.

The woman's carbine barked again . . . again . . . and then a third and fourth time, each bullet snapping and throwing brush or pluming dirt and pine needles. A pinecone bounced down the slope to roll up against his right boot.

"I apologize, miss!" Climbing to a low crouch, Sartain scuttled back down the slope like a schoolboy who'd just been caught peering through the half-moon hole in the girl's privy door.

Only when he'd hopscotched the dam and was back on the same side of the creek as his horse did he start to wonder who she was and what she was doing out here. That, he supposed, was no more his business than what he'd been watching her do.

His ears were still red as he approached the camp. It didn't help that Boss turned to him with what he couldn't help believing was an admonishing cast to the horse's copper-eyed gaze. Boss gave his tail a sharp, derogatory switch. Of course, there was no way the horse could know what Sartain had been caught doing, but some folks thought horses had a sixth sense, and the way Boss pawed the ground as though openly jeering his master, Sartain was beginning to wonder.

"Ah, shut up. If you'd seen her . . . and seen how well set up she was . . . you'd have ogled her, too."

With a sense of genuine shame, and hoping he hadn't scared the woman too badly, he broke camp, first kicking dirt on his fire and kicking the rocks onto the dirt, making sure the flames were thoroughly out. Then he gathered his gear.

Her image stayed with him, however, as he rode back out to the main trail and resumed his journey. You didn't find too many women as good-looking as she out here. Of course, he'd found Belle, who was this young lady's equal, but gals like Belle and the blonde were generally few and far between. The western frontier—and especially mining country—was notoriously hard on women.

This lass must have been some prospector's daughter. She'd probably been having an afternoon in the mountains by herself, enjoying some rare, precious time away from her otherwise endless chores—only to have her sojourn ruined by some degenerate ogling her from the brush while she'd stolen a few minutes to relax and cool off.

Sartain cursed himself for a low-life, but he couldn't help chuckling. She might have been a rarefied beauty, but she knew her way around a rifle, and she'd damned near kicked him off with a bullet, too. Maybe he'd learned his lesson.

"The next time you come upon some blonde-headed forest sprite bathing her titties in a creek, just ride on, old hoss!"

He snorted another laugh and then started scrutinizing the trail, focusing on the task at hand.

The trail continued to twist, turn, and rise ever higher, stone fingers of eroded rock towering over him, high above the sun-splashed tops of the firs, pines, and tamaracks. Occasionally, the trail flattened out as it snaked through an open valley or across a clearing, but it soon rose again.

All that first day on the trail, aside from the blonde forest sprite, he didn't see another soul. He also didn't see many tracks on the trail he was following, either. A few shod horses had made their stamp on the two-track trace, and two or three light wagons, but that was all.

Apparently, the Weaver's Meadow Trail didn't see much traffic, though Sartain knew that gold and silver had long since been discovered in the Sangre de Cristos, and he suspected plenty of miners and prospectors had staked their claims up here. Somewhere. It was a vast range, however, studded with deep hanging valleys, many forests and parks and beaver meadows divided by crags, and dogleg canyons, and The Revenger just didn't happen upon any of them.

He also didn't come upon any obvious sign of a holdup or an ambush, either.

That night, he camped in a high mountain park, near a stream at the edge of a fir and spruce forest. There was plenty of elk and moose scat along the creek, and seeing a couple of bear prints reminded him to keep his Henry close at all times. He had no hankering to become some bruin's slow supper.

He fished for trout in the stream, catching a couple of pan-sized brook trout, which he fried with lard, mountain sage sprigs, and some wild onion in his iron skillet. He fried corn cakes in the same pan. Sitting Indian fashion near the short, leaping flames that snapped and crackled and perfumed the air around him, he washed the sweet, tender meat and thin, crusty cakes down with coffee brewed on his iron tripod.

In typical high-mountain fashion, the night was clear, cold, and as black as the inside of a glove despite the seeming nearness of the stars glittering above the pine tops. Before retiring, he had a few sips of the Sam Clay bourbon he always carried in a hide flask, to cut the chill. He added a few small branches to his fire against the knife-edged cold and set a few more broken branches nearby, which he could feed to the flames from time to time during the night.

He slept in his heavy wool coat, wrapped in his blankets, his Henry close beside him.

The cold night with its smells of stone and the cold creek and frosty grass closed over him.

He slept so soundly that he didn't even dream, though the intermittent cries of coyotes and wolves from the crags looming over him were dreamlike in their smoky comings and goings.

The next day, just after noon, he had his first real sign that he wasn't alone in the mountains. A rifle spoke from an escarpment above and on his right, and the bullet blew him from his saddle.

CHAPTER 8

Sartain flew headlong into the brush on the left side of the trail, the ambusher's shot still echoing. That side of the trail dropped into a wooded canyon, and when The Revenger hit the ground, he rolled several times down the hill before fetching up against a tamarack bole, the branches of the tree several feet above his head.

Cursing and slapping his right hand over the bullet burn across the front of his left arm, he twisted around and stared back up the trail. The shooter's rifle barked twice more and then a third time, the bullets thumping and cracking into the brush just above him. Up on the trail threading the canyon and a large, black escarpment jutting on the trail's opposite side, Boss was pitching wildly and buck-kicking.

The rifle cracked again. A bullet plumed dust near one of the buckskin's pounding hooves.

"Boss, high-tail it, ya damn fool!" Sartain yelled, gritting his teeth and waving his good arm angrily.

As though in compliance with his rider's wishes, Boss dropped onto his front hooves and wheeled, knocking the saddle down his side and giving Sartain a good look at the Henry still in its scabbard. At the moment, The Revenger would have given his eyeteeth to have the sixteen-shooter in his hands. Loosing another enraged whinny, Boss kicked his rear legs straight out behind him once more and galloped back down the trail in the direction from which he and Sartain had come.

Ignoring the blood oozing from the rip in his right shirt-sleeve—the wound was merely a burn, though it smarted like twenty bee stings—Sartain palmed his LeMat, which he was happy to find hadn't slipped out of its holster in his tumble down the slope.

Staying low, he looked up through the evergreen brush to see the ambusher maneuvering around on top of the dark crag. The shooter wore a tan Stetson, a yellow neckerchief, a white-and-red checked shirt, and a rifle from Sartain's vantage. The hat appeared the same shape as that his ambusher of the previous night had been wearing.

Likely the same man.

Now as the shooter hunkered low and extended his rifle once more, Sartain pivoted to his left and ran along the side of the slope.

The bushwhacker's rifle screeched, bullets tearing up dirt and pine needles just upslope from Sartain. Another slug hammered a pine tree. Yet another clipped a branch and sent it hurling toward The Revenger, who kept running until he launched from the balls of his boots, diving forward, and hit the ground behind a large, deadfall tamarack lying parallel with the trail and the escarpment looming above it.

The rifleman atop the escarpment triggered several more rounds, but all were well wide of their target. Apparently, the man had lost track of his quarry. There was something green about this shooter, another thing that told Sartain he was the same shooter as before.

Sartain lifted a careful look over the top of the deadfall. He couldn't see the shooter now; there was nothing but clear sky above the bulging, cracked face of the escarpment, which loomed about a hundred feet above the trail. Straight above Sartain was a vestibule of sorts in the formation's facing side. It was a cleft in the rock that appeared to run from top to bottom, and was about wide enough to conceal a man The Revenger's size.

Quickly, before the rifleman could adjust his position, Sartain heaved himself to his feet, leaped the deadfall, and scrambled up the bank. As he crossed the trail, he cast a quick look up toward the top of the escarpment. He didn't see his bushwhacker, but a couple of stones buzzed through air to his right, thumping into the brush at the base of the scarp.

Sartain gritted his teeth, expecting another shot. None came, and he gained the cliff wall with a deep sigh of relief, panting from the run and removing his neckerchief to tie it around the bullet burn. The rocks had no doubt come from the shooter shifting position, but there was no indication he'd spotted his quarry.

Staring straight up at the bulging wall of rock looming over him as though a massive, fat finger pointing at high, thin swirls of cloud in the cobalt sky, he stepped back into the niche he'd spotted from the slope. It leaned back into the formation, likely a softer spot in the rock that had eroded more quickly over time than the rest of the granite.

It was strewn with rocks of all shapes and sizes and showed the erosion of rainwater tumbling through its middle, sweeping the rocks and debris this way and that. Even a few gnarled shrubs were trying to grow up out of the thin, stony soil.

Both sides of the scarp sort of swelled out around it, concealing it, offering cover to a man wanting to climb up there and shake hands with the son of a bitch trying to perforate his hide. Sartain knew it was risky. If the shooter anticipated the move, the shooter could simply wait near the top of the makeshift rocky chute and drill Sartain a third eye when he poked his head up out of the hole.

But there was a good chance the man wasn't aware of the chute. From up top, he'd have an entirely different view of his position, and he'd probably be expecting Sartain to remain below, waiting for the shooter to show, which he might eventually do. Or he might wait until dark and simply slip away to come at The Revenger again in a similar cowardly fashion.

Sartain quietly spat dust and pine needles from his lips. He'd eaten a good bit of both in his rumble town the slope. Looking up the steep cleft in the scarp, he thought it was best to end this chapter in his visit to the mountains right here. The shooter was likely the same man who'd ambushed him in Silverthorne, which meant he was a persistent if hapless cuss.

Besides, Sartain was not only piss-burned the way any man would be, getting shot out of his saddle, but he was damned curious, too.

He holstered his LeMat, snapped the keeper thong over the hammer, grabbed a finger of rock sticking out of the side of the chute up near his right shoulder, placed his left boot on a shelf of sorts, and hoisted himself up into the chute. Now he was five feet above the ground and a little winded. Sweat cut through the grime on his cheeks.

He was on the first leg of his journey.

That first step was the hardest. After that, it was mostly a matter of finding secure rocks and the occasional shrubs to use as steps and handrails. He had to move around bellies of rock bulging out of the greater rock wall to his right and, doing this, he left himself exposed for a few seconds each time to possible fire from the top end of the gap.

He kept an eye on that gap as he continued climbing, trying hard not to make any noise. A few times he caused slight rock-slides, but nothing too prolonged or loud, and each time he did, he pulled his LeMat and aimed it toward the patch of cloud-scalloped blue above, ready to shoot the bushwhacker if he showed his head.

He continued climbing. The window on the sky grew wider

and brighter above him.

He was six feet from the top. A step from one rock to a cleft in the bulging wall on his right, and he edged his head up out of the chute. He looked around, aiming the cocked LeMat straight out in front of him. The top of the escarpment was all bulging, cracked rock from which a couple of scraggly cedars grew from fissures.

The air was fresh, almost cool, the sun like honey warmed on a stove.

The only movement was the breeze brushing over the various humps and piles of ancient volcanic rock, jostling the cedars. Holstering the LeMat, he used both hands to hoist himself up out of the chute.

Standing atop the escarpment, in a crease between low hills of solid lava, he unholstered the LeMat once more and started moving slowly along the crease to his right, sliding his gaze from left to right and back again, stopping occasionally to swing full around. He moved into a deep corridor between two ten-foot-high mushrooms of solid stone. Ahead, a shadow moved across the stone floor, sliding from his right to his left.

He saw the shadow of the front of a hat, and he stopped, tightening his grip on the pistol, raising it.

Behind him, something screeched so loudly that it seemed to come from inside his own head. He heard the windy rustle of wings, and spun in time to see a large crow sweep down toward him from a higher mound of stone, the bird's beady eyes bright with anger, beak opening and closing as it loosed its ratcheting screams.

The bird just started to pull up and away from Sartain when he started to spin back around.

Too late.

Something both icy and hot slammed into his right temple like a pugilist's resolute fist, laying him out cold.

His brain became an exposed, sputtering nerve that some faceless demon was probing with a dull, rusty nail in a room as black as the inside of a coffin. The demon was chuckling while poking that nail against the frayed, dancing nerve, and while Sartain cursed and groaned and tried to pull his head away, he couldn't quite manage it. Something was holding him down on a marble slab while that demon continued its diabolical torture, chuckling all the while.

By increments, the pain lessened. Inexplicably, he was aware of the taste of whiskey on his tongue and its burn spreading throughout his belly.

The pain continued to abate, and when he started to smell the smoke of a fire and the aroma of cooked beans and boiling coffee, he opened his eyes. A young blonde woman sat across a fire from him. She held his shirt in her hands, and she was poking a needle through the left sleeve. A thick wing of honey-gold hair hung down over her right eye, obscuring her face, but when she lifted her head slightly, glancing over at him, she dropped the shirt and needle on her lap and picked up his LeMat.

Leaning back away from him, she extended the heavy revolver in both hands and ratcheted the hammer back.

"You just stay right there," she said testily. "Or I'll drill you with your own gun!"

Sartain studied her. She was the young woman who'd been bathing in the creek. The one who'd taken issue with his indiscretion and pumped several rounds from an old Spencer rifle at him. Now she sat just across the fire, the sky awash with the pastels of dusk showing through the tall, columnar pines behind her, from beyond a pinnacle of black rock jutting from a near ridge.

He glanced at his arm. A bandage of feminine material, maybe part of a chemise, was wrapped tightly around it. There was no bloodstain. He was aware of a bandage of similar material wrapped around his forehead, though he was too weak to lift his arms to investigate further.

He cleared his throat, ran his dry tongue across his dry lips, and said, "I'd pay ya a pretty penny." Wincing and groaning, he found the strength to press three fingers to his hammering skull, trying to quell the demon's prodding. "Go ahead—shoot."

She studied him over the slightly quivering barrel of the heavy weapon in her hands. Her eyes were hazel, nose long and fine. Her face was round, she had a cleft in her chin, and her smooth cheeks were tanned the color of varnished walnut. Her honey blonde hair was bleached from many hours in the sun, giving her an earthy, slightly wild air. Her eyes, too, added to this feral quality about her. Those two wide-set, blue-green orbs were like a doe's eyes—a doe with a fawn to protect.

Threatened, wary, ready to action if necessary.

When she didn't say anything but just continued to study him like a doe sniffing the wind, he said, "Oh, put it down. I ain't in no condition to go anywhere, much less make a play for you. And if you were so damn suspicious, why all the fuss?"

"What're you talkin' about?" she asked. Her voice was raspy, a little husky—too raspy for such a cherubic face, though it complemented her earthiness.

"You know—the bandages. The fire." He looked at the sewing in her lap. "My shirt."

Faintly sheepish, she lowered the LeMat. Handily, she depressed the hammer and rested the pistol, barrel down, in the V that her two bare feet formed, tucked beneath her. They were poking out from beneath her skirt tented across her lap and bent knees.

Like her face and hands, her feet were tan. She obviously went without shoes a lot. Her stubby toes were dirty. Pine needles clung to the pink pads.

Sartain remembered her pale, cherry-tipped breasts swinging

to and fro as she'd washed them, and felt a very faint electrical charge sweep through him.

"Just passin' the time," she said, picking up his shirt, needle, and thread. "Waitin' to see if you was gonna live or not. If you were gonna die, I figured it only proper to bury ya."

"Right nice of you to do that for a man you caught spying on you."

Her cheeks flushed as she went back to work sewing a patch over the hole in his shirtsleeve. "Yes, it is."

CHAPTER 9

"What the hell happened?" Sartain asked the girl.

"What do you mean?"

"Who shot me? How'd you find me? How . . . come that fella with the rifle didn't finish me off? He put enough work into it."

His mind was sluggish. He was exerting a lot of energy fighting the pain of the bullet crease. At least, he figured it was a crease. It must have carved a nice trough across his temple, maybe nicked the bone. He'd been grazed similarly before. It was painful, but he'd live, though he might not want to for a few more hours.

The girl hiked a shoulder while she poked the needle through Sartain's shirtsleeve. "Never seen him. He must've figured you was dead and left you to the carrion eaters."

"How'd you find me?"

"Heard the shootin'. I was up on the ridge yonder." She jerked her sewing needle back over her left shoulder. "Rode down here, found you, found your horse, and hobbled him with mine."

Sartain had heard the faint munching of horses cropping grass. He looked beyond the girl, saw that the backside of the escarpment blended almost perfectly with the slope angling down from the evergreen-carpeted ridge five hundred feet above. That explained how the rifleman had got up here—a hell of a lot more easily than Sartain had.

She glanced over her work and over the fire's leaping flames at The Revenger. "You hungry?"

He shook his head. All he felt was pain and nausea. He wanted to sleep but wondered if he could with the hammering in his head.

"How 'bout a cup of coffee?" She canted her head toward a brown bottle near the base of rise of rock to her left and arched a brow. "I have whiskey."

"I'd take the whiskey."

She reached for the bottle, tossed it to him over the fire. He had to make a quick grab for it, and she seemed to enjoy that, spreading her mouth in a slightly devilish grin before lowering her gaze again to her work. Sartain sucked a sharp breath through his teeth against that faceless ogre hammering away at his brain plate.

He popped the cork, took a couple of soothing swallows. He'd hardly got the cork back into the bottle before the dark spirit of sleep, however painful, reached up and pulled him back down into its fold.

When he woke again, it was morning, and she was dropping a load of deadfall branches down beside the flames dancing in the fire ring. As she did, her shirt billowed away from her chest, as did the undershirt beneath it, and he caught a glimpse of her tender breasts.

"Hey!" she scolded him schoolmarmishly.

"Oh, shit," Sartain groaned. "That time wasn't my fault. I just opened my eyes and you were—!"

"Here." She lifted both shirts to her neck. "Have you a good long look so you can stop skulkin' around, thinkin' about 'em."

"I wasn't skulkin' around . . ." Sartain let his voice trail off. What was the point of lying? "They are truly spectacular. Thank you."

She let her shirt fall back down to her belly. "I have a feelin' you're a fella who's seen quite a few of 'em, ain't ya?"

This was not the conversation he wanted to be having first thing in the morning after another cold, restless night's sleep. "At the risk of incriminating myself to someone who has me at a great disadvantage here . . . me bein' unarmed and in the foggy-headed state I'm in . . . I'd just as soon withhold responding to the query until I'm capable of taking quick, evasive action. In case you go for your Spencer again."

He caught her smiling before she turned away, walking off down the sloping, lumpy stone floor of the escarpment and disappearing from view.

Meanwhile, the fire danced beside him, flicking its welcome warmth against him. His own coffee pot hung from a tripod over it, the water whooshing as it heated. Gray ash fluttered around it, caught in the steam puffing up from the spout. He could tell by the cold dampness of his blankets that it had frozen last night and the frost had just recently burned off. The sun was warm as it rose over his right shoulder, just now edging its buttery light into the camp.

She returned with another armload of wood, flushed, breathing hard with the effort. Her hair was down and unbrushed, hanging prettily all around her. Her charcoal skirt buffeted around her legs, which he could tell were slender. She was certainly a nimble, athletic girl. She wore thick socks and men's black lace-up half-boots.

She bent over with the wood again and dared him with a look from beneath her blonde brows. Sartain looked away and tried to whistle, but his lips were too dry.

She crouched to set some of the new branches on the fluttering flames. "Coffee?"

"Please." He saw his canteen resting against his saddle. She must have placed it there. It was also full, he realized, lifting it. He removed the cap and drank. The water in it was so cold and fresh, he feared it would crack his molars. He took several long pulls, thirsty, and then returned it to his saddle. He didn't see his rifle or LeMat anywhere.

As she used a leather swatch to remove the pot from the hook and pour him a cup of the coal-black brew, she said, "Don't worry—they're safe. And they'll be returned to you in due time."

He took the cup from her with both hands. "What's due time?"

"When you're ready to ride out of here."

"I'll be ready today." Sartain blew on the piping hot brew, took a sip, burning his tongue and wincing. "I'm feelin' fine as frog hair."

She scowled at him, as though he were the dumbest thing she'd laid eyes on. "Frogs don't have hair."

He took another sip of the coffee, swallowed. "No, but you got some sproutin' out of both ears."

"What?"

"Sure enough. You probably never noticed. But you got a couple of old-man tufts!" He'd had a feeling that the only way he could get her to let her formidable guard down was through humor—at risk of offending her and getting shot with his own LeMat, of course.

She stared at him, not quite sure she should believe him. Then she clapped her hands to her ears, scowling. "I do not!"

Sartain grinned.

She lowered her hands and threw herself down against him, laughing. "You're just a silly one!"

"No, no," Sartain said, placing two fingers on her chin and directing her face to his. "You're the silly one." He kissed her. To his surprise, she did not pull away but squirmed closer, wrapping one leg over his and mashing her mouth harder against his lips.

She wrapped her arms around his neck and kissed him for a

long time, groaning, squirming, making little grunting and chuckling noises. She pulled away, giving him a sly look.

"Is this what you had in mind all along?"

"No." It wasn't a lie. In fact, if someone had told him she'd be so ready and willing to tongue-wrestle with him after yesterday's embarrassing little debacle, he'd have laughed heartily and deemed that person ready for the crazy farm.

"Come on, now—be honest," she said, poking a finger into his ribs.

"Well, now that you mention it."

He drew her closer. While the mood change was shocking, it did distract him from the pain in his head. He kissed her, and she readily returned the kiss once more before pulling abruptly away.

"All right, mister. That's far enough." She laughed. "See—I knew you were up to no good. A charmer with a dozen hands—that's what you are!"

"What's your name, anyway?" he asked, holding her warm, pliant body in his arms. She smelled musky and earthy, and also of wood smoke and pine. "What the hell are you doin' out here all by yourself?"

"Me?" she said, friskily touching her index finger to his nose. "Folks call me Crazy Mary." She touched her nose to his, crossing her eyes at him. "How 'bout you, Mr. Hands?"

"Sartain. Mike Sartain."

"Well, hello there, Mr. Mike Sartain. You sound funny—you know that?"

"Funny?"

"Yeah, you draw your words out real looong and give most of 'em a sorta *swirl*. Sorta musical."

"Do you like it?"

"I do like it!"

"Tell me somethin', Mary—why do folks call you 'Crazy Mary'?"

"Ain't it rather obvious?"

Sartain frowned, as though she'd surprised him with the question. "Not one bit."

She shrugged and looked at the fire. "I don't know. Some folks say I'm touched in the head. They say it happened after the mine collapse and my pa and two brothers was killed, back when I was just nine years old.

"Ma—she was the first one to go soft in her thinker box. We lived in our cabin up near Ute Ridge—just the two of us. We didn't have nowhere to go, nothin' much else to do, so we stayed on at the place. Ma—she hanged herself from a pine tree in the front yard one mornin'. Yep, she sure enough did. Lan' sakes, I was never so surprised to wake one mornin' and stumble outside to see her hangin' there, just starin' at me, tongue swelled up like a fist in her mouth!

"First off I thought it was a trick. Or a joke of some kind—you know, like the kind you play on people? But Ma never was like that even before Pa and the boys died, and even less like it after.

"Well, I cut her down, just let her drop. And then I wheeled her in a barrow up to the hill where we buried Pa and the boys, and I planted her there, too. I stayed on at the cabin—"

"All by yourself?"

"Sure. Who else would be there?" Mary asked him. "No, it was just me an' the mule, Aunt Sarah." She snickered. "Named her after our Aunt Sarah because she's got a similar stubborn streak. Hah! So, it's just me an' Aunt Sarah now, and I ride down to Silverthorne every once in a while to buy, sell, or trade. I forage for roots and stuff, make my own medicines, pilfer eggs from birds' nests, snare rabbits, shoot deer on occasion, though they're so cute when they're little.

"That's what I rubbed into your forehead and arm—my concoctions. It's made of snakeroot, mule pee, pinesap, and tea boiled from shadbark berries. I just got some fresh. An' gettin' back to your question—I been overhearin' folks call me Crazy Mary for years now. Several years, anyways. I don't really understand it, but, yeah, I guess I'm crazy. Livin' alone will make you different. Anyways, I don't mind. I reckon we're happy enough—Aunt Sarah and me. We get along."

She stared off, squinting against the brightening sunlight and the smoke billowing against them. Sartain studied her, his heart swelling for the pretty, lonely girl. She was right—living alone will make you "different." He knew that from personal experience. That's why he tried not to stay alone for too long at any given time, but always drifted on back to the vengeance trail.

"I told you about me," Crazy Mary said. "What about you, Mike. Who are you, anyway?"

"Me?" Sartain blew on his coffee. "I'm a loner. Drifter. General no-account."

"Plenty of them in these parts," Mary said matter of factly. "What're you doin' up here? Lookin' for work up at the Painted Lady—somethin' like that? You got big arms." She wrapped both hands around his left bicep and squeezed, rubbing her cheek against him. "I bet you could really swing an' ax or skin a mule team!"

"No, I'm up here lookin' for that stolen gold, Mary."

Mary frowned. "Stolen gold?"

"Yeah, the gold that was stolen a couple months ago from Sheriff Higgins and his deputy, Jasper Garvey. They were haulin' it down from the Painted Lady to the Wells Fargo office in Silverthorne, only they never made it. Neither one's been seen or heard from since . . . and neither has the gold."

Mary looked horrified. "That's terrible!" She shook her head, turning her mouth corners down. "But that's how life is, Mike.

Greed rules the day. Human lives are even more worthless than the lives of fish and other critters, includin' grub worms. To be honest with you, I can sort of see why."

"Well, to be honest with you, Miss Mary—my own thoughts on the human tribe ain't all that different from your own. But I was sent out by the sheriff's daughter to find out what happened to him, and to deal some frontier justice to those who stole that gold."

"Do you think the sheriff's dead?"

"Mostly likely."

"His deputy, then, too, I suppose?"

"I suppose. Unless it was the sheriff's deputy who killed the sheriff and stole the gold."

"See what I mean about humans bein' barely above grub worms!"

"I do, indeed." He glanced at her. She seemed to range far and wide in the Sangre de Cristos. There was a chance she might have seen something suspicious regarding the stolen gold. "You didn't see anything, I take it, Mary? Or any strangers in the mountains?"

"Nope, not a thing, Mike." She rose and removed the coffee pot from the tripod over the fire. "More?"

"Sure."

As she crouched to refill the cup he held up for her, she said, "I sure do feel sorry for Miss Belle, though. Don't know how she's gonna manage without her pa."

"Oh? You know Belle, Miss Mary?"

"Sure, I do. I venture down to Silverthorne four, maybe five times a year. Stay in one of her rooms when I'm flush. She treats me nice and old Northcutt, he's quite a cook!"

Sartain chuckled. "He is at that."

"You hungry, Mike? You'd best eat somethin'. Help you heal."

Sartain sipped the coffee. The girl brewed a powerfully potent pot of mud. That first cup was chewing on his insides. "You know, I think I could eat somethin'. Don't go to any trouble, though, Mary. I think I'm well enough now to tend to myself. I have plenty of jerky and biscuits in my saddlebags."

"Oh, hush!" Mary returned the coffee pot to the hook over the fire. "I'm gonna fix you a fresh pot of my good crow and bean stew. You'll love it!"

"Crow, Miss Mary?"

"Crow meat's delicious!" the girl intoned, wide-eyed, rubbing her belly. "You never had crow before?"

"Nope." Sartain shook his head and tried to smile. "Can't say as I have."

"You just sit tight. One was cawin' so loud this mornin', he woke me before sunrise. I think I know where he is." She set her coffee cup on a rock. "I'm gonna go fetch him for the stew pot!"

"Be careful, Mary," Sartain warned. "That bushwhacker might get to wondering if he really left me for dead and come back to check on me."

"Oh, don't you worry about that." Mary grabbed her rifle, set it on her shoulder, and started off toward the woods, but then stopped and glanced over her shoulder at Sartain. "The whiskey bottle's just to your left there, Mike. Help yourself. Don't worry—I won't tarry!"

She winked and sauntered away.

CHAPTER 10

Sartain had to admit the crow stew wasn't bad once he got past the idea of the dark, stringy, chewy meat being crow. He half-hoped the crow was the one who'd spooked him into falling prey to the bushwhacker's bullet.

He'd eaten plenty of squirrels during the war, when there hadn't been much else around, and he just pretended he was eating squirrel meat. Then it went down rather well. It helped that Mary had spiced it with wild onions and sprigs of wild mint and thyme. He chased every few bites with whiskey-laced coffee, and the meal was at once nourishing, invigorating, and soothing.

During the meal, he'd looked across the small fire on which the coffee pot stayed warm, to see Mary staring at him furtively. When their eyes met, she flushed, chuckled, and lowered her gaze to her plate.

Sartain wasn't sure what to make of the strange, beautiful girl. He concluded that the handle she'd been tagged with was, while not very charitable, most likely accurate. He found himself feeling a deep tenderness for her. She did seem relatively happy, however. If he was to ever go insane, he hoped it would be after the same, carefree fashion as Crazy Mary.

He was feeling well enough now, the ache in his head merely a moderate if still occasionally pulsating discomfort, to help her with the post-meal chores. Sartain dressed in his denims and freshly washed and mended shirt and gathered up some of the dirty dishes. He followed Mary down the slanting crown of the escarpment and into the grassy woods bordering it. He followed Mary along a trail that dropped down into a shadowy gorge where a tumbling creek formed a small, storybook waterfall amidst the ferns and pines.

Mary had hobbled her mule and Boss on the far side of the stream, where the grass grew deep and lush, and Boss appeared to be getting along fine. Spying his rider, however, the buckskin bobbed his head and whickered.

"The sign of a good man is a horse that likes him," Mary said, favoring Sartain with a fond glance. "That's what my pa always said."

They washed the dishes in the stream beneath the falls and then went back up to the camp and set the utensils out on the rocks to dry in the sun and warm, dry, high-mountain air. Sartain was a little tired from the journey into the ravine, so he decided to turn in for a nap in the shade.

He'd decided to rest another day and to resume his quest for the missing gold bright and early the next morning. Mary also decided to take a nap and threw her bedroll down about ten feet from his.

He slitted his eyes a few times and caught her staring at him pensively. He wondered what she was thinking about back behind those deep, soulful hazel eyes of hers. But then, it was hard to know what a crazy person thought about anything. Sartain had known men who'd been "touched" after their bloody experiences during the War, and they'd seemed to be straddling two worlds—one foot in the so-called real world and the other foot in their folly-stricken minds.

Sartain wondered for a time who his ambusher had been. The thought had been jerking at him ever since he'd awakened with his head aching. Most likely, he was the same bastard who'd fired that rifle at him in town. And, again most likely, they'd meet again soon. Only Sartain hoped the next encounter would be on his terms and not on his bushwhacker's.

Nothing like a notch in the noggin to make a man sleep.

Sartain woke feeling as though he'd slept for twenty years. Blinking, he sat up. It was late in the afternoon but still warm. The sun slanting down behind the western ridge cast as many shadows as a dreamy, fuzzy, salmon-lemony light. He realized what had awoken him. Someone was singing somewhere off in the distance.

Sartain glanced at where he'd last seen Mary. There were only her blankets . . . and her dress and her shirts . . . her boots and her socks.

A warm hand cupped The Revenger's balls, squeezing gently.

The singing continued. He recognized Mary's voice. The singing was soft and melodic but he couldn't make out the words. He caught only a few brief bars here and there on the warm, velvety breeze brushing over the escarpment from the woods. If she was naked, she was probably down at the falls, bathing, as she seemed in the habit of doing.

He'd best remain right here on the rock. She'd probably taken her rifle.

Looking around, he saw that his own rifle and LeMat were now leaning or lying near where he'd been napping. The rifle was in its leather scabbard, and the LeMat was snugged down in its holster, the cartridge belt containing .44-caliber rounds as well as several shotgun wads, coiled around it. His over-and-under derringer with gutta percha grips rested beside the LeMat, sitting on his freshly laundered and neatly folded neckerchief. His folding Barlow knife, which he usually carried in a boot, lay nearby.

The big LeMat's silver finish and pearl grips shone beautifully in the sunlight. She must have cleaned the piece. Something told him she'd cleaned the other two guns, as well.

He tossed his blankets aside, rose, stretched long and luxuri-ously, and then began gathering some wood together in the stone ring for a fire. He could do with some coffee.

The singing, like the sonorous strains of dancing forest sprites, continued to career gently up from the loamy gorge. Occasionally, Sartain could also hear the soft rumble of the falls. The girl's singing, the birds, the gentle breeze, and the soft rush of the falls were like siren songs calling Sartain to the gorge.

He kept remembering how she'd looked, taking her sponge bath in the creek, just before she'd started slinging lead at him. Finally unable to bear it any longer, he pulled on his boots, donned his hat, slipped the derringer into his vest pocket, and strolled down the top of the scarp and into the woods. He fol-lowed the winding path down into the gorge.

He looked around. There was nothing but the creek and the trees and the little falls tumbling into a wide black pool abutted by two large granite boulders. Chickadees peeped. Somewhere a mourning dove was giving its mournful song. Mary's own music had dwindled until now he could no longer hear it at all.

"Mary?" Sartain called.

Nothing.

Then he thought he heard her giggle. The singing resumed very quietly until it almost sounded like wind chimes tinkling softly above the pulsating rush of the creek, which dropped quickly through the bottom of the gorge, heading for even lower ground. The singing seemed to be coming from above the falls, in a nest of evergreen shrubs and pines.

Sartain told himself to turn around. He had no business down here.

But then he heard the faint, ghostly giggles again, and they were like a moist feminine tongue in his ear. Compelled by the primal urges that keep all men boys, Sartain followed a game path up around the falls and onto higher ground. He looked around.

A pool lay before him—a wide spot in the mossy rocks and trees that gathered the water flowing from the slower moving creek above it and that ran through a relatively flat beaver meadow into a pool. A deep one, judging by the oily blackness of its water. Pine boughs and ferns dropped over the swollen pool that gurgled quietly over the ledge to Sartain's right forming the falls.

The girl's singing and chuckling had stopped.

"Mary?"

The brush snapped softly behind him. Something round was pressed against the small of his back. Sartain jerked with a start. He glanced over his right shoulder to see Mary standing behind him, naked, dripping wet, and pressing the barrel of her old Spencer carbine against him. Her hair hung wet around her shoulders, tendrils licking up around the pale globes of her cherry-topped breasts.

She said with a cunning grin, "I thought you learned your lesson about spyin' on girls while they're bathin'!"

Sartain raised his hands shoulder high and said, "Some men never learn."

"You heard me callin', didn't you?"

"That's right."

"It was my siren call."

"It surely was."

Mary lowered the rifle and leaned it against a pine bole. "Join me?"

As he turned to face her, she stepped toward him, smiling beguilingly up at him, her gaze flicking around his chest and down his arms to his waist and up again.

Sartain cleared the phlegmy knot in his throat. His urge was to begin undressing, but, despite the hammering in his loins, he resisted it. The girl was touched. No descent man would take advantage of that.

"No." He shook his head. "I heard you down here, just wondered . . . thought maybe you were in trouble. Needed help. That's all." He smiled, winked. "I'll head back to camp. I'm buildin' a fire. You're gonna need one, once you're . . . hey . . . now," he said. "What're you doin' down there?"

She slowly lowered herself to her knees and was unbuttoning the fly of his denims.

She looked up at him from beneath her brows. "Shhh."

Somehow, they ended up in the water together.

Sartain rolled over to loll in the slow current beside her, his broad chest rising and falling sharply from the exertion. "Mary, that wasn't your first time, was it?"

"No." She turned to him, wrapped her arms around his chest, and tucked her face hard against his neck. "There was only two others, and I don't think you could even really call it an honest roll in the hay, if'n you know what I mean. I mean, the poor boy was just too excited. This was a long time ago, you understand. Several years back, before my family died and it was just my ma. Both o' them suitors, if you could call 'em that—hah!— were miners' sons, moonin' around our shack of a night."

She ran her hand across the hard slabs of his chest and then down across his flat belly, lolling now as they were both lazing in the chill water of the pool. "I was just curious, so I let 'em. It wasn't nothin' like it was here, now . . . with you. I'd sort of let myself stop thinkin' about it, since those first two times didn't amount to much. Now, though, I got a feelin' I'll be thinkin' about it all the time!"

She laughed huskily, lustily, and pressed her lips to his cheek.

"You're right nice, for a big man," she said, snuggling against him. "I like you, Mike."

"I like you too, Mary."

CHAPTER 11

It was good dusk, with only a little fuzzy orange light angling through the forest, when they finally dressed and made their way together, hand in hand, back to their encampment atop the scarp.

Sartain built a fire while Mary went off to check the rabbit snares she'd set earlier, returning only five minutes later with two large jackrabbits. She dressed and skinned the two beasts, carefully saving the fur with which she intended to line her winter boots, and threw together a wonderful stew. After the meal, they sat languidly by the fire, sipping coffee laced with Sartain's favored Sam Clay bourbon.

"Where you headed next, Mike?" she asked after they'd sat in silence together for nearly a half hour, staring at the dwindling flames.

"Up to the Painted Lady, I reckon. Figured I'd talk to the owner or the superintendent or somebody, see if they had any leads about who might have attacked Higgins and Jasper Garvey. Sometimes a disgruntled former employee will do such things to get back at their former employers . . . and to line their pockets while doing so. I'd think it was as simple as just another holdup or the lawmen themselves running off with the loot . . ."

Sartain let his voice trail off as he thought about the bushwhacker in Silverthorne. The man with the horse. Most likely the same man who'd laid him out here, left him for dead.

Who was he? How was he tied to the robbery? In one way or

another, he had to be tied to it. And he must be wanting to snuff The Revenger's wick before Sartain ran him and/or the gold down.

Whoever he was.

Something told Sartain he might find the man up at the Painted Lady, though he wasn't quite sure why he thought so. But the man was obviously hanging around the country near Silverthorne. He'd either followed Sartain into the mountains, or he'd been waiting for him, anticipating his move.

For some reason, he very badly wanted The Revenger scoured from the gold's trail, and no doubt learning this man's motives would bring Sartain one step closer to that strongbox, and to learning the fate of Sheriff Stephen Higgins and his deputy, Garvey.

"You be careful up at the Painted Lady, Mike."

Sartain looked down at her snuggling against his chest. "Why's that, Mary?"

"Dangerous folks up there. Not only the people who work for the mine. But there's a whorehouse up there that attracts all sorts of bad men and bad doin's. Brings in the men from the mines all across this side of the Sangre de Cristos, and it's well known that a good many of the men who step foot in the Painted Lady Saloon and Dance Hall end up leavin' boots first. Drunkards and evil fornicators, the lot of 'em. That's how my ma described 'em, and she forbade me to ever go near the place."

"Drunkards and fornicators," Sartain said, raising his coffee cup and sniffing the whiskey-laced steam. "Ahhh."

Mary giggled.

"Mike?"

"Mm-hmm."

"Can we do it just once more before we turn in?"

Sartain groaned.

★　★　★　★　★

When he woke the next morning, Mary was gone.

He sat up, blinking in the mid-morning sunshine, feeling like a cork-headed fool. Not only had he slept way past dawn, which was when he'd wanted to get up and start traveling, he hadn't even heard the girl rise, gather her gear, and leave the camp!

Sure enough, when he'd tossed away his blankets and walked down to where they'd picketed both Boss and Aunt Sarah close to camp, only Boss was there, staring at Sartain as though wondering if they were going to pull their picket pins sometime today, or was his rider going to waste another day lollygagging and trifling with that hussy?

Sartain doubted he'd ever slept as soundly as he had the past couple nights. He hoped it was only due to having his scalp creased and his ashes hauled so thoroughly by Miss Mary down by the creek and elsewhere, not that he was getting trail soft. When a man who hunted other men for a living—and was in turn hunted himself—started getting trail soft, his time on earth would soon come to a hard, bloody end.

Then again, Mary had no doubt figured Sartain needed all the rest he could get, with his wound and all. She'd probably taken extra care to move around quietly as she'd packed up. She'd built no fire. As at home in these mountains and forests as any stalking mountain lion, Crazy Mary could move quietly, indeed.

Sartain had found that out yesterday when she'd rammed her Spencer against his back.

Still feeling fatigued from the head wound as well as from his torrid coupling with Mary, Sartain took time to build a fire, make coffee, and eat a few morsels of jerky while Boss ground oats from the feed sack his rider had hung from his ears. When Sartain had finished his second cup of coffee, he felt ready to ride. He kicked dirt on his fire, gathered his gear, saddled Boss, and mounted up.

The ambush had cost him a couple of days, but he admonished himself to continue to take his time scouring the Weaver's Meadow Trail up to the Painted Lady. Those two days wouldn't amount to much in the scheme of things. Two months had already passed since the holdup. The culprits' sign couldn't get much fainter than it already was. If he didn't study the trail thoroughly, patiently, he'd likely miss something important.

But he found nothing all that day. By the time he started hearing the metronomic slamming of the mine's stamping mill and started smelling the rancid odor of the smelting plant, the sun's belly was getting poked in earnest by a high, northern pinnacle of twisted rock that was not hard to identify as Bayonet Ridge. He'd been told the mine lay in the shadow of Bayonet Ridge, and there was no mistaking the sound or the smell.

He and Boss climbed on through the forest, growing cooler and darker by the minute. He checked the buckskin down atop a ridge and stared into the broad valley below—a scoured-out chunk of forest along a rocky creek snaking along the base of the ridge Sartain was on. Situated on this maybe two city-block-long stretch of flat, cleared ground was a large gaudy hotel whose sign The Revenger could read even from this distance of a hundred and fifty or so yards as the crow flies: THE PAINTED LADY SALOON AND DANCE HALL.

He had to squint to make out the letters below the main sign stretched across the building's second story: "Richard H. Maragon, Mine Proprietor and Superintendent."

Just the man Sartain wanted to see.

Sartain touched spurs to the buckskin's ribs, and they followed the trail down from the ridge and into the outskirts of the little settlement that was as colorful on one hand as any painted lady. On the other hand, it appeared as roughhewn and seamy as any other mining camp Sartain had ever ridden into. And he'd ridden into a few.

On the roughhewn side were three long, L-shaped buildings, probably bunkhouses for the miners, flanked by two barns and several corrals, the ground around the corrals cluttered with large ore drays used for hauling the raw ore from the mines to the stamping mill and then to the smelter. The commotion of that industry could probably be heard from one end of the valley to the other.

The mine sat about two thousand feet above the town, and from the trail leading down the ridge toward the town the large ore wagons clattered behind braying mules. There was also the relentless stamp of the mill. Loud piano music clattered away from inside the Painted Lady Saloon and Dance Hall.

The saloon itself was the main splash of color in the otherwise humble little settlement. But now, as Sartain rode along the trail that had become the settlement's main drag, he saw another bird of striking plumage in the white, pink, and spruce-green Victorian house sitting nearly directly across the street from the saloon. The house was three stories high with a broad porch abutting two sides and liberally adorned with gingerbread trim. The main, street-facing gable was open. As Sartain stopped Boss to scrutinize the impressive place, which he'd bet the seed bull belonged to the mine owner, Maragon, a figure moved in the open gable.

The figure was a woman in a fancy, fawn-colored waistcoat over a ruffled blouse secured to the woman's ivory neck with a brooch of some kind. She'd been sitting in a chair against the front wall, reading, but she'd set her book aside and risen. She was walking to the front of the gable, where she stopped to stare down through the open air into the street at the newcomer.

Sartain's heartbeat quickened. The woman was as well put together as the house. She was strikingly attired, but she was just as strikingly *naturally* attired, as well. Her hair, a rich indigo, was pulled back into a loose chignon and trimmed with red ribbons. Her face was pale and classically sculpted, her mouth wide and as red as the last crimson splash of a Colorado sunset. The bosoms pushing out from behind the white silk blouse and tweed waistcoat were, by all indications, firm and full and proud as deacons' wives, but also jeering.

"You can look," such a bosom said. "And you can dream all you want about touching. But that dream is all the closer you'll ever get."

Everything about this woman screamed money and upbringing.

As she stared heavy-lidded down from her gable perch, a haughty queen glowering down from a pedimented castle wall at her soiled, toiling subjects, Sartain smiled and pinched his hat brim to her.

She blinked slowly, with the automatic, cool disdain of her ilk when in the presence of an obvious inferior, and asked tonelessly, "Who are you?"

"Who am *I?*" Sartain said, brashly taking her in. "Who are *you?*"

A certain bellicosity always surfaced when he found himself being looked down a snooty nose at—even though this gal probably had every reason to feel superior.

Abruptly, she turned away, sat back down in her wicker chair, and took up the book she'd been reading when the latest plebian had ridden into her domain.

"Just tryin' to make conversation," Sartain grumbled and turned Boss over to the saloon from which the piano music was still clattering.

He tied the buckskin to one of the three hitchrails fronting the place, shouldering him in between two docile-looking geldings, and loosened his latigo and slipped his bit. There was relatively fresh-appearing water in the zinc-lined stock tank

fronting the rail, and Boss took no time dipping his snout—
after he'd glanced at both geldings, making sure they knew who
was the new boss of the rail, that was.

Both geldings snorted and shifted slightly away from the stallion. They'd received the message.

Sartain slipped his Henry from his scabbard. Mine settle-
ments were notoriously aswarm with thieves. "Drunkards and
evil fornicators, the lot of 'em," as Crazy Mary's late mother
had described them. Well, she could add thieves to the list.

As Sartain mounted the porch steps, a gun exploded.

Instantly, he had the Henry in both hands and a round
levered into the action.

CHAPTER 12

A man bellowed from inside the Painted Lady.

The piano chimed to a crashing halt, as though the player had slammed both hands onto the keys.

A man bellowed again, like a cow that had stepped into a gopher hole. Otherwise, an eerie silence drifted out over the tops of the heavy, ornate oak batwing doors. Sartain crossed the wide front porch and cast a cautious look over the doors.

Inside, the two dozen or so customers, sitting at tables or standing along the well-appointed bar and mirrored back bar running along the far wall, were all turned toward a large, round table in the middle of the room, about fifteen feet from Sartain and slightly to his right.

One man at the table was standing, his hand extended over the table toward another, seated man. Charcoal-colored smoke billowed over the table. The seated man threw his head back and opened his mouth, loosing another bellow that echoed loudly around the drinking hall.

"Bastard!" he screamed, his eyes flashing angrily beneath the narrow brim of his opera hat.

A long-faced, middle-aged gent, he was dressed in a flashy black and burgundy three-piece suit. He slid his chair back, rose stiffly like a gentleman in a snit, heaved himself heavily to his feet, and began walking toward Sartain. He tripped over a chair leg and nearly fell, but then he got his feet set and continued walking loose-hipped and knock-kneed, as though drunk.

All eyes followed him, as did those of the man who'd been standing and extending his hand over the table.

The man walking toward Sartain said, "Let it be known that Norman W. Teagarden the Third was murdered in cold blood by the snake Wendell Green in the Painted Lady Saloon!"

The man standing by the table raised his hand again, showing the two round maws of the silver-chased derringer in his fist. He wobbled drunkenly and slurred his words as he yelled, "Turn around and have another one at no extra charge, Teagarden!"

Sartain stepped around Teagarden, who was only four feet away from him, and raised the Henry to his shoulder, aiming quickly. The sixteen-shooter roared like a cannon.

The snake Wendell Green wheeled as though caught by a throw rope, triggering his little popper through a window just right of Sartain. Green fell over his chair, howling, throwing the derringer away to clap his right hand to his bloody left shoulder.

"He shot me!" the wounded man screamed, flopping around on the floor, his lower legs draped over his overturned chair. He was short and burly and dressed in the hickory shirt, canvas trousers, and high-topped, hobnailed boots of your typical miner. "He shot me! You seen him—he shot me!"

Half the sitting men had gained their feet. Several had reached for sidearms but quickly let their hands drop away from their holsters when Sartain loudly rammed another shell into his Henry's chamber, the spent cartridge clanking to the wooden floor behind him, and slid the barrel from left to right, covering the room.

A door opened on the balcony over the bar, and a dark-haired, mustached, craggy-faced man stumbled out onto the balcony, yelling, "What the bloody hell is goin' on down there

233

now? If you men insist on killing each other, kindly do it outside so I can get some sleep!"

"Mr. Maragon!" the wounded man shouted, still on his ass and clutching his bloody shoulder. "That bastard with the Henry shot me for no good reason!"

Maragon switched his bleary-eyed gaze to Sartain. His craggy face was as pale as flour, and he appeared to be blue around the eyes. He had a thick, British accent. "You there," Maragon said, pointing a beringed finger at the stranger. "Kindly lower that weapon."

Sartain obliged the man, but he only lowered it to his right hip. He kept it cocked and aimed at the room.

Maragon said, "Mister Green says you shot him for no good reason."

"Oh, I don't know," Sartain said, his voice even, his gaze cautiously roaming the room. "I'd say a drunk man waving a loaded and cocked pistol in my direction is a good enough reason. Besides"—he glanced at Teagarden, who lay belly down at Sartain's boots—"a bullet to ole Teagarden's back would have been overkill."

A large blood pool was growing on the floor beneath Teagarden.

"Teagarden done tucked another ace into the deck we was playin' with, Mister Maragon!" Wendell Green was furious, spittle flecking his lips. "I had every right to shoot him!" He glanced at a sign tacked to a ceiling support post about ten feet away from Sartain. It read: "POKER CHEATS AND CARD SHARPS WILL NOT BE TOLERATED HERE!—THE MANAGEMENT"

"That's right," Maragon said, staring at Sartain but speaking to Green. "If you can prove he was cheating, you did have the right to shoot him."

"But that bastard with the Henry shot me anyway!"

Sartain flared his nostrils at the man but he kept his voice pitched low with soft-spoken menace as he said, "If you don't stop your caterwauling, you're going to get another one." He aimed the Henry at Green. "Now, where would you like it?"

Green screamed and flopped onto his back, holding his hands in front of his face as though to shield himself from a bullet.

Maragon closed both his hands over the balcony rail before him. He was dressed in a red velvet robe with what appeared a marten fur collar. He looked well bred and flush, but he also looked badly hungover. "Mister, who are you?"

The Revenger let the Henry droop toward the floor, though he remained ready to bring it into action if he needed to. "Sartain. Mike Sartain. I'd like a word with you, Maragon."

Maragon studied him, his bushy, dark-brown brows beetled with incredulity. "Ah, shit," he said, recognizing the tall stranger with the Henry repeating rifle. "The stinking Revenger!"

Mutters rippled through the crowd.

"Well, that's not my full, given name," Sartain said. "But I reckon it'll do." And true enough, given his doings of the last few days . . .

"Who you looking for, for bloody cryin' in the King's bleedin' beer?"

"No one here." Sartain scrutinized the room once more, narrowing one eye. "At least, I don't think it's anyone in this room. Could be wrong."

All eyes were on him now. They'd heard of him, of course. Most folks had—at least those who'd spent more than a few months on the frontier. Word of his trail of death had spread fast, and it continued to spread. One day, someone would backtrack those stories to his doorstep, wherever that happened to be at the time, and his trail of death would end with his own.

For some reason, the idea didn't frighten him in the least. In fact, maybe an end to his compulsion would be a welcome relief.

"See that door over there?" Maragon asked.

Sartain followed his gaze to a door at the top of the carpeted stairs that ran up the room's left wall.

"I'll meet you in there in three minutes." Maragon looked around the main drinking hall. "Billy, Worm! Tend Teagarden and clean up the blood. Someone get Green over to that old, drunk sawbones. Tell the sot to send me the bill." The mine/saloon/dancehall-owner smiled devilishly, his eyes slanting up at the outside corners so that his pale, craggy face resembled that of an English satyr. "I'll be taking it out of Green's pay."

Green didn't respond to this. Sitting up now, he merely cupped his hand over his shoulder and gave Sartain the hairy eyeball, though when The Revenger looked at him, he wrinkled his nose and averted his eyes.

Maragon swung around, his robe billowing out around him, disappeared into his room, and slammed the door behind him. Sartain's eyes swept the room once more. Seeing no one who looked like they'd try to avenge Green, he depressed the Henry's hammer, set the rifle on his shoulder, and climbed the staircase to the door Maragon had indicated. He gave the door a single, perfunctory knock with the back of his left hand, opened it, and stepped inside.

Closing the door behind him, he found himself in a large, ornate office with a rug so deep he felt he was stepping in mud, and a large desk that appeared made out of cherry or maybe some rare wood from Europe. The size of a large ore dray, its legs were carved so that they almost looked like moose antlers. File cabinets and wooden shelves surrounded the desk, as did a deep, leather sofa and a fireplace, cold at the moment.

A brass clock, also likely imported, ticked on a wall above a glassed-in humidor the size of a small china cabinet. Sartain's mouth watered. The room smelled of expensive leather and tobacco soaked in port or brandy and maybe rum. He couldn't help himself. He walked over to the cabinet and stared through the glass at the several open boxes of cigars the size of dynamite sticks and ranging in color from coffee brown to butterscotch.

Footsteps sounded. The room was open to the right, beyond the fireplace, and now Maragon walked through the opening and into the office, running pale, arthritic fingers through his thick, wavy dark-brown hair that was graying at the temples.

"Help yourself," he said. "Take two. Hell, take a third one for the road."

"Who said I was going anywhere?"

Maragon sighed and flopped into the red leather chair behind the massive desk. Sartain had been right about the man—he was, indeed, blue around his eyes, beneath which bags the size of tobacco sacks sagged. "Look, Sartain, I got enough problems without having a crazy vigilante raising hob with my miners."

Sartain pulled open the cabinet door and took Maragon up on his offer of three cigars. He chose a trio with paper wrappers labeled in Spanish, slipped two into his shirt pocket, and took a third one over to the guest chair with him. He sank into the chair before Maragon's desk, and the mine owner slid a cutter and a wooden matchbox toward him.

"I'm not here for your miners," Sartain said, clipping the end off the cigar. "At least, not if none of 'em stole your gold."

"My gold?"

"That's why I'm here." Sartain touched a leaping match flame to the cigar and slowly rolled the cigar in the flame, drawing the aromatic smoke and blowing it out the side of his mouth and his nostrils. The cigar tasted of old book leather and apple wood and possibly well-aged bourbon. "Damn, that's good!"

"It should be. It cost a pretty penny. You say you're here about my gold? Who sent you? I already have a Pinkerton—"

"You must be doin' all right for yourself, Maragon," Sartain said, leaning back in the chair and blowing a plume of the rich smoke into the well-appointed room. He noticed an oil painting hanging on the wall to his left. Sartain was no art connoisseur, but it looked like an original oil to his untrained eyes. It also looked old and expensive.

"I do all right," Maragon said grumpily. "At least, I did . . . at one time. Losin' that strongbox hasn't helped any. Look, Sartain, I may appear eighty, but I'm only forty-five. Born and raised in East London. Fought my way up from the street and through the ranks of a shipping company. Married the boss's daughter. Got sent by the boss out here in the middle of the western frontier to run his stupid gold mine. Bought this place as an investment. Frolicked with a whore I shouldn't have. My wife is young and beautiful. Oh, bloody hell—how beautiful she is! Just the same, I like a Negro girl now and then, and I poked the wrong one and ended up with Old Joe. Poked a half-breed Apache girl—just couldn't resist the girl's big, black eyes—and promptly came down with a case of the morning dew. I've also contracted consumption. And to top it all off, my wife has kicked me out of the house—that house right over there!"

He turned his chair to look out the window over the couch and beside the clock. "You saw the one when you rode into town. You couldn't miss it."

"Couldn't miss the woman in the open gable, neither. If that's your wife, good Lord, man—what's wrong with you? Contracting both syphilis and gonorrhea so you can't sleep in your own *bed*?"

Sartain couldn't help chuckling at the sad irony of Maragon's life.

"I appreciate your sympathy."

Again, Sartain shook his head.

CHAPTER 13

The mine owner flushed with anger.

"I'm a fish out of water, for chrissakes! I'm a million miles from home. Of course, Mathilda came with me, but she tends to be a little stuffy, if you get my drift. I'm a man whose blood has always run hot. When I landed out here, I thought the least I could do was let my hair down a bit."

Maragon rose and grabbed a bottle of Spanish brandy and two tumblers off a filing cabinet. "Anyway—back to my gold." He splashed brandy into both tumblers, slid one to Sartain, sipped from the other one, and sagged back into his chair. "Why are you after it? I've posted no reward. I have a Pinkerton out there now, sniffing around the mountains for it. Haven't heard from him in several days, so I'm hopefully assuming he's on to something."

"I'm sniffing around for that strongbox as a private favor to Belle Higgins from Silverthorne."

"Belle Higgins?"

"Sheriff Higgins's daughter."

"Oh."

Maragon downed half his brandy in a single knock. He set the tumbler down and hastily refilled it. He looked like a man who'd found water again after a long time wandering parched in the desert. "Christ, I try to stay off the stuff. Doesn't mix well with the tincture of mercury I take for the pony drip. 'A night in the arms of Venus leads to a lifetime on Mercury,' as they say."

He lifted his glass to Sartain, smiled drunkenly over it, and knocked half of the brandy back. He sighed and smacked his lips. "There are worse ways to die than drunk. Anyway, Belle Higgins wants you to find her father—that it?"

"Pretty much. She thinks possibly his deputy, Jasper Garvey, killed her father and made off with the gold."

"Or her father might have made off with it," Maragon pointed out. "I never really trusted that man. Of course, in my business, it's hard—as well as foolhardy—to trust anyone."

"The rumors that Higgins stole the gold himself, either alone or in cahoots with Garvey, have made their way to Belle. And she doesn't like it. She wants me to sniff out the truth."

Maragon nodded, fiddling with his half-empty glass on the desk. "Well, hell," he said, raising the glass in a salute of sorts. "The more the merrier." He slammed that drink back, as well.

He was racked by a brief but violent coughing fit, wiped his mouth with a blood-spotted handkerchief that he produced from his robe, and leveled a rheumy-eyed gaze at Sartain. "If you can find that strongbox, Mr. Revenger, I will fortify the reward Miss Belle Higgins has offered you for doing so with another thousand."

Sartain sipped his brandy, followed it up with another puff from the tasty cigar, blowing the smoke in a slender plume over Maragon's head. "The cigars and the brandy will do me. I don't do what I do for money."

"Why turn down a thousand dollars?"

"Because I don't like being tied to it."

Maragon arched a brow over a bloodshot eye. "Or to anything?"

"Or to anything."

"You just live to kill then, I take it? Like what all the newspapers have said about you?"

"To kill those who need killin', Maragon. For those who can't do the killin' themselves."

Maragon studied him, quirking his mouth corners up from beneath his bushy mustache. "You're insane, aren't you, Sartain? You must be."

"Most likely. The nice thing about bein' insane, though, is you're always the last to know." Sartain finished off the brandy and waved his hand over his glass when Maragon extended the bottle toward him.

"Well, shit," said the mine owner. "What can I help you with?"

"I'd like to know if you suspect anyone other than Higgins and Garvey, and I'd also like to know which route they took down the mountain when they lit out with the gold."

Maragon sighed and stared at the bottle, considering whether to have another drink. He turned to look out the window toward his house and cursed. He picked up the bottle, refilled his tumbler, and again extended the bottle to Sartain, who again waved it off.

"For all I know, my wife had it stolen." Maragon chuckled. "Wouldn't put it past her."

"Why would she do that?"

"To ruin me. Both financially and in the eyes of her father, so the old bastard would see fit to let her divorce me. Oh, he knows about the Cupid's itch, but I suspect the old boy is carrying one or two of those afflictions himself." Maragon turned his chair slightly to take another brooding look toward his house. "No . . . I would not put it past my dear Mathilda. As cunning as she is beautiful."

Sartain studied his cigar. He thought that his visit with Maragon would narrow the parameters of his search effort. Instead, he was finding them widening. At least he could probably learn which trail the gold had been lost on. He repeated the question to the unhealthy, unhappy mine owner.

"They took the Old Ute Trail. Leastways, that's what all the men around here call it. It's the northern trail. Meets up with the Weaver's Meadow Trail about two miles northeast of Silverthorne."

Sartain had seen where the trails intersected down in the valley.

"Well, that explains why I saw no sign on the southern trail."

"It would, indeed." Maragon frowned and directed his gaze to the bandage wrapped around Sartain's forehead, beneath his hat. "Say, there . . . can't help wondering . . . what happened . . . ?"

"Someone tried to give me a pill I couldn't swallow. First in Silverthorne, then on the trail up here. Fortunately, my bacon was pulled out of the fire by a pretty young blonde who happened to be out roaming the mountains."

"Crazy Mary." Maragon smiled.

"You know her, I take it."

"Everyone in these parts does. Keeps to herself despite the fact every miner on my roll would like to . . . uh . . . take a roll with the gal. As far as I know, she hasn't tumbled for a one of 'em. Most unattached girls in this neck of the mountains end up here, workin' for me. I once invited her to try her hand at the fine art of love-for-pay, and she told me she'd rather lie with a bobcat than a man any day of the week."

Maragon chuckled. "What does that leave her—women?" He laughed again. "Keeps to herself up on Ute Ridge, in her family's old mine shack. Doesn't show herself around here much, but I hear she rides down to Silverthorne fairly often." He sipped his drink. "Odd girl."

"So I gathered."

"What she needs is a good poke, if you're askin' me. I wouldn't mind bein' the one to give it to her, neither . . ."

Sartain felt the warmth of anger rise beneath his collar. He liked Mary, crazy or not, and it graveled him to hear her talked about in Maragon's off-hand but likely customarily insulting fashion.

Having got what he needed from the man, Sartain peeled the coal off his cigar and rolled it into the ashtray. He stuffed the half-smoked stogie into his shirt pocket for later and rose from his chair. "Obliged for the information. I'll check the trail out tomorrow."

"You're welcome to stay here, Sartain. I have plenty of rooms, plenty of beautiful women. They'll come downstairs in an hour or so, around five. Considering that your endeavor here in the Sangre de Cristos might very well benefit me, the night as well as the girl—or girls, if you prefer—will be free of charge."

"No, thanks. I shot one of your miners. Miners are a close fraternity. I'm likely to get a bullet in the back while I'm enjoyin' your girl . . . or girls. Thanks anyway." Sartain donned his hat, strode to the door, and picked up his rifle.

"Where will you stay, then?" Maragon asked, perplexed. "This is the only hotel on the mountain. The rest of the shacks around here are bunkhouses for my miners."

"I'll find a place out in the high and rocky," Sartain said, pinching his hat to the man. "My horse and I prefer it out there."

He went down and bought a bottle at the bar, watching his back in the bar mirror. His preferred drink was Sam Clay, brewed down in the green hills of Kentucky, but he'd nearly gone through his cache and he didn't even bother to ask for it here.

He bought a bottle of brandy, figuring the bottom-shelf Who Hit John here was probably concocted in a washtub out in one of the barns, with a shovelful of mule shit for flavor.

A swamper scowled up at him from where he was scrubbing

Green's blood off the floor, though it appeared to Sartain that he was only making the stain larger. The Revenger touched his hat brim to the man and headed outside. He dropped his bottle into a saddlebag pouch, slid his rifle into its scabbard, and stepped up into his saddle.

As he passed Maragon's flashy house, a woman's English-accented voice said, "You down there!"

Sartain checked Boss down and stared up at the open gable. Maragon's wife, Mathilda, stared down at him.

"You down where?" Sartain said.

She widened her dark-brown eyes in anger. "You down *there*."

"Oh, me down *here*. Why didn't you say so?"

"I just did."

"You're right," Sartain said, doffing his hat and smiling up at her. "You did. I'm just the contrary sort."

"You make a lot of noise for a stranger just riding into a place."

She must have meant the report of his Henry earlier. "Yes, ma'am, I do have that tendency."

She scowled and touched her temple. "Your head—does it hurt?"

"What—this? Nah. I've hurt myself worse shavin' of a mornin', Mrs. Maragon."

"You're The Revenger."

"Word spreads fast."

"Faster than a wildfire. Especially after you just ride into a place and shoot a man."

"Well, in my defense, he needed shootin'."

"Where are you headed, Mr. Sartain?"

"For the high and rocky."

She frowned. God, she was a piece of work. She must have been around twenty-five and with a face that could have been carved out of ivory by a master craftsman fashioning the likeness of a goddess straight out of a gilded cloud. Sartain wasn't accustomed to having his heart flutter like a boy's with a schoolyard crush, but it was doing that now. It made him feel light-headed, like the street was rising and falling like slow ocean waves around him.

"Whatever that means . . ." she said.

"It means I'm headin' out to set up camp for the night."

"No need to do that. I have plenty of room here. My husband is no longer allowed on the premises, and it's just myself and my housekeepers, Lyle and Edna."

Sartain was genuinely surprised by the invitation. "Mrs. Maragon, are you inviting me, a stranger, to spend the night in your home?"

"Indeed I am. Besides, you're not really a stranger, Mr. Sartain. Why, I've read about you in all the papers."

"No doubt. But, still . . . what could be your reason?"

"I need to speak with you privately. Possibly at some length."

Yes, Sartain thought. He was getting a whole lot more information than he bargained for here at the Painted Lady.

"Just so we don't shock the miners out of their boots, why don't you ride on out of town and return after dark? Ride around to the barn in back and stable your mount. Knock on the back door. I'll receive you there."

Sartain couldn't help casting a cautious look toward the window of Maragon's office in the second story of the Painted Lady. He could see nothing but the reflection of the sun, however.

"Can I at least inquire what you'd like to talk to me about, Mrs. . . . ?" Sartain let his voice trail off. She was no longer looking down at him. Apparently, he'd been dismissed.

He cast another sheepish look toward the Painted Lady then touched spurs to Boss's flanks. "Your wish is my command, Your Highness."

CHAPTER 14

Sartain followed the stream into the country west of the makeshift mine settlement. He gathered a little wood and built a fire, over which he brewed coffee while Boss cropped grass nearby along the stream.

He considered what Maragon had told him about his wife. And then he wondered what Maragon's wife wanted to talk to him about. Not that he had any problem talking to a woman who looked like Mathilda Maragon. Women like her didn't come with every mountain. But he had to keep his head. She was Maragon's wife, despite her having barred the mine owner from their home.

Odd for a married woman—especially a married woman of her social standing—to invite a strange man into her realm and offer him a bed. What if she offered herself, as well? Would he turn her down?

Fat chance of that happening. She might have invited a stranger into her home, but that was a far cry from inviting him into her bed. Besides, he needed to stay focused on what she had to tell him. She'd no doubt discerned that he was here about the gold.

As the sun dropped behind the western mountains, Sartain kicked dirt on his fire, tightened Boss's latigo, and climbed back into the saddle. Fifteen minutes later, he rode back into the Painted Lady settlement and swung around behind the house to the log barn and corral flanking it.

246

The barn's windows, one on either side of the broad doors, shone with watery light. As Sartain stepped down from Boss's back, one of the large doors squawked outward and a bespectacled old man appeared, half-silhouetted by the lantern light behind him, and said, "Mr. Sartain?" He had a blanket draped cape-like about his fragile shoulders.

Sartain had slid his hand to his pistol grips when the old man had appeared so suddenly, but now he dropped his hand to his side. "That's right."

"I'll tend your horse, Mr. Sartain. The madam awaits you in the house."

"All right." Out of habit, The Revenger reached for his Henry.

"That won't be necessary, sir," the old man gently chided him. "I'll stow it away safely here in the barn."

Sartain removed his gloved hand from the Henry's stock, pinched his hat brim to the old gent, gave Boss's neck a parting pat, and sauntered down a brick path curving through large, dark sycamores toward the house. Most of the first-story windows appeared to be lit, making the house resemble a large, ornate, glittering jewel set against black velvet.

Sartain mounted the narrow rear porch. He'd tapped on the back door just once when the door opened and another old person appeared in the doorway. This was an elderly woman in a plain housedress and apron, with her silver-gray hair piled in two buns atop her head. Like the old man, she wore spectacles. From behind her wafted the smell of cooking food—dark, well-seasoned meat and gravy and possibly a fresh-baked pie, Sartain's keen sniffer told him, causing his mouth to water and his stomach to give an eager kick behind his cartridge belt.

"Yes, come in," the old lady said.

As Sartain doffed his hat, he gave his boots a scrape on the hemp mat and stepped inside a short hall dimly lit by a bracket lamp. A dark, varnished staircase rose sharply on his right to disappear into the wainscoted ceiling. On his right, a broad doorway opened into a large kitchen from where all those wonderful smells were originating. Steam rose from pots on a black range and, indeed, a pie of some kind was cooling on a wooden table, near a butter churn.

"Mrs. Maragon is waiting for you, Mr. Sartain," the old woman said, closing the door and latching it with a slight grunt and a wince. "Right this way."

Sartain followed the old woman, whom he assumed was Edna as he'd assumed the old man in the barn was Lyle, along the twisting hall, up a very short flight of blue-and-gold carpeted stairs, and through two French doors into what appeared a drawing room appointed with heavy, ornate furniture, a walnut liquor cabinet, books, a baby piano, and a neat brick fireplace before which Mrs. Maragon herself was seated in a big armchair upholstered in cowhide. The chair nearly swallowed the woman, but as Sartain entered the room behind Edna, she rose and turned to him, holding a cut-glass tumbler in one hand.

Sartain's heart gave that schoolboy flutter again as his eyes raked the woman who looked even more beautiful than before, dressed as she was in a deep, dark-green velvet gown so low cut that it could hardly contain her boisterous bosom. Pearls dropped down to just above her deep, pale cleavage.

Her dark-brown hair, held in place atop her head by a comb crusted with tiny jade and crimson jewels, fairly sparkled in the light of the popping fire that danced the fragrance of forest pine into the room that otherwise smelled of leather and varnish and the molasses aroma of fine busthead.

The room also smelled of the woman herself. Lilac with an understrain of cinnamon and orange blossoms. There was that flutter in Sartain's chest again. Tiny, gold javelins jostled in the woman's dark-brown eyes and were reflected off the diamond earrings dangling low against her neck.

Edna said with what sounded like faint reproof, "Mrs. Maragon, Mr. Sartain."

"Yes—thank you, Edna."

Edna gave her dimpled chin a cordial dip, not smiling or meeting Sartain's gaze, as she turned away from the couple and ambled back through the French doors toward the kitchen.

"Hello, Mr. Sartain."

"Mrs. Maragon."

She smiled broadly, showing all her perfect white teeth, those javelins dancing even more furiously in the lovely eyes. "You like the gown, I take it."

Sartain flushed and twirled his hat on his finger. "Was I staring?"

"No need to apologize. What woman would take offense at being appraised so obviously favorably by such a handsome and storied man?" She turned and seemed to fairly float in her billowing gown toward the liquor cabinet. "A legendary wanderer of the western frontier . . ."

"I'll be hanged if I don't sound fascinating."

"Bourbon?" She was at the liquor cabinet, holding an upper, glass-paneled door open, glancing over her shoulder at him.

"How did you know?"

She pulled a bottle off the top shelf and showed him the label: Sam Clay.

Sartain gave a lopsided grin. "How did you know?"

"Something in the way you roll your syllables." She set a goblet down on the cabinet table. "Water?"

"I'm not gonna bathe in it."

"A neat man."

"Is there any other kind?"

When she'd poured his drink and refreshed her own from a fancily labeled brandy bottle, she walked back over to the fire, gave him his bourbon, and gestured at the leather chair matching her and also facing the fire. "Please have a seat, Mr. Sartain."

When he'd eased into the chair, she sat down, as well, half-turning to him in her own chair. The chair's leathery masculinity accented by contrast her petiteness and voluptuous femininity. She turned her right leg under the left one and crossed the left one over her right knee, demonstrating her dexterity and showing the long, cleanness of both legs under the velvet gown drawn taut against them.

She sipped her brandy and rested her right elbow on the chair arm, boldly scrutinizing him.

"Tell me, Mr. Sartain—did my husband send for you?"

Sartain sipped the bourbon, let it loll on his tongue for a few seconds, savoring it, before swallowing. When it hit his belly, he swore he could smell the verdant hills of Kentucky wafting in through a window though no windows were open, as the Colorado mountain night was chilly.

"No, he did not."

"Then why are you here?"

"I'm looking for the gold and those who might have stolen it."

"So my husband didn't send for you?" she asked again with a dubious arch of her brow.

"No, ma'am—he did not."

"Who did, then, if I may ask?"

Sartain shrugged. "I don't reckon there's any reason why you shouldn't know. Belle Higgins put me on the gold's scent."

"Ah, the sheriff's daughter."

"There you have it."

"Well, that makes sense." Pensively sipping her brandy, Mathilda Maragon stared into the dancing fire as though considering her next words.

Sartain sipped his own delicious drink, savoring it. The fire felt good, as the night had turned chilly, and the bourbon was sweeping that warmth all through him. He was curious about what Mrs. Maragon had on her mind—why, specifically, she'd asked him here—but he'd be patient and let the lady herself get around to it. He couldn't help sneaking glances at her, sitting there to his left, angled slightly toward him and the fire both.

Her hair was as rich and thick as freshly whipped chocolate. Her eyes were luminous, the flames dancing on her corneas. Her lips were rich and red and full. He couldn't help imagining how they'd feel and taste, pressed against his own. Her breasts were heavy, weighing down the corset of the ornate, velvet dress. Shadows danced across her cleavage.

Slowly, she turned to him, and he pretended he hadn't been staring at her, fantasizing about her.

"Mr. Sartain," she said abruptly, "I think it may well be very possible that my husband himself is responsible for the stealing of that gold."

That rocked The Revenger back on his metaphorical heels. He scowled his incredulity. "Why on earth would he steal from himself?"

"He wouldn't really be stealing from himself. He'd be stealing from my father. My father and three other investors own the Painted Lady. Richard is given a commission on each ton of gold he mills and a salary."

"The gold in the strongbox would be quite a haul for him, in other words."

"Yes, it would supplement his income quite nicely. Also, he would be spitting in the eye of my father. He would be spitting in my eye, as well."

"Right."

"I take it he told you about our relative estrangement."

"Yes."

"He tells everyone," she said, laughing mirthlessly but loudly, her fine cheeks flushing. "The simple fool. Did he also tell you he's diseased?"

"Yeah, he told me about that, as well. He doesn't look good. In fact, I'm no doctor, but I'd venture to say he doesn't have long left."

"You don't need four years at Harvard to see that. Which means he doesn't have anything to lose. He hates my father because my father is paying him 'pennies and pisswater'—those are Richard's own words—and he hates me because I won't allow him in the house anymore, let alone our bed."

"I can see how that may be the most painful punishment of all."

Mathilda studied him, both brows raised. And then she flushed again and smiled seductively. "Yes, well, be that as it may . . . I believe he hired someone to steal the gold and secret it away somewhere in these mountains. I don't doubt that he'll disappear in a couple of weeks. He'll go dig up his gold and head to Mexico or San Francisco and spend the rest of his days living high on the hog—eating, drinking, and fornicating to his heart's delight."

It was Sartain's turn to be taken aback. He'd never known such a highbred filly to use such language. Spoken by those succulent lips in that high-toned English accent, the word sounded downright elegant.

Forcing himself to stay focused on his mission, he said, "Ironically, Mrs. Maragon, your husband thinks you were the one responsible for stealing the gold."

She widened her eyes in surprise and fingered the pearl necklace that hung like a tongue over her bosom. "Oh, really?" She laughed. "That's priceless. And wonderful." She paused, thinking it over. "Oh, yes—I like that indeed. So he doesn't just see me as some jewel he acquired through a business transaction. He suspects me. Maybe even fears me a little." She looked at Sartain. "What do you think, Mr. Revenger? Do you think I stole the gold?"

"Yes."

She smiled slowly, delightedly, letting her fingers drop from the necklace and slide down over the mouth of her cleavage. "Really?"

"I'll suspect everyone, Mrs. Maragon. Until I find it."

"Oh," she said, a little crestfallen. "Well, that I can understand, though I would have liked it better if you suspected me most of all. For a time, anyway. That would have made the evening all the more fun and intriguing."

Sartain met her simmering gaze as she tapped two fingers against her cleavage. He felt his pants grow tight as she made love to him from across the three-foot gap between them, with only her eyes and those two fingers caressing the V-shaped space between the tops of her breasts. She bounced her left foot as it hung down from her opposite knee.

"Mrs. Maragon?" Edna's voice startled them both of their pregnant silence.

Mathilda let her hand drop away from her bosom. "Yes, Edna?"

"Dinner is ready, Mrs. Maragon."

Sartain thought the housekeeper might have put an ever-so-slight accent on the Missus, as though to remind them both that Mathilda was married.

"Wonderful!" Mrs. Maragon rose. "Shall we, Mr. Sartain? Or may I call you Mike? I think we've come to know each other well enough to be on a first-name basis, don't you?"

"I do indeed," Sartain said, his bullet-burned temple throbbing with mannish attraction.

CHAPTER 15

Halfway through the delicious meal served at a long table draped with a snow-white silk cloth and trimmed with crystal and fine china that sparkled like diamonds in the candlelight, Mathilda cleared her throat and turned to Edna standing off her right elbow: "Edna, would you and Lyle please prepare the bedroom next to mine for Mr. Sartain? He'll be spending the night with me. And heat water for a bath, will you?"

Edna glanced across the table at Lyle, who was standing behind Sartain, holding a china gravy boat and ladle.

Edna asked, "A bath for you or Mr. Sartain, Mrs. Maragon?"

Mathilda smiled through the candlelight at Sartain. "For both of us. In my room. In fact, you might as well skip the second room. Make sure my room is presentable, won't you?"

Sartain choked on a bite of the potatoes to which Lyle had just added a liberal dollop of hot elk gravy. Mathilda smiled at him from across the table. Edna stood staring down in shock at her mistress before glancing conspiratorially at her husband once more and saying, "Well, then." The old woman's sagging, craggy cheeks were mottled red. "I guess we'd better get started, Lyle."

"Yes, you may be excused," Mathilda said.

The two retreated to the kitchen in a silent snit. Sartain heard the range door squawk open and the thumps of wood being added to the firebox.

He wiped his mouth with a cloth napkin and said, "You're

taking much for granted, Mrs. Maragon."

"Am I?"

"How do you know I'm that kind of a boy?"

She forked a small chunk of meat and gravy-drenched potatoes between her full, red lips, and chewed. "A woman can tell these things."

"Word will spread like that wildfire mentioned earlier."

"Yes, it will, won't it? Sort of the way word of my husband's infidelities have spread like that very same wildfire mentioned earlier."

"I see."

"Are you offended?"

"At you using me to seek revenge on your lecherous husband?" Sartain sipped his wine and set his glass back down on the silk tablecloth. "I am not called The Revenger for nothing, dear Mathilda."

She leaned back in her chair, laughing. "I think we're going to have a bloody good time together this evening, Mike. I haven't had a good . . . *time* . . . for over a year."

"You might just kill me."

She made no attempt to lower her voice as she said, "Shall we forego dessert? Maybe save it for the wee hours of the morning as a post-coital treat? I for one don't like to make love on an overfilled belly."

"My sentiments exactly."

Mathilda turned and called through the kitchen door, "Edna, we're skipping dessert. Hurry with that bath, will you, please?"

The only response was something fragile shattering on the floor.

Mathilda smiled devilishly at Sartain and shrugged a shoulder as she chewed.

A half hour later, when they'd finished their coffee and another glass of wine, they rose from their chairs and retired to the second story. Mathilda pushed open the door to her bedroom, and walked in, Sartain following, staring at her backside with appreciation. He was partial to women with full figures.

She grabbed a rear poster of her large, canopied, four-poster bed and swung back toward him. The bathtub steamed to her left. It was a large, ornately painted copper affair with a high back. Lamplight reflected off the dark surface of the water and off the steam rising from it, humidifying the room.

Sartain closed the door.

"Well, then," she said, glancing at the tub. "Last one in's a rotten egg."

When they were finally finished rocking together, and the bed had finally stopped hammering the wall, she sagged against him, kissed his chest, and then slid down to lie curled beside him. They were both panting and breathing as though they'd sprinted a mile with a horde of Apache warriors close on their heels.

A soft knock sounded against the door.

Edna's firm, even voice: "Mrs. Maragon?"

"Yes, Edna—what is it?"

"We'll be leaving now. Lyle and me. We're finished here, ma'am. We cannot work in a house of such sinfulness."

"Yes, I understand, Edna. Stop back tomorrow and I'll give you the time I owe you plus a generous severance."

The only sound on the other side of the door was Edna's footsteps heading down the hall toward the stairs.

Sartain looked at Mathilda. "Now you've done it. Who's going to shovel out this dump?"

She laughed.

"You don't care?"

Mathilda rubbed her cheek against Sartain's hair-matted

chest. "Don't need 'em. Richard hired them when we first came here. I never needed them but didn't have the heart to release them when I released Richard. They'll get along. They'll probably return to Denver, where they're from. They never much cared for this crude, remote place."

They dozed together for a time, and then they took a long, leisurely bath together in the lukewarm water.

Half-dressed, they slipped downstairs for coffee, bourbon, and dessert, and then returned to Mathilda's room and slept the sleep of the dead.

Sartain woke to a noise. Not moving, but only opening his eyes, he saw that soft, blue morning light was pushing through the bedroom windows. He also saw Mathilda walking toward him, wearing a sheer, powder-blue wrap. Her hair was still mussed from sleep. He couldn't see her face because of her mussed hair and the dim light, but she moved with such a furtive air that he did not react but merely kept his eyes slitted, watching her.

Before they'd drifted off to sleep, he'd hung his gun from the near bed poster. Slowly, Mathilda moved toward it, taking one slow step at a time, moving soundlessly save for the slight swishing of the wrap against her bare legs.

She stopped only a foot away from Sartain. Sliding her hair back from her cheek with her right hand, she extended her left hand toward his brown leather holster. She wrapped her hand around the LeMat's ivory grips and slowly slid the revolver out of the sheath.

As she aimed the gun toward Sartain, she touched her thumb to the hammer, as though to cock the weapon.

The hammer hadn't started to go back when Sartain lashed out with his own left hand and wrapped it around hers, turning the barrel away from him.

Mathilda gave a startled cry. "Mike, you're hurting me!"

"I'll take that." Sitting up, he wrapped his right hand around the barrel and pulled the LeMat free.

Mathilda took a stumbling couple of steps away from him, shaking her hair out of her eyes. "Mike, it's not what you think!"

"Oh? You weren't about to blow my brains out?" Sartain dropped his feet to the floor, holding the LeMat on his thigh and scowling angrily at her. "What is it, then? We have an intruder downstairs? Rats?"

"No, there's no intruder," Mathilda said. "And, no, there are no rats. I just saw it there . . . and . . . I was curious is all. I've never been around many guns. I was raised in London and Boston, and until I got out here, I'd never seen so many guns. Still have never held one in my hand. Especially one like that. Beautiful . . . and yet one that has probably killed many men."

Sartain studied her. She stared back at him between the mussed wings of her hair, most of which she'd shoved behind her head. He believed her. At least, he thought he did. When it came to women like her—beautiful, well-bred, well-educated women—he had to admit he was not swimming in his usual waters.

Maybe after last night, he wanted to believe her. He had a penchant for romanticism, which was probably due in no small part to the hot Cajun blood coursing through his veins.

Besides, what motive would she have for killing him?

Judging by her screams, he'd done fairly well last night in the ole mattress sack.

Or, as her husband suspected, was she responsible for stealing the gold?

"Sorry," he said, rising and flipping the LeMat in the air, catching it by its barrel. He walked over to her and held the heavy gun out to her, pearl grips first. "Old habits die hard. Here. It's all yours."

She stepped toward him, shoved the gun aside, and reached

down for him. "I've changed my mind. There's another gun here I'd really rather play with."

CHAPTER 16

His male desires sated, and his belly full of the oatmeal and eggs Mathilda had cooked for him, Sartain kissed her good-bye and went out to the barn. He grained and saddled Boss and led the horse out around the house to the main street, both sides of which were still concealed in purple morning shadows. The sun had not yet risen from behind the eastern peaks.

The street was nearly deserted, just a few men leaving the mine bunkhouses and drifting over to what Sartain assumed was the cookhouse. Heavy smoke issued from the building's two chimney pipes, flattening out over the pitched, shake-shingled roof. The hammering of the stamping mill sounded all the louder in the otherwise peaceful morning stillness, and the rancid odor emanating from the smelter was all the more cloying.

Sartain took a minute to check Boss's bridle straps, and then climbed into the saddle. As he turned Boss west along the street, he spied movement on the porch of the Painted Lady Saloon sitting kitty-corner to the Maragon house. Sartain stopped the buckskin as Richard Maragon himself drifted out of the porch's heavy shadows and dropped down the steps and into the wan morning light.

He was wearing his red velvet robe with the fur collar again. His face was as white as paper, its stark contrast making his dark-brown hair appear almost black. He drew on a half-smoked stogie, blew the smoke out, and said above the reverberation of the stamping mill, "You have a good time last night, Sartain?"

Sartain merely pinched his hat brim to the man and touched spurs to Boss's flanks.

Maragon said loudly, angrily behind him, "You find that gold and bring it back here and maybe, just *maybe* I won't sic some rabid dogs on you as payback, *Revenger!*"

Sartain just kept riding but stopped when he saw Mathilda standing out on her open gable again, as she had been when Sartain had first seen her. She stepped up to the rail, facing her husband, and said, "You send any dogs after him, Richard, you worthless sot, I'll pay those dogs double what you paid them to hang *you* right here on the street between my house and your brothel. And then I'll burn your brothel to the ground."

"You stay out of this, Mathilda! It doesn't have anything to do with you. It's between me and him!"

Mathilda threw her pretty head back, laughing. "Last night had everything to do with me and Mister Sartain, Richard. Don't tell me you couldn't hear my love cries." She placed a mock-reflective finger on her chin. "But then, how would you know they were mine . . . since you've never heard them before!"

Chuckles rose beneath the hammering rumble of the stamping mill. Sartain glanced behind him to see several miners in felt watch caps and canvas coats and trousers standing on the street between the bunkhouses and the cook shack. Some stood on the cook shack porch. They were all either smoking or drinking coffee or both, and they were all facing Maragon, elbowing each other and chuckling.

Maragon swung around to face them, pumping an angry fist in the air. "You men either get to work or draw your time and get the hell out of my town! Do you hear? Or get the hell out of my town and don't ever show your faces around the Painted Lady again!"

His voice rose so shrilly that it cracked.

Cowed, the miners hustled into the cook shack.

Sartain again touched spurs to Boss's flanks and headed for the open country beyond the mining settlement. He glanced over his right shoulder. In the open gable, Mathilda waved and blew him a kiss.

He pinched his hat brim to her.

Sartain made his slow way along the gradually descending Old Ute Trail, rising over windy, rocky passes and falling through lush, timbered valleys. He was especially careful now, more thoroughly scouring the trail, because he knew that this was the trail Higgins and his deputy had taken down the mountains toward Silverthorne.

The first day he didn't see a thing. Because of his slow, thorough progress, he rode only about six or seven miles before the sun fell far enough that shadows obscured the trail, and he camped for the night. The next day, just after he'd stopped around noon to water Boss and to refill his own canteen at a stream, the sun flashed off something bright and shiny.

He twisted the cap onto his canteen, walked over to where a gnarled cedar jutted near a rock half its size, and dropped to a knee. He reached down and plucked the spent brass cartridge casing from the ground beneath the cedar, and held it up to inspect it—a relatively short cartridge compared to the Colt .45 or the Schofield, the two most common revolvers on the frontier.

This cartridge, about the length of Sartain's index finger from the first joint to the tip, had likely propelled a 210 grain bullet from a Smith & Wesson Model 3 "Russian" revolver.

Propelled the bullet into what?

He looked around. A few yards away, he saw something else.

A splash of brown across another cedar.

He pocketed the cartridge, walked over, dropped to a knee again, and ran the brown-stained needles of the cedar between his right thumb and index finger. The brown stain crumbled and dropped away. It owned the texture of ever-so-slightly damp cinnamon.

It was blood that had been fresh maybe four, possibly five days ago. There was more of it on the ground three feet away.

As Sartain investigated the blood-stained rocks and sand, he saw that several branches of a shadbark shrub had been snapped. They were sagging to the ground, not quite dead yet, as though something heavy had fallen on them. Around the shadbark, the dirt and sand was scuffed, and grooves had been carved into the ground, showing intermittently amongst the brush and trailing off along the stream.

Standing by the creek, Sartain looked off toward where the grooves disappeared down a gentle slope between low, stone escarpments tufted with juniper and cedar. The stream dropped down the declivity, as well, chuckling, flashing darkly in the stark noon light. The Revenger's heart quickened.

A body had been dragged down there.

He glanced back at the sun-washed trail showing beyond the pines and mentally laid out what might have happened. A man or men had left the trail to water their horses at the stream, just as Sartain himself had done, and the man or men had been bushwhacked. One had taken a bullet, and maybe the other one had dragged the wounded man to safety. Or to what he'd hoped had been safety . . .

Sartain's breath came faster. His blood was charged. He finally had some sign, a clue.

He walked over to where Boss stood at the edge of the creek, water trickling from his snout as he studied Sartain dubiously. The buckskin knew his rider's blood was up. Sartain patted the mount's neck, slid his rifle from his saddle boot, pumped a round into the action, lowered the hammer to half cock, and rested the barrel on his shoulder.

He fished the second of Maragon's stogies from his shirt pocket, nipped off the end, and fired a match to life on his thumbnail. Sometimes when he was on a hot trail, he smoked a good cigar. The smoking soaked up some of his excess energy and helped him think.

When he had the cigar drawing to his liking, he tossed the match into the stream, heard the clipped sizzle, and patted Boss's neck once more. "You stay, boy. Keep an eye skinned and call out if you see anything."

He was thinking about the bushwhacker who'd carved what would probably be a permanent notch in his left temple a couple of days back.

Puffing pensively on his stogie, he followed the intermittent trail through the brush along the creek.

Where there were no furrows from what Sartain figured were a pair of men's boots, there were scratched rocks and broken sage branches. He followed the trail through mixed cedars, piñons, and juniper scrub down the declivity that dropped more steeply. He soon found himself in a deep, cool canyon walled in by shelving stone mesas.

Here the water ran faster as it traveled down the steep slope.

Beneath the low roar of the tumbling creek, a high screech sounded. Anticipating a gunshot, Sartain stopped suddenly and raised the Henry, thumbing the hammer back to full cock.

But then he saw the large, mottled brown eagle take wing from a mound of rocks about fifty yards away. The bird gave another angry screech as it flapped its heavy wings and slanted skyward over Sartain's head, the *whir-whir-whir* of its wings audible fleetingly above the creek's hollow, gurgling roar.

Sartain eased the Henry's hammer back down and dropped deeper into the canyon. He pulled up beside the mound of rocks.

It was not a natural cairn deposited here by floodwater. The sun-bleached, water-polished rocks, most about the size of a wheel hub, had been hauled up from the wide creek bed and placed here where the creek had once run and where it still probably ran in the spring, violent and bone-splintering cold with fresh snowmelt.

No brush had grown up around the rocks, which meant they hadn't been here long. There were brown patches of blood here and there on the rocks and sage tufts and cedar limbs.

Sartain drew on the stogie, blew the smoke out, and rolled the cigar around between his lips as he looked carefully around the canyon, wondering if his bushwhacker had trailed him here. It had become suddenly darker, though it wasn't much after noon, and a cool wind rife with the smell of rain scuttled through the cut, chilling the sweat on his back.

He looked up to see angry-looking storm clouds sliding over the canyon, beginning to block the cobalt blue of the high-altitude sky.

"Shit," The Revenger said around his cigar.

He'd been lucky so far. He'd had to contend with no rainstorms on his journey from Silverthorne, though brief but often violent afternoon squalls were part and parcel to the high country this late in the summer, edging toward August. It looked as though he was in for one now, however.

Quickly, he leaned his rifle against the cutbank, dropped to his knees, and began lifting the rocks from the cairn, setting them aside. Someone had piled a lot of rocks here, as though they'd wanted to keep whatever they'd been concealing from ever being found by man or beast, though the eagle had obviously been curious.

In fact, the eagle had been more than curious. Sartain winced as he removed another rock and set it beside the cairn, staring down at the disembodied eyeball he'd just uncovered. It was a copper-colored eye with a bloody spot where the eagle's beak had plucked it from its socket. It trailed a long, frayed, bloody string of sinew.

The eagle had poked its head and beak down deep amongst the rocks and found a tasty morsel. Now Sartain made a face as the sickly sweet stench of decay wafted up from the rocks, filling his nostrils and threatening to pinch his wind. He swallowed and, continuing to work, breathed through his mouth to muffle the odor.

He lifted a couple of more rocks and revealed part of a wool vest and a blue shirt as well as a faded red neckerchief. He lifted another rock and revealed a face. The face was puffy and pale, and its lone eye stared up past Sartain as though in hushed surprise.

The nose was long and sharp. Beneath it was a light-brown mustache. A puckered blue hole shone in his forehead. Blood had oozed out of the hole to drip across the man's forehead in a thin, crusted brown line.

Sartain removed the rest of the rocks from the body—a man about his size, dead less than a week. He was beginning to bloat and he stank to high heaven, but he was dressed in a store-bought three-piece suit. He wore brown stockmen's boots and spurs. Pinned to his checked brown vest, just above a gold watch chain, was a copper shield on which PINKERTON DETEC-TIVE AGENCY was engraved. To the right of the badge was another bullet wound surrounded by thick, dried blood.

The smell was so overpowering, Sartain had to step away from the body and draw a couple of deep breaths of the fresh air that smelled even stronger now of the coming storm. Lightning flashed in the western sky, and thunder rumbled above the creek's roar.

Cloud shadows danced across the creek bed.

Cupping a handkerchief to his mouth, Sartain went back to the body and started going through the man's pockets.

He found a wallet that contained twenty-three dollars in greenbacks. Obviously, he hadn't been killed for money. In a front pocket of his broadcloth trousers Sartain found six bits and half a comb as well as a brass matchbox on which the letters *CM* had been engraved. In another pocket he found a small, pasteboard-covered and -backed notebook. There were some penciled scrawls inside—some that looked like a train timetable, and the name "Maragon" followed by "Painted Lady."

Otherwise, Sartain saw nothing of insignificance with his perfunctory flip-through. He'd give the pages a more thorough scrutiny later, when he was away from the poor man's death stench.

The man wore a shoulder holster, but there was no gun in it. He had a knife sheath sewn into the well of his right boot. It contained a long, slender blade, slightly rusted and with a wooden handle. It didn't appear to have ever seen much use. The man also had a small .41-caliber pocket pistol with gutta-percha grips in a pocket of his brown tweed coat. In that same pocket was another badge.

Sartain stared down at it, frowning.

"Silverthorne Deputy Sheriff," he muttered, reading the words engraved on the five-pointed star.

Sartain flipped the badge in his hand, pondering.

Had the Pinkerton come upon the body of Deputy Jasper Garvey? If so, where was the body of Sheriff Higgins? Unless Higgins himself had killed Garvey and taken the gold . . . ?

Sartain pocketed the badge. As he relit the stogie, he spied another cairn in a slight depression, closer to the creek and partly hidden by a deadfall aspen.

"Higgins?" Sartain muttered aloud around the stogie, blowing smoke out his nostrils.

He hurried over and, ignoring the thunder and the cold rain beginning to spit at him, began removing the rocks from the top of the cairn. He'd removed only a few when he stopped and stared down at the badly swollen and misshapen face of a middle-aged man with a thick, gray-brown mustache in the old Dragoon style.

The stench was like a fist to the jaw. Sartain breathed into his arm. The Dragoon mustache was about the only distinguishing feature he could make out, for the body had been vituperating for a good two months, and the birds, worms, and maggots had been working on the bloated carcass. It appeared that the dead man had only a few wisps of thin, sandy gray hair combed straight back over the top of his lightly freckled head, with straps of fuller hair on the sides.

He had a bloody hole in his neck just left of his throat, and another in his right shoulder.

The man's lips were stretched far back from his long, yellow, tobacco-edged teeth in a death snarl. Keeping his mouth pressed against his arm, his eyes watering as though against a strong onion, Sartain looked around on the man's clothes for a badge that should read TOWN SHERIFF OF SILVERTHORNE.

He found none.

But judging by this dead man's age, he had to be Higgins.

Sartain straightened quickly, strode several yards from the body, and removed the handkerchief from his mouth. Drawing fresh air into his lungs, he stared across the stream and wondered just what he'd found here. What would these two dead men tell him if they could?

A shadow slid over the rocks and gravel to his right. Something told him it wasn't a cloud shadow. The rain and wind were cold, but they weren't what caused the short hairs at the back of Sartain's neck to rise. A spur chimed faintly.

The maw of a gun pressed against The Revenger's spine at the small of his back. Dread pooling like hot mud in his belly,

Sartain lifted his hands.

"Let me guess," he said. "Jasper Garvey?"

CHAPTER 17

The man behind Sartain gave a high-pitched laugh. "How in the hell did you know, Sartain?"

"Can I turn around?"

The man unsnapped the keeper thong over Sartain's LeMat and slipped the big popper from its holster. "Slow."

Open hands raised to his shoulders, Sartain turned around to face a young man about six inches shorter than he was. His face would have been handsome if not quite so round, his eyes set not quite so close together. His cheeks owned a three- or four-day growth of sandy beard, and a thin, long goatee drooped from his chin. A skimpy mustache mantled his upper lip. His nose and the nubs of his cheeks were pink and peeling from sun blisters.

He'd been spending a lot of time outdoors of late.

He'd backed up and shoved Sartain's LeMat down behind his twin cartridge belts. His Russian .44 was aimed at Sartain's belly. He was grinning, showing small, crooked, yellow teeth. "So . . . you're The Revenger."

"So . . . you're the appropriately named Jasper Garvey."

"One an' the same." Garvey canted his head a little to one side. "How'd you know it was me?"

"I only found your badge. Not your body. Higgins wasn't wearing any badge. At least, I'm assuming that smelly carcass with the bad neck wound over there is Sheriff Higgins."

"That's him, all right."

"You must have pinned your badge to the sheriff's shirt, thinking that's all anyone would find after the scavengers had finished with him and strewn his bones around this canyon. They'd think Higgins had killed you, the poor innocent deputy, and made off with the gold. It would be him any investigators would be looking for, and you'd be free to spend all that gold by yourself."

Garvey was still grinning. "That's pretty close to the size of it, all right." A fine rain fell at a slant, and thunder rumbled loudly, causing the ground to shudder. The rain was pelting him, whipping his longish hair and neckerchief around his cheeks.

"You didn't expect a Pinkerton to find him before the scavengers could go to work on him. The nights up here are cold, and the light probably doesn't last long in this canyon. He didn't rot and draw the carrion-eaters as fast as you'd expected, so you came back recently and buried him. Or maybe you dogged the Pinkerton out here, shot the detective, and buried Higgins."

"You're right smart. I reckon you earned your reputation. Too bad I gotta kill you now."

"What the hell are you hanging around here for, Garvey? Why aren't you in Mexico by now, spending that gold on tequila and *senoritas*?"

"A man has his reasons." Garvey raised the cocked Russian and narrowed one eye as he aimed at Sartain's forehead. "You scared? You should be, because you're gonna die in about two jangles of a whore's bell."

Sartain flicked a glance behind Garvey. "Oh-oh."

Garvey started to turn his head, wrinkling the skin at the bridge of his nose. Then, realizing that Sartain was only trying to distract him, he started to smile.

But the instant's distraction was enough for Sartain to make his move, since he had nothing to lose. He'd bulled forward and grabbed the Russian just before the former deputy had got the revolver leveled on him again, and shoved it straight up.

It thundered between the two of them, the blast feeling like two open hands slapped against Sartain's ears, which instantly started ringing. Distantly, he heard another crack. It might have been the thunder but then it might not have been, because he found himself staring at Jasper Garvey's blown-out right temple.

The kid's arms went slack in Sartain's grip, and Garvey stared at him with a vague look of befuddlement, as though he wanted to ask, "What just happened?"

His arms slid out of Sartain's hands, and the kid crumpled at Sartain's boots, blood and white brain matter oozing out that fist-sized hole in his temple. As thunder peeled and lightning flashed, Sartain spied a human-shaped silhouette and a familiarly shaped tan hat on the sloping stone ridge looming behind Garvey. He also spied a rifle barrel being brought to bear on him, and leaped to one side too late.

He hadn't seen anyone on the ridge when he'd distracted Garvey, but someone really was up there . . .

Shit.

The bullet tore hotly into Sartain's right thigh. He grunted, ground his teeth against the burn—it felt as though a hot railroad spike had been driven into his flesh—and then he wheeled as another gun crack sounded amidst the storm.

A bullet spanged off a rock to his right. He grabbed his Henry from where he'd leaned it against the deadfall aspen, and dove behind a large, pale boulder that was now being lashed with the wind-blown rain.

Two bullets hammered the rock's far side, too close together to have come from the same weapon. There were at least two shooters.

Sartain's ears were still ringing from the blast of Garvey's

Russian. That, his pounding right thigh, and the storm served to confuse and disorient him. Quickly, as the rifles atop the ridge continued to blast away at his covering rock, he wrapped his neckerchief around the bullet wound in his right thigh and consciously fought to regain all his faculties.

When he did, he rose to a crouch, trying to ignore the hammering pain in his leg, and edged a glance around the rock's left side.

There was a small flash atop the ridge, and Sartain drew his head back behind the rock as a bullet sang past him, the rifle's report half-drowned by the storm. Sartain snaked his rifle around the rock and fired at where he'd seen the rifle flash, loosing a mini-barrage and watching rock shards fly from the lip of the ridge.

He thought he heard a woman scream, but then he wasn't sure because the rushing roar of the rain, wind, and thunder filled the canyon. Fearing he wouldn't have the strength to keep up the fight much longer and knowing there was a chance he'd pass out from pain and blood loss, Sartain waited for a particularly loud, earth-shuddering thunderclap, and ran out from behind the rock.

He hop-skipped, dragging his bad leg, as fast as he could, to a gap in the ridge wall, below where he'd seen the rifle flashes.

Grunting and cursing, the wind and rain lashing him, he climbed the boulders littering the gap, holding his Henry in one hand. The leg burned and throbbed. He could feel the blood leaking out around the neckerchief and mixing like oil with the rain soaking him. He was only halfway up the ridge wall when the thunder and lightning stopped suddenly, and the wind died as though it had been the end of a long, violent exhalation.

The clouds parted and shafts of washed-out, golden light angled down from the sky, bathing the dripping rocks and showing Sartain the top of the ridge nearly straight above him. He stopped, raising the rifle. But then he lowered it.

He stared at the blonde hanging down from a jutting block of granite. She lay on her back, and she hung over the rock, arms and wet hair dangling straight down below her, toward Sartain. Her hazel eyes were open. Blood stained her forehead where Sartain's bullet had drilled her. Her Spencer repeater had fallen to hang up against a rock about ten feet below her.

She was wearing a red-and-white checked wool shirt and a yellow neckerchief. A man's brown felt hat lay near the rifle.

"Mary," Sartain whispered in the sudden silence, broken only by the soft gurgling of the rain running and dripping down the rocks around him.

The man who'd creased his temple had been wearing similar attire.

No, the woman who'd ambushed him.

Crazy Mary.

Why?

From somewhere atop the ridge came a horse's energetic whinny and a female voice yelling throatily, "Hi-*yahhh!*"

Shod hooves clattered on rock, and brush crackled beneath the horse's galloping hooves. The sounds dwindled quickly as horse and rider apparently descended the ridge's opposite side from Sartain. And then there was just the dripping rocks and Crazy Mary staring down at him from the lip of the ridge above, her eyes wide and glassy in death.

"Mary," Sartain said, shocked and puzzled. He felt as though he'd been sucker-punched in the heart.

The answer lay with the other rider—whoever she was.

Mathilda Maragon? Could her husband's suspicions be true?

Sartain scrambled as quickly as he could down from the rocks and boulders, falling several times and cursing his aching leg. He hurried back toward Boss, the sky growing lighter and the chill burning off with the intensifying sun, steam rising from the ground around his feet.

When he got back out to the trail, he called for the buckskin and looked at the trail itself. The mud shone with fresh tracks heading on down the mountain, in the direction of Silverthorne. Hooves thudded and brush snapped, and Sartain turned to see Boss moving toward him from where he'd apparently taken shelter in the heavy timber.

Happy to see his rider and relieved that the short but powerful mountain storm had passed, Boss shook his head and snorted and then lowered his snout to sniff Sartain's bloody leg.

"Thanks for alerting me to trouble, pal," Sartain raked out, sliding his rifle into his scabbard and cursing while trying to gingerly heave himself into the saddle. "Really appreciate that!"

The horse must have been more preoccupied with the storm, which he'd likely heard building long before Sartain had, than sniffing the wind for danger to his rider.

As if to announce just that, Boss whickered and shook his soaked head again, rattling the bridle bit in his teeth.

Thanks to the mud, the fleeing rider was easy to track. He or she—or whoever in hell the ambusher was—rode straight on down the main trail, twisting and turning with the lay of the mountains.

About a mile from where Sartain had left Crazy Mary and Jasper Garvey, his quarry had swung off the main trail onto a single-track horse trail that headed off into a forest of firs, aspens, and pines. Soon, a muddy creek bubbling with the recent rain swung into sight from the woods on Sartain's right to follow the trail. Ahead, a patch of gray appeared.

It was a stone cabin with an abutting, falling-down pole corral.

Sartain stopped Boss and stared cautiously toward the hovel—likely an old prospector's cabin. A saddled horse stood in the corral just left of the place. A shadow moved in the window left of the half-open door.

His heart lurching, Sartain neck-reined Boss around sharply and dashed into the creek as smoke puffed in the dark window. The rifle's hollow report echoed as Boss splashed across the creek and lunged up the opposite bank and into the relative sanctuary of thick forest.

Sartain rained Boss to a halt behind a large, moss-patchy boulder and a sprawling spruce, and eased tenderly out of the saddle, trying to put as little weight as possible on his right foot. The rifle cracked two more times, and then a third time, the bullets plunking into the ground and spanging off rocks near the creek.

Grimacing against the pain bayoneting up and down his right leg, Sartain shucked his Henry from his saddle scabbard and told the buckskin to stay. The horse was wide-eyed and fidgety about the gunfire, and he shifted his weight around but otherwise stayed put. Sartain hobbled out away from the rock, heading straight ahead along the stream on a course that, if he kept going, would place him at the cabin's left end. There was more cover from the large spruces, pines, and boulders in this direction, and more shade.

He stopped behind a spruce, cast a look toward the cabin.

Rain-washed, sparkling sunlight angled down through the trees to burnish the gray, shake-shingled roof patchy with thick tufts of wet green moss. The chinking had disappeared from around some of the stones comprising the walls, showing black gaps. Sartain tensed when a rifle barrel slid slowly out the window to the left of the shack's front door.

Like a snake's tongue, it seemed to be probing the air for a target.

Sartain felt the burn of anger well up from the wound in his leg as well as the annoying, ever-present ache in his temple.

Time to find out who Crazy Mary's accomplice was.

The Revenger raised the Henry, quietly levered a round into the action, snaked the barrel around the side of the spruce, and cut loose with five shots, one after another, the cartridge casings arcing back over his right shoulder to clank against each other behind him. Shards from the stones around the window casing flew in all directions, showing copper in the clean sunshine.

The rifle disappeared from the window. A scream rose from inside the shack. The scream was a woman's.

Another woman's.

A familiar voice, muffled by the shack's walls, said, "Damn you, Mike!"

Sartain frowned, stared down the Henry's smoking barrel toward the window. "Belle?"

CHAPTER 18

The girl sobbed.

Sartain stepped slowly out from around the spruce and, holding his cocked rifle at port arms, and keeping his eyes on the window and door, dragged his right boot toward the cabin. His mind was swirling like the creek he crossed. Twenty feet from the cabin, he slowed his pace, approaching from the end facing the creek, ready for that rifle to be thrust out the window or the open door.

He moved a little faster when he heard soft sobs coming from inside.

He moved to the worn patch of ground in front of the door, aimed the Henry straight out from his right hip, and stepped as quickly as he could through the door. He stepped to the right, pressed his back against the wall, out of the light from the door.

The cabin was empty, the floor strewn with dirt and dead leaves.

Empty except for Belle sitting on the floor, her back to the small, stone fireplace a little larger than a charcoal brazier. A Winchester carbine and a sand-colored Stetson lay on the floor near her men's stockmen's boots. She was dressed in a wool shirt and denims. Trail gear.

To her right was the strongbox.

Golden sunlight angling through a window to Sartain's left laid a trapezoid across the box and the girl's legs. She was breathing hard, groaning and holding a hand against her right side.

"Congratulations, Mister Revenger," Belle said in a pinched voice. "You did your job right well. Did exactly what I asked you to do."

She patted the closed strongbox on her left and smiled grimly.

Sartain hobbled over and kicked the lid up, let it drop back behind the box. Six gold ingots shone brightly in the sunlight.

Sartain shook his head, thoroughly befuddled. "I don't get it, Belle. You, Crazy Mary, and Jasper Garvey . . . ?"

"You didn't know my old man. He was a devil. When he found me an' Mary together one night, after he'd come back to town after chasin' bank robbers, he whipped us both. Damn near shredded the skin on our bare asses."

Belle grunted, winced, briefly showing her teeth. Blood oozed out the hole in her side, pooling on the floor beneath her. "So we decided to take the gold shipment and head East, buy us some frilly dresses and live high on the hog together. See us some opera shows in New York City an' the like."

Awkwardly, Sartain dropped to his good knee beside her, set his rifle down, and untied her neckerchief. He wadded it up and started to press it against the hole in the girl's side. She waved his hand away, shook her head.

"Don't bother. I'm a goner. Took a ricochet. Tore me up pretty good inside. I ain't gonna be able to spend an ounce of that gold." She laughed, but there was no humor in it. "When I sent for you, I was really outsmarting myself, wasn't I?"

Sartain just stared at her.

"I figured no one would suspect I had anything to do with it . . . if I hired you to track down the robbers. That way, when Jasper cleared you from our trail, me an' Crazy Mary could take off with the gold, and we wouldn't have to worry about anyone followin' us. I was just heartbroken on account of Pa's killin', so

I turned the saloon over to Northcutt. Everyone would see how I just needed to go somewhere to lick my wounds . . . start a new life for myself."

"Why did Mary take that shot at me in town?"

"She was jealous. Gets that way from time to time. She said she heard us together, saw what we were doin' through the keyhole in my door. She was gonna ride on back to the mountains but then turned back and fired that shot through the window. That was just Mary. Crazy Mary. I love her, though." Belle sobbed. "Poor, sweet, Crazy Mary . . . Then, when she saw you on the trail, she decided to take another shot. And then, when she saw you up close, she decided to see what all the fuss was about . . . between you an' me."

Belle laughed again, and then she sobbed some more and grunted against the pain.

"And Jasper?"

"Oh, I couldn't kill my own pa, as much as I hated him. I promised him some of the gold if he shot Pa on the way down from the Painted Lady. Told him how me an' Mary would be extra nice to him . . . if you get my drift, Mike."

"Yeah, I get it. Why'd you shoot him?"

"I was fixin' to wait till he'd shot you, but I got a nervous trigger finger. He wasn't no use to us anymore—Mary an' me. We were tired of entertainin' him."

Belle laughed briefly, insanely, scrunching up her eyes. She grabbed Sartain's wrist. "It wouldn't have been easy . . . watchin' you die, Mike. After the other night. But, you see, we just had to do it. There was no other way. We loved each other, Mary an' me, though I know that sounds strange—us both bein' girls an' such. But we loved each other just the same, though we both enjoyed you. Now, there was a time!"

The girl paused, tears glittering in her eyes. Her breathing was growing more strained. "I really hope you're gonna be okay,

Mike. I'm awful sorry about that bullet in your leg. Mary fired that one, I think. Just the same, it could have been me, and I'm not a very good shot, I'm afraid."

"Ah, Belle," Sartain said, frustration and sadness welling in him. "Belle, Belle, Belle!" He smoothed a lock of hair back from her tear- and sweat-damp cheek. "Look what you done to yourself, girl. To both you and Mary." He sat down beside her, drew her tautly, warmly against him.

"Maybe it's better this way," she said, and pressed her lips to his neck.

They sat there together for several minutes, neither saying anything more. Finally, Belle jerked once, convulsively. She quivered, gurgled, and sighed. She died there against his side.

Sartain ran his hand through her hair, fighting back tears of his own.

Outside, the clattering of wooden wheels rose. He looked out through the open door to see a chaise buggy jouncing toward him along the creek. The driver was a woman. There was no mistaking the curves or the rich black hair bouncing on her shoulders beneath the broad brim of her brown felt hat.

Mathilda Maragon wore a black leather jacket over a white blouse, and her black-gloved hands deftly handled the reins of the palomino stallion hitched to the chaise. She pulled up in front of the shack, set the brake, looked around, stared through the open door, and then climbed down from the buggy.

She strode beautifully up to the door and stared inside.

Her red lips parted but she didn't say anything for a time. Then she walked slowly inside and stood staring down at Sartain and Belle, who was still resting her head against his side.

"Oh, Mike," Mathilda said. "I saw Crazy Mary at the Painted Lady earlier with a young man obviously trying to conceal his features. They appeared to be following you. I was worried, so I finally hitched up the chaise and . . ."

Slowly, his voice heavy and sad, he told her all about it.

Mathilda said she'd send some men from the Painted Lady settlement to bury the bodies and retrieve the gold.

And then she helped the heavy-hearted Sartain out into the chaise, bandaged his leg with a cutting from a blanket, and gave him a couple of shots of brandy to dull the pain in his leg. They rode back along the creek, Boss following, his bridle reins tied around the saddlehorn.

"It's not your fault, Mike," she said as he leaned far back in the quilted leather seat.

"No, it's not, but I still feel like hell."

"You won't feel like hell for long." Mathilda reached over and patted his knee. "Soon we'll have you all fixed up. Of course you'll have to stay with me while you recover. My nursing skills are not half bad."

She turned to give him a smoldering look, her cheeks dimpling, dark eyes briefly blazing beneath the brim of her hat.

Sartain gave a slow smile.

ABOUT THE AUTHOR

Born in North Dakota, bestselling western novelist **Peter Brandvold** has penned over seventy fast-action westerns under his own name and his penname, Frank Leslie. He is the author of the ever-popular .45-Caliber books featuring Cuno Massey as well as the Lou Prophet and Yakima Henry novels. Recently, with his first young-adult western, *Lonnie Gentry,* and its successor, *The Curse of Skull Canyon,* he began publishing with Five Star. Head honcho at "Mean Pete Publishing," publisher of lightning-fast western ebooks, he lives in western Minnesota with his dog. Visit his website at www.peterbrandvold.com. Follow his blog at www.peterbrandvold.blogspot.com. Send him an email at peterbrandvold@gmail.com.

The employees of Five Star Publishing hope you have enjoyed this book.

Our Five Star novels explore little-known chapters from America's history, stories told from unique perspectives that will entertain a broad range of readers.

Other Five Star books are available at your local library, bookstore, all major book distributors, and directly from Five Star/Gale.

Connect with Five Star Publishing

Visit us on Facebook:
https://www.facebook.com/FiveStarCengage

Email:
FiveStar@cengage.com

For information about titles and placing orders:
(800) 223-1244
gale.orders@cengage.com

To share your comments, write to us:
Five Star Publishing
Attn: Publisher
10 Water St., Suite 310
Waterville, ME 04901